FALL FROM GRACE

DAVID MENON

A DCI HOYLAND MYSTERY

First published in 2012

This book is copyright under the Berne Convention. All rights are reserved. Apart from any fair dealing for the purpose of private study, research, criticism or review, as permitted under the Copyright Act, 1956, no part of this publication may be reproduced, stored in a retrieval system, or transmitted, in any form or by any means, electronic, electrical, chemical, mechanical, optical, photocopying, recording or otherwise, without the prior permission of the copyright owner. Enquiries should be sent to the publishers at the undermentioned address:

EMPIRE PUBLICATIONS
1 Newton Street, Manchester M1 1HW
© David Menon 2012

ISBN 1901746 852 – 9781901746853

Printed in Great Britain.

'...to Julie and Tony G for showing me the meaning of the word 'family' and to all those friends who've shone some much needed light into my period of black ink darkness over recent months... eternal gratitude and love...'

'...and to anyone who Falls from Grace whilst fighting long and hard just to make sure you survive ...'

...And once again thanks to Maddie and the extended French side of my family for their revolution and for the delicious way they cook rabbit!

...And to my good friend Janet Keene for truly getting the story.

ACKNOWLEDGEMENTS

TO ASHLEY, John, Sadie and the rest of the team at Empire for giving me this opportunity and for running the coolest publishing house from the coolest office in the shadow of Old Trafford cricket ground. I think this now makes me part of the whole 'Madchester' scene and I couldn't be more proud.

When you've a moment or two, check out the website www.republic.co.uk. 'Republic' is the organisation that campaigns for the replacement of the monarchy in Britain with an elected Head of State. Listen to the argument and join the debate.

You can reach me by one of the following thoroughly modern methods.

www.davidmenon.com

www.facebook.com/davidmenon

www.twitter.com/#ifanyonefalls

www.facebook.com/sarahoyland

CHAPTER ONE

HE'D ALWAYS BEEN known as Dr. Sprightly. Gerald Edwards had been a G.P in the North Derbyshire town of Glossop for the best part of fifty years until he retired on the same day that his beloved Margaret Thatcher was forced out of office by her spineless comrades. He would never forget the tears on her face as she made her way to the car outside number ten. She'd been betrayed and as far as Gerald was concerned they should all have been ashamed.

He could no longer ride his bike into town but he could still walk down the hill with the best of them, although going back up took a little longer these days. As he got closer into town he exchanged greetings and short conversations with various people he passed along the way. His son and daughter had both followed in his footsteps into medicine and taken over the health centre out on the Buxton road that he'd started back in the sixties. All the family, his grandchildren included, were known around the town and most people also mentioned his dear wife Joan who'd passed away some years ago. It was for Joan that he kept up his routines. It was for her that he never left the house without wearing a tie, a jacket and his shoes polished. She wouldn't have wanted him to have given up on himself. She'd been a dutiful wife and he owed it to her memory to keep up his appearance like she'd have wanted him to.

He bought some apples, pears and bananas at the greengrocer and put the three brown paper bags into the shopping bag that he'd kept in his pocket. He then went to the cake shop and bought a Victoria jam and cream sandwich that would probably last him two or three days, though his youngest grandchild Nicholas always called round on his way home from school. His other grandchildren were all at university.

He went into the newsagent and bought his copy of that day's Telegraph. He didn't linger much in the newsagent these days. Since Mr. and Mrs. Singh had taken it over he didn't care to. What on earth would he have to talk about with these Asian merchants? What could they say that would be of any interest to him?

As he came out of the newsagent he stepped back to let a lady through. She was of a similar age to himself, though probably a little younger, and as they exchanged a smile they were both gripped by a flash of recognition that took them a very long way back. He could see what was happening in her eyes and he walked on briskly pretending not to notice that she had fainted.

Sara Hoyland knew she didn't have to make much of an effort to look good. Her crystal blue eyes, high cheek bones, small yet pronounced mouth and natural blond hair meant that she was regarded as something of a stunner. She could throw anything on, just like she'd done this morning with a plain white t-shirt tucked into stone washed denim jeans and finished with a black leather jacket, and she still looked better than some of her colleagues who'd spent hours pouring over what would be the right thing to wear. She put a brush through her shoulder length hair and rubbed some moisturiser into the flesh of her face. It was an expensive moisturiser, her one concession to the finer art of female make-up techniques, and then she was ready to leave her warehouse apartment across the road from Piccadilly station on the east of Manchester's city centre. She'd sometimes thought about moving out to one of the southern suburbs like Chorlton or Didsbury, but her social life revolved around the city centre so what would be the point? Until she met a man she wanted to settle down with she would stay in her apartment which, despite the economic crisis, had still on paper, made her quite a packet. And besides, she liked being in the city surrounded by noise and activity. She wouldn't know what to do with peace and quiet.

She parked her car outside the Serious Crime division headquarters on the Chester New Road, not far from her hallowed ground of Old Trafford. If anything was sure to make the scales fall from her eyes it was the teasing by City supporters that none of United's fans were actually from Manchester. Sara was a Mancunian down to her fingertips, born and brought up in a family that was steeped in the traditions of God's own football club for God's own city. Being the youngest and the only girl meant that the obsession of her Dad and her older brothers had been instilled in her from the moment she could speak. It was only her and her Dad who went to the home games now and they'd always been close so they relished the Saturday afternoons on their own. Her brothers, all with kids and mortgages the size of Greenland, couldn't afford it anymore. Screw all the City fans. It was just pure jealousy and if United didn't end up top of the league this season then she'd rather see Blackpool there than bloody City!

She ran up the three flights of stairs and along the corridor to where she knew she had to make a good impression. Her Mum and Dad were so proud. Their little girl had made it through the ranks to Detective Chief Inspector and one of the youngest in the country. They still worried themselves sick about her being a serving police officer on the streets but they'd been telling anybody and everybody that their daughter was up there with the best and still a year away from being thirty.

She took a deep breath and knocked on the door of the Superintendent.

'Come in!'

She opened the door to see Superintendent James Hargreaves, sat at his large desk. They knew each other but she'd never worked directly for him. She knew he was highly regarded at the station for playing it straight with his team. She also knew that he had a reputation as something of a ladies' man. He was married with two teenage children but it was an open secret that his marital status didn't stop him having a little fun whenever the opportunity presented itself. Currently he was alleged to be seeing a WPC who was twenty years younger. He'd tried it on with Sara once but she'd been able to laugh him off, which clearly hadn't caused him any offence seeing as he'd been on the interview panel that had decided on her promotion. Sara was by no means a prude. She loved sex. But married men could keep it in their trousers as far as she was concerned. She'd been there, done that, got the broken heart and burned fingers and she was never going back there again.

'Ah, Detective Chief Inspector Hoyland,' Hargreaves said warmly. He stepped from behind his desk and shook hands with her, 'now how does that sound?'

'Great, sir' said Sara, beaming. 'Really great.'

Sara once again took in the short black hair, the six foot burly frame and the twinkle in the Superintendent's eyes. There was certainly a lot of charm to go with the unquestionably handsome looks and she understood his success with the women. It was rumoured that he was pretty well blessed in the third leg department too and for a moment she wondered if she should've shagged him when she had the chance, just the once, just to see what he was like as a lover and how big his tool really was. Then she told herself to snap out of it. This was the first day in her new job and it wasn't the time to think like a girl.

'Your promotion was well deserved, Sara,' said Hargreaves. 'Your record is exemplary. A brave and trustworthy officer. That's exactly who I need on my team'.

Sara could feel herself blushing, 'Well thank you again, sir'.

'A fast tracker without having been on a fast track,' said Hargreaves. 'One of the best clean up rates of any officer in the city.'

'Well, I'm proud of that, sir, of course I am,' said Sara, 'but now I'm just looking forward to getting on with the new job'.

'Good,' said Hargreaves, 'but first I want to introduce you to your new DI who'll be your second in command. His name is Tim Norris. Do you know him?'

Sara counted on all her powers of resilience to stop the mention of Tim's name from causing the walls of her world to cave in on her.

Paul Foster was manager of the Salford community services centre in the Broughton area of the city. He'd been asked to manage it by the leader of the city council because he was known for setting his own rules and using his imagination to solve problems instead of relying on a book of regulations. The centre was unique because it brought together under one roof all aspects of social services along with an NHS dentists practice, a GP surgery and mini treatment centre, a group of counsellors and therapists, a branch of the Citizens Advice Bureau and a firm of solicitors that handled legal aid work. Paul also led the team of social workers based there. There were the usual internal political tensions like there always was when you try and get different empires together for the benefit of the greater good, but Paul could handle that and indeed, loved the challenge of it. If his instinctive decision-making got under the noses of his more empire protecting colleagues then his instincts told him he was doing the right thing.

He was on his way to a call on the Tatton estate. Formerly owned by the council but now owned and managed by a not-for-profit housing association, it had been built in the 1960's and was a grey labyrinth of high rise blocks of flats, maisonettes and so-called family homes. He knew the estate like the back of his hand. It was his patch and there were a minefield of problems on it but Paul was a revolutionary who would never accept that nothing could ever change for the better. He was known as being tough. He took issue with many of the residents who saw it as their right to have a flat screen TV but not their responsibility to get their kids to school. They'd been indulged by too many in his profession. He'd once overheard a colleague telling a parent how 'impressed' she was with her for getting her child to school every day for a week. That was the trouble with some of his colleagues. They let people off too easily. Getting your child to school every day should be normal and not worthy of comment.

He rang the doorbell of No.6 Kendal Way. Lorraine Cowley opened the door. She'd been expecting him.

'You'd better come in,' said Lorraine.

Inside there was stuff all over the place, some of it recognisable as nappies and baby clothes, some of it a complete mystery, all of it scattered with no apparent reason or order. Stomping through it all was Lorraine on her wafer thin flip flops. Her black shorts were tighter than tight and her stomach hung over them like a slab of meat on a tray that wasn't big enough for it. The hem of her white t-shirt was dangling way in front of her distorted frame and her neck had disappeared into a sort of area that connected her chin to her chest. She was a couple of years younger than Paul but she looked far older and she was already a grandmother twice over. Her greasy hair was scraped back in a savage ponytail making her face look even fatter. She'd never gone out to work. Instead she'd had three children by different fathers all of whom the state paid for just like it now paid for her children's offspring.

Paul followed her through to the kitchen where one of her teenage daughters was sat, or rather slumped, at the table, chin resting on hands supported by elbows bent on the table. She was smoking and sipping from a mug of what Paul took to be coffee and she looked completely disinterested in life. She was watching her toddler daughter run naked around the small space with a dummy in her mouth and a bag of crisps in her hand. The toddler looked at Paul and smiled. He winked at her and she giggled the way little people of her age do. He bent down to her.

'Hello, Candice,' he said, warmly, 'do you remember me?'

'And you are?' her mother asked.

Paul asked as he straightened himself up and turned

round. 'I'm Paul' he said. He held out his hand but Anita didn't respond. 'I work at the social services centre up at Broughton. We have met before. You're Anita, aren't you?'

'Yeah, and I do remember you. You tried to get me to have my baby adopted.'

'I said it was one of your choices.'

'And I said that half the girls in my street had got babies and I wanted one too.'

'You're nearly seventeen, aren't you Anita?'

'So?'

'So if you could find yourself a job you could make use of the nursery we've got at the centre.'

'Oh no she couldn't!' Lorraine insisted, 'she's staying here to look after Candice.'

'Why?'

'Because it's her right!'

'Sorry Lorraine but since when did it become the right of those not in work to have children that they expect those in work to pay for? Did that pass me by or what?'

'It's just another attack on the poor and helpless.'

'You may be poor, Lorraine,' said Paul, 'and there may be all kinds of reasons for that. But you're not helpless. Now, how's your Michaela getting on?'

'Alright, although it's no thanks to you.'

'Lorraine, she's fifteen, she needed to get back to school.'

'She needs to be here looking after her baby!' Lorraine insisted, 'instead of which you made her go back to waste more of her time listening to useless teachers'.

'They're not useless, Lorraine, they're dedicated to helping your kids'.

'Rubbish!'

'Where is the baby by the way?' asked Paul.

'Upstairs asleep,' said Lorraine, 'and our Michaela has got nothing to do with you, whether she goes to school or not.'

'I'm afraid she has,' said Paul, 'she's a minor, she's underage, and she has everything to do with me.'

'You threatened me with jail unless I made her go back to school.'

'And I'd do it again for the sake of Michaela,' said Paul, 'but we've also got another matter to discuss.'

Lorraine had made a complaint against her GP who was a colleague and friend of Paul's in the community services centre. She said that Dr. Fergus Keene had refused to proscribe drugs to her eight-year-old son Sam who she claimed had A.D.D. Dr. Keene, on the other hand, had told her that her son was not suffering from A.D.D and therefore did not need the drugs. Lorraine had kept Sam off school that day and Paul went through to the lounge to talk to him.

'He needs something to calm him down,' Lorraine insisted between drags on her cigarette. Since Paul had arrived she'd never had one out of her fingers just like she'd never put down her mug of the hot brown liquid she called coffee.

'And why do you say that, Lorraine?' Paul asked.

'Well you can see,' she said, 'he's all over the bloody shop.'

What Paul could see was a little eight-year-old boy called Sam who was very easy to engage with once someone took an interest in him. He spent half an hour talking with Sam, asking him about school and what he liked to do there. Sam told him that books and reading were his favourite things and that had opened up a conversation about Harry Potter. Sam said he was halfway through the fifth book which didn't surprise Paul considering all his school reports stated that his reading ability was a good three years ahead of his age. Sam was able to give him a full resume of all the leading Hogwarts characters. Paul thanked God for JK Rowling. Her books had gone way beyond the simple limits of entertainment. They were reaching into the minds of boys like Sam and taking him light years away from the gloom of his reality.

'It's no good him reading if he can't behave,' said Lorraine who didn't seem too impressed by her son's knowledge of the world of the boy wizard. She hadn't said anything whilst Paul and Sam were talking. She'd just looked round and glared a few times.

'Lorraine, what can we do for your son without resorting to drugs?'

'Drugs are what he needs to calm him down!' Lorraine insisted, 'My nerves are shot to pieces because of his antics.'

'You want us to drug him into not being a bother to you? Is that what this is all about, Lorraine? What kind of country do you think you're living in? When are you going to take proper responsibility as a parent?'

'My girls have never been any trouble to me, not even for one single second! But him...' she stabbed her finger in the air in her son's direction '... he's been a pain since the minute he was born!'

'So both your daughters having babies when they were underage isn't a problem but your son showing an interest in getting educated is?'

'If you put it like that.'

Useless bitch, thought Paul. Lorraine's daughters were turning into extensions of herself whilst her son clearly had the potential to be something different and that's what

Lorraine couldn't cope with. So she had to demonise him, isolating him within the family and pushing his behaviour into proving her point. It wasn't the first time Paul had seen this kind of abuse. Kids on estates like the Tatton aren't allowed to be bright. There was too much peer pressure to hold them back.

'Dr. Keene says that Sam doesn't need drugs,' said Paul.

'But what about my human rights?'

'What?'

'Well him getting the drugs is about me getting my human rights.'

Paul could've read the riot act with her on that one but knew it would be no good. People like Lorraine attached herself to the idea of human rights like a heat seeking missile but she had no idea what it was really all about. It was just the latest avoidance of responsibility excuse and it made his blood boil.

'This is not about you or your human rights, Lorraine.'

'Well what is it about then?'

'It's about your son.'

'My pain in the bloody arse, you mean.'

Paul took a deep breath, 'Look, don't you ever talk to Sam?'

Lorraine screwed up her face, 'Talk to him? What do you mean?'

Give me strength, thought Paul, 'I mean talk instead of shouting, yelling and chastising? Do you never just sit down and talk to him? Do you ever show any delight in something he's done? He's been fine whilst I've been here talking to him and more importantly, listening to him. He's calm and he's happy.'

'He is when he's got his head in some stupid book.'

'You should be proud of his reading ability, Lorraine. Have you read his school reports?'

'I've got better stuff to do with my time.'

'Well if you did you'd see that his reading ability is about three years ahead of his age. Aren't you proud of that?'

She shrugged, 'No, means nothing to me, to be honest.'

'Don't you even take an interest in what he's reading?'

'No.'

'So you don't even know if what he's reading might be inappropriate for an eight-year old?'

'Look, what is it you're saying exactly because you are so doing my head in. I asked you here to help me and my family.'

'I am trying to help you Lorraine, if you'd only see it.'

'You could've fooled me.'

Paul knew he was heading down the road to trouble with this one but he didn't care. Lorraine was holding her family back. She hadn't achieved anything in life and she didn't want them to either. It was classic. He'd seen it so many times.

'I don't think Sam is the problem, Lorraine.'

'So what, you're saying I am?'

'He's a bright lad, Lorraine and he'll make something of himself if you, his mother, encourage him.'

'Make something of himself?' she scoffed, putting down her mug on the carpet by her feet and pointing her finger again. 'I'll tell you this now, I'm not having him getting fancy ideas. You're just wasting my bloody time coming in here and telling me to sit down and talk to him. Well I tell you, I'll go to any bloody doctor until I get them drugs!'

'Lorraine, he doesn't need drugs. I'm going to put you down for parenting skills classes.'

'What?'

'I think you'll get a lot out of it and that'll make Sam happier,' said Paul. 'We all need help from time to time. The classes will be at the centre and you attend the first three on your own then the rest together with Sam.'

'Do I get any extra benefit for going?'

Paul was exasperated. 'No, Lorraine, you don't. You just get to be a better mother to your son.' He noticed that Sam looked like he was about to start crying. 'What's wrong, Sam? What's up, mate?'

'I told you,' said Lorraine, 'he's a flaming nuisance!'

'He is if that's what you want to make him, Lorraine, but a change of attitude from you could make it all so different,' said Paul who then turned back to Sam. 'I'm going to see your head teacher, Sam. I want to see if she can organise some extra reading classes for you because I know that makes you happy, doesn't it?'

Sam nodded, 'So you'll come back and see me?'

'Of course I will. We're mates now.'

Lorraine still hadn't said anything.

'Lorraine? What are you thinking?'

'I'm thinking that if I'd wanted Jeremy Kyle, I'd have gone on the bloody telly!'

CHAPTER TWO

LADY ELEANOR HARDING knew that her time on this earth was running out. She'd already done well to last as long as she had given the excessive lifestyle she'd spent years enjoying. She'd just turned ninety and the will was still as strong even though the body yelled out at her to be more sensible. She still held her parties, although she tended to sit them out these days and watch everyone else having a good time with all the merchandise she'd provided. She still drew up the guest list. Charles and Camilla came up regularly for shooting parties and they always brought an entourage with them each time. Charles was so fortunate to be with his paramour at last after that other stupid slip of a girl had tried to disrupt their obvious happiness with something as ridiculous as love. How fortunate it was for all concerned that her interference in the royal tradition of duty had been curtailed in a Paris tunnel.

'Dinner will be in an hour, your ladyship.'

Colin Bradley, her head of household staff, popped his head round the door and left again after making his announcement. She liked Bradley. He'd been with her for years and he was a good sort; obedient, loyal and she could tell him any old bollocks and he swallowed it whole like a whore desperate for cash. Except that lately he'd been getting rather moody. Ever since she'd told him he couldn't have a pay rise he'd been acting like he'd just failed his exams. Oh, he'd get over it. Even without a pay rise he knew how much his bread was buttered working for her and at least he wasn't one of the homosexuals. She had no objection to that sort in principle but these days they demanded to be treated as equal which she found exceptionally disturbing. Even her own late husband Ronald, a rampant homosexual who'd paid off more blackmailing threats than he could keep a count of, even he would never have approved of such open defiance of the acceptable order that's everywhere today.

She picked up her copy of the Manchester Evening News that Bradley had left for her on the small table beside her chair. She gasped as she read the front page article. Poor Dieter was in trouble. His house in Glossop had been besieged by vultures from the press. The poor man wasn't even able to open his front door and all because some stupid Polish bitch who should've kept her mouth shut had decided to use these modern times to exact her revenge. How dare she do such a thing! Couldn't she have left the past where it should be? Eleanor felt the tears begin to moisten her cheeks. It was typical of Dieter that he hadn't called her to ask for help. He'd always been too proud. Well she was going to help him. He wasn't going to face this on his own.

She called Dieter on the phone and then she pressed her call button on the small console set she carried with her at all times. Bradley appeared moments later wearing his best appeasing smile. She gave him his instructions, said she'd already spoken to Dr. Edwards who'd given her directions to a narrow road behind his house where he would wait for Colin. She told him to go straight away.

'Eleanor!' called Dieter a couple of hours later as he was led down the hall by Colin who then made his escape. Watching these two coffin dodgers act like Mills and fucking Boon was just too sickening for words.

'Dieter! Forgive me for the clandestine nature of my provision of sanctuary but there seemed to be no other way of rescuing you from the reality of being Gerald Edwards.'

'My dear lady, I left Gerald Edwards behind in Glossop. To be called Dieter again and never have to go back to Gerald Edwards … well God in Himmel it feels so good!'

They embraced and held on tightly to each other. Although they'd been lovers for seventy years they hadn't lived together since the end of the war. Despite the reality of their marriages to other people, they'd met up once a month all the way through the decades to celebrate their spiritual and romantic union. Dieter was no stranger in her house. But now as she looked at him her heart skipped like it had done on that day back in 1940 when she'd first met him. He was the love of her life and she was overwhelmed that now they could enjoy a proper reunion.

'I can't let you go to prison, Dieter,' said Eleanor, 'that would be too awful to even contemplate especially as it would all be because of that vile Pole. You must stay here until the dust settles and you become yesterday's news.'

Dieter held Eleanor's hands, 'It will be like the old days.'

Eleanor smiled the way a woman does when she's looking into the eyes of her one true love, 'It most certainly will.'

'My dear lady, I shall never be able to repay you. My children, they… well they have disowned me. They wondered why this… this woman was so insistent. They're professional people. They're not stupid. I couldn't lie to them anymore'.

'Do they know you're here?'

'Yes. And I'm afraid that made it worse.'

Eleanor caressed Dieter's face with her hand. 'Oh my poor, poor Dieter. We shall explain everything to them once this is all over. You're their father. They'll understand in time.'

'They've always believed that their mother was my only true love.'

'It will be hard for them to take, but then again, the truth often is.'

Dieter stroked the side of her face. 'I can't believe I'm back here with you after all these years. I knew that our love would draw the circle one day.'

'These are dark circumstances that have brought us back together but I'm glad nevertheless. But losing you twice in one lifetime…' her voice faltered as she fought back the tears. He always did have such a gentle touch, '… well that would be the end of me'.

'And we can't have that. I am here now and we shall never be parted again'.

Paul Foster picked his parents up from the bungalow at South Shore in Blackpool that they'd retired to five years earlier. As he drove them up the promenade he was amazed that some owners still advertise their 'select' holiday flats. What was that all about? Did people have to sit an exam before staying there or something? Then there were the hotels offering their 'world famous English breakfasts.' World famous English breakfasts? He shook his head and smiled.

'We've had many a happy holiday in this town,' said Paul's father, Ed, sat alongside him at the front, 'don't you remember, our Paul?'

Paul's memories of his childhood family holidays in Blackpool weren't as happy as his father thought they were but he'd never told his father about it and now he never would.

'Yeah, Dad,' said Paul, smiling. 'They were good times.' He looked in the rear view mirror at his mother who was sitting on the back seat. She said nothing.

They carried on up the Fylde coast along Blackpool's North Shore and by the time they got up to the town of Fleetwood at the top end of the coastal peninsula, the sky had completely cleared and the sun was high. Paul parked in one of the nose-in spaces on the esplanade from where they could see right across the vast open space of Morecambe Bay to Barrow, on the edge of Cumbria, fifty miles or so to the northwest.

'You'll still need the blanket over your legs despite the sun, Dad,' said Paul, 'there's quite a breeze blowing out there.'

'There always is up here,' said Ed.

Paul took his Dad's wheelchair out of the boot and set it up for him. He then helped him out of the passenger seat of his car. His father's face contorted with pain as the cancer inside him fought against his every move and Paul was careful to take his time, holding his father still for a second or two to give him a breather when the pain seemed to overwhelm him. He got him into his wheelchair and carefully folded the blanket over his legs, making sure his feet were resting on the footplates. His father squeezed his hand in appreciation.

'We're all set then,' said Paul, 'shall we eat first or go for a walk?'

'Let's eat,' said Ed, 'I'm a bit peckish to tell you the truth.'

'Well it's a treat to hear you say that these days, Dad, so eating first it is.'

Paul's mother stood there with a face like a wet weekend and Paul knew that she'd only get worse as the day went on, especially after she'd had a couple of glasses of wine. He wished she'd stayed at home.

There were several little cafes offering the kind of lunch they'd come up for but Paul knew his Dad liked to go into the big hotel that dominated the esplanade on the corner where the tramway to Blackpool turned towards the port. The hotel had once been the terminus for trains that would bring passengers up from London on their way to Scotland. The early days of the railways had lacked the kind of engineering that could excavate the necessary tunnels through the Lake District and so the passengers were transferred to boats to take them across the bay where they'd pick up another train to take them on to their Scottish destination.

A container ship was loading up in the port that wasn't enormous but it was big enough to dominate the narrow stretch of water between Fleetwood and Knott End-on-Sea on the other side of the estuary. When he was a child, Paul had wanted to escape to Knott End on the little boat that crossed over the estuary to it, but when he got older he dreamed instead of running onto one of the ships and becoming a stowaway. He thought the high seas would offer him sanctuary from his mother's hand, her fist, her fingernails breaking his skin and drawing blood, her teeth biting into him like a dog attacking an intruder. But then he learned that the ships only went as far as the Isle of Man or Northern Ireland and neither of those two places seemed far enough away.

At the front of the ground floor of the hotel was a long bar that served food. Paul wheeled his Dad in and found a table halfway down. He went up to the bar and ordered three lots of fish, chips, and mushy peas, and three glasses of the house white. When they'd finished their food they were ready for more drinks. Paul went back to the bar and ordered two more glasses of wine for his parents and an orange juice for himself.

'What are you doing with that stuff?' his mother wanted to know.

'Drinking it, Mum.'

'Well why haven't you had a glass of wine like me and your Dad?'

'Because I'm driving, Mum, and one is enough.'

'Ponce,' she snarled and then turned back to the couple at the next table with whom she'd been talking.

'Mary,' said Ed, wearily, 'please, not today.'

Paul started talking to his Dad about the football. His Dad was an avid, lifelong Liverpool supporter but the team hadn't been doing consistently well this season and his Dad blamed it on the way football seemed to be less about the game these days and more about a celebrity circus for the footballers and their high spending girlfriends.

'I think you're right, Dad,' said Paul.

'Your Uncle Doug will be over on Saturday to watch the game against Middlesbrough with me.'

'Middlesbrough are a striker down aren't they?'

'Yeah, so in principle it should be a breeze for Liverpool.'

Mary turned from the conversation she'd been having

with the couple at the next table and snarled once more at Paul. 'why the hell are you talking about football?'

Paul took a deep breath. Would she ever stop? 'Because I like football, Mum. You know that.'

Mary laughed sardonically, 'You like footballers more like!' She turned back to her new friends and pointed her thumb at Paul, 'he's a shirt- lifter.'

'Mary!' Ed warned.

'What? Is he ashamed of himself? He bloody well should be.'

'No, I am not ashamed of myself, Mum, though I know that disappoints you.'

'He's got some boyfriend in the Army you know,' said Mary, turning back to her new friends who were now looking very uncomfortable, 'he's out in Afghanistan and hasn't been heard of for weeks on end. But they're not going to bother about bringing some bent piece home in a body bag, are they? I mean, it stands to reason. The Army's no place for that sort and the public aren't going to waste any sympathy.'

'Mary, that is enough!'

'It's alright, Dad,' said Paul who didn't want his Dad getting upset, 'it's alright.'

It wasn't alright. It wasn't alright at all. Paul was going out of his mind with worry about Jake who was a Lance Corporal on tour with his unit in Southern Afghanistan. The last time Jake had rung Paul, almost four months ago, he'd told him he wouldn't be able to ring him for a while and that he'd just have to be patient. But Paul had gone way past the stage of being patient. The worry was like a living hell. He and Jake had been seeing each other for four years and he ached for news that Jake was okay. Almost every night he had nightmares about what might have happened to him, what some evil thugs could be doing to him if they'd got hold of him. He'd been on missions before, but had never been out of contact for anything like this length of time. Paul couldn't ring anyone, not the Army, not the MoD, because Jake wasn't 'out' to his comrades. He wasn't out to his family either and they knew nothing about his relationship with Paul.

'You've heard nothing from Jake then, son?' asked his father. He'd met Jake several times and liked the bloke. He thought he must be in the thick of it now though judging by what was on the news every night, 'I forgot to ask before, I'm sorry.'

'It's okay, Dad, I understand and no, I've heard nothing.'

Paul swallowed hard. He wanted to burst into tears but that would give too much ammunition to his mother so he'd save that for when he got home later.

'Thirty-five years old and still living in a two-up, two-down house because he insists on staying in a job where he helps all the scum and the dregs of society,' his mother scorned, 'how bloody pathetic is that?'

'It's not pathetic, Mum,' said Paul who could hold his own against her but was sick of having to do so. He felt like he'd been doing it all his life, 'and they're not the dregs of society.'

'Of course it's all so different with our daughter Denise,' Mary boasted, 'she lives in a beautiful big house down in Berkshire. Oh yes, her husband, my son-in-law George, he's got a top job in the city. They have a very good life.'

'And Denise has only been to see Dad once since he got ill and that was only for a couple of hours one afternoon, during which she watched the clock the whole time.'

'Shut your stupid mouth!' his mother scolded.

Paul closed his eyes to quell his anger. When he opened them he saw that his father had fallen asleep but still he lowered his voice as he turned to his mother.

'Mum, when was the last time your darling daughter even rang up to see how her father was?'

'She's very busy,' said Mary, quietly.

'Yes of course she is, Mum. She's got nails to paint and magazines to read. Of course she's far too busy to spend time with her dying father.'

'George has a very important job and they can't just drop everything to come all the way up here,' said Mary, 'you're talking out of the back of your head as usual.'

'I don't deserve the crap I take from you, Mum' said Paul, his emotions hardening to her. 'I make a hundred mile roundtrip three times a week to see to Dad and to give you some support, and I do it gladly, but all you do is kick it straight back in my face and yet our Denise who never calls you and never comes anywhere near gets put on a bloody pedestal.'

'Don't you dare bad mouth your sister!' she warned.

'And what will you do if I carry on, Mum? Are we going to go back to the old days? Are you going to make me go without my tea and tell Dad when he gets home from work that I've already eaten? I lost count of the nights I went to bed hungry because of your cruelty. Are you going to pour boiling water over my hand until the skin starts to peel off and then tell Dad how clumsy I am? Are you going to lock me in the cupboard under the stairs for hours on end knowing how claustrophobic I get? Are you going to beat the shit out of me but only on my body so that Dad won't see? Do you remember what you always used to say to me? You used to say that if I told Dad I'd get it all ten times worse the next day. I will never forget any of it for as long as I live.'

'I did it for your own good.'

'Oh yes that's it,' said Paul, shaking his head in absolute disgust, 'the standard excuse used by parents who assault their children.'

'You were always far too sensitive,' she sneered, 'I needed to toughen you up.'

'Oh there goes another of the stock excuses. Keep on going down the list, Mum, I'm all ears. I'd hate to live in your world. It must be a very twisted place.'

'You don't know the half of it.'

'Really? Well what I can't work out is what made you hate me so much? What could I have done? I was only a child for God's sake and you never did any of it to our Denise. That's what hurts me more than the abuse itself. You singled me out and you still do and our Denise stood by laughing just like she does now.'

Sara Hoyland and Tim Norris had once been part of the same social gang, a group of about twenty who'd all hung out together before life had moved most of them into the settling down stage. Everybody had always expected Sara and Tim to get together as more than friends one day but then Tim met a nurse called Helen whom everybody acknowledged was gorgeous and lovely and beautiful and 'so right' for Tim. It had mightily pissed Sara off at the time that they all seemed to forget the feelings she had for Tim. Then, when fate gave her a reason never to forget what the rest of them seemed to have discarded, she distanced herself from them and now had a whole new set of friends. Tim had married Helen and by all accounts they were very happy. She was pleased for them. She just didn't want her nose rubbed in it.

'It is good to see you again, Sara,' said Tim as they sat in her office. He meant it even though he knew that this could cause complications. But there was a certain comfort in seeing Sara again after all these years. The sudden nature of their parting all those years ago had left things rather untidy. Maybe they could be given a second chance at least at the friendship side of what they'd shared before, although he did want to know why she'd suddenly slipped out of his life. The fact that they'd slept together after being such close mates for all those years had been a mistake that they'd both acknowledged at the time.

'Sounds like you've been having to think about that and convince yourself.'

'Don't be like that,' said Tim, 'I didn't walk away from you. It was the other way round.'

'How's Helen?'

So, thought Tim. That's the way it's going to be. Any talk of the past and the conversation is closed down.

'She's well, thanks.'

'You must've been married ... what, five years now?'

'Five years next month.'

'Is she still nursing?'

'Yes but she's part-time now,' said Tim. 'We're trying for a family'.

'Right,' said Sara who really hadn't wanted to hear that, 'I see.'

'And you?'

'Me what?'

'Are you with anyone?'

'No' said Sara.

'Serious?'

'Why would I lie to you?' said Sara, defensively.

'Oh I didn't mean that, I just … I just thought you'd have met someone.'

'I don't need anyone to take care of me, Tim.'

'No, of course you don't,' said Tim, 'I didn't mean it that way. Look, Sara, is this going to be a problem for us? You and I working together?'

'It's a bit early days to be thinking about potential problems, isn't it?' said Sara.

'I was also thinking about the squad.'

'I'm not saying that seeing you again isn't a little unsettling,' said Sara, 'It's certainly not what I need when I'm starting a new job. But that's the situation and we're going to have to get on with it.'

'Isn't that a little … cold?'

'Look, Tim, we were friends for years and then one night we gave in to all those feelings we'd been trying to ignore. Then you told me the next morning it had all been a big mistake, that it was one of those things that two people who are close friends should never do'.

'I thought we'd both agreed that it had been a mistake?'

'Your recollection is different to mine,' said Sara, 'you just assumed that I agreed with you and I was too devastated by your attitude to argue with you. Then after you'd met Helen there didn't seem much point in me hoping anymore.'

'Hoping?'

'That you'd have a change of heart,' said Sara, 'all of our mutual friends embraced Helen with open arms and I felt like they'd all stabbed me in the back. They just seemed to ignore the fact I'd had feelings for you all those years. Because of Helen I lost you and all my friends in one foul swoop.'

Tim rubbed his hand across his face, 'I didn't realise you felt that way.'

'I don't believe that, Tim,' said Sara, 'you couldn't have been that blind.'

'Sara, I'm sorry.'

'And I was pregnant.'

Tim felt like his heart stopped for a second. 'You were what?'

'I was pregnant with your child,' said Sara who despite the tremor she could hear in her voice was feeling remarkably good about finally getting things off her chest.

'What did you do?'

'I had him adopted.'

Tim was reeling. He hadn't counted on a knife being taken to his past when he turned up for work this morning.

'You had our child adopted without even telling me about him?'

Sara could've slapped his face, 'don't start playing the 'our child' card, Tim, please. I couldn't take that.'

'Sara, if I'd known …'

'…What? If you'd known I was pregnant? You'd have dumped Helen and married me? No way would I have been second best just because I was carrying your child.'

'It wouldn't have been like that.'

'Yes it would!' She hissed.

The aggravation was getting to Tim. 'You should've told me!'

'No I shouldn't,' said Sara, 'you were head over heels in love with Helen and I didn't want to bring up a child on my own. But I can tell you this, there isn't a day goes by without me thinking about my baby. I see little boys of the age he'd be now and sometimes it's like a dagger through my heart. So don't you dare lecture me, Tim. Don't you dare lecture me.'

'Oh I'm not going to lecture you,' said Tim, unconvinced by Sara's emotional entreaty, 'I just want you to give me a reason not to hate you for denying me my right to be my son's father.'

'I can't do that, Tim,' said Sara who was struggling to hold her ground in the face of Tim's obvious fury, 'but perhaps this is an appropriate time to remind you that I'm your superior officer.'

'Oh don't try and pull that one,' Tim sneered.

'You've got two choices, Tim,' said Sara, hardening to her task, 'I hope for your sake you choose the right one.'

'That sounds like a bloody threat to me!'

'That's because it is,' said Sara, 'I won't allow you to bring our personal history into what we have to do professionally.'

Tim angrily retorted, 'Well, when you're holding my balls in your claws I've got no choice.'

'That's right, Tim,' said Sara, 'You've got no choice.'

CHAPTER THREE

'SO WHAT IS THIS Obama person doing as President?' said Dieter as he and Eleanor enjoyed a drink before lunch. 'Only working for the coloured people?'

'A negro as President of the free world,' said Eleanor with her face contorted as if she'd just been shocked by a bad smell, 'it's just too awful to even contemplate.'

'But it's real, liebling,' said Dieter, 'far too real for either of our likings.'

'We need another Hitler to come and sort out these Muslims just like he so bravely tried to sort out the Jewish problem.'

'But he paid such a heavy price for it,' said Dieter, 'so did my poor friends in the east of Germany who had to live under Soviet tyranny for all those long, painful years. The wrong side won the war, Eleanor. You know I've always believed that and I always will. We're all now the victims of communist, liberal teachings. Hitler would never have allowed the Muslims to have their say on anything. They'd have been silenced good and proper.'

It so amused Eleanor when Dieter's accent fell between the clipped German tones he could reveal in front of her and the relaxed Derbyshire drawl of his adopted life. He'd be a challenge for any impressionist.

'What are you smiling at, my love?' Dieter asked.

'I'm smiling at you Dieter,' said Eleanor, her hand wrapped in his. 'You've brought the joy back into my heart and at our time of life that's quite something.'

Dieter kissed her hand. 'It most certainly is.'

'I've had Bradley prepare your favourite meal,' she told him excitedly. 'Roast knuckle of pork with mashed potatoes.'

'Ah that will take me back to my childhood in Munchen,' said Dieter, wistfully. He hadn't been back to Germany since his excursion to England at the beginning of World War Two. He had brothers, sisters, but he'd never attended any family funerals, christenings, or weddings. The deal he'd come to negotiate, brokered by Eleanor, had never been concluded and his family had all been told that he'd perished in an English gaol. He did sometimes wonder if any of his brothers or sisters were still alive. 'I expect it's changed somewhat since I was last there a lifetime ago.'

'Just like everywhere else,' said Eleanor, 'have you heard from your children?'

'They've both called, yes,' said Dieter, feeling more than just a twinge of guilt at what he'd done to his family. 'So has my youngest grandson Nicholas. He's eleven and we're especially close. I miss them all terribly. Dearest Eleanor, even though they won't see me, I can't stay away from them for very long. I have to try and explain to them. I can't just leave it like this.'

It hurt Eleanor to hear Dieter speak those words. She could never claim to have had any kind of maternal instinct when it came to her daughter Clarissa but that didn't mean that she'd been happy with the way things had turned out. But Dieter was different. He adored his family and they'd clearly felt the same before all this business had blown up. That meant that he was way ahead of her.

'Just give it a few days,' said Eleanor, 'you're still all over the news.'

'I still can't quite believe that this is all happening,' said Dieter. 'I just can't believe it.'

'You don't regret it bringing us back together?'

'Of course not my darling Eleanor,' said Dieter who kissed her hand again. 'You know that. But to try and extradite me after all this time?'

'We have to put our faith in God, Dieter.'

'It's all we can do.'

'Every time we celebrate the Mass'

'Eleanor, I haven't missed one Sunday celebrating the Mass in the seventy years I've been in England,' said Dieter. 'But what am I going to do whilst I'm here?'

'There's a local priest I know who needs funds for a new church roof,' said Eleanor. 'He'll help bring you closer to God whilst you're here.'

'Are you sure, Eleanor? Nowadays the rules are very different from when Father Heaney used to come here every Sunday during the war.'

'My darling Dieter,' said Eleanor, 'whether it's nineteen forty-one or twenty eleven, money still talks louder than any human voice.'

The last thing Sara had wanted was to start a new job in the kind of atmosphere that now existed between her and Tim. She hoped that it would pass and that Tim, being a grown man and a highly professional police officer, would have the emotional resilience to come to terms with what she'd been carrying around for the last five years. She knew she'd hurt him very badly and she couldn't help that now but in the meantime there were other members of the squad who she had to get to know and build relationships with and detective sergeant Joe Alexander was one of them.

When they got to Gatley Hall, Sara wound down her

window and spoke to the security guard who was at his post in the small cabin outside the front gates.

'I'm Detective Chief Inspector Hoyland and this is Detective Sergeant Alexander, Greater Manchester Police serious crime squad,' said Sara as they both held up their warrant cards for the CCTV camera perched just above them. 'We're here to see Dieter Naumann. Could you let us in, please?'

There was a gap of almost a minute before the gates were opened and they were able to proceed.

'Take your time, mate,' said Sara before driving them through and beginning the mile-long drive down the tree-lined road that led to the 200 room grand house itself.

'I'll bet you never thought that your first case would be the requested extradition of an alleged Nazi war criminal, ma'am?' said Joe who initially was quite impressed with the new DCI. She was one of the few high ranking female officers who didn't behave as if she had strapped a dick to herself every morning before coming to work. Neither was she an ice Queen. She seemed human. She had warmth and a sense of humour. Joe had taken to her instantly.

'I must admit, Joe, I didn't,' said Sara. 'But as far as I'm concerned, however old these people are, they should be brought to justice even if they have to be helped into the dock on a zimmer frame.'

'My sentiments exactly, ma'am,' said Joe.

'And listen, when there's nobody else around, call me Sara.'

'Okay, Sara,' said Joe, 'thanks.'

'How long have been in the squad, Joe?' asked Sara who had a good feeling about Joe. He seemed genuine and without an agenda of some kind. That was refreshing in officers at his level.

'About eighteen months,' said Joe, 'Sara.'

'You didn't go for promotion?'

'I don't think I'm ready yet, Sara. I like to know my current job inside out before I go for another one. Perhaps I shouldn't admit it but I'm not fiercely ambitious.'

'Who is on the squad?'

'Well …'

'… I'm sorry' said Sara, 'I'm putting you on the spot and that's unfair.'

'No,' said Joe, 'I understand why you ask. And I'd say it was Steve Osborne who could be described as that.'

'I'd better watch my back when he's around then.'

'Something like that,' said Joe.

Joe thought that Sara seemed like an intelligent person who didn't make crass judgements about people. But still he felt self-conscious about what she might be thinking about him personally. He existed on a diet of beer and curry. It was one of the reasons why his GP had told him that unless he lost some weight he was in danger of becoming a diabetic. His ideal weight for his height was 75 kilos and he was clocking in at 105 kilos. It pissed him off somewhat. He didn't think he looked that big and besides, he saw many others, including colleagues in the police force, who were bigger than him and had larger overhanging stomachs. That really did piss him off. Were they all being told by their doctor that unless they went on a diet and started a regular routine of exercise then they might end up prematurely dead? So what if he could no longer fasten the trousers of a suit he'd bought two years ago for his cousin's wedding. Did it make him a bad person? The answer was that he wasn't a bad person, far from it, but he was considered to be overweight so that meant he didn't have much luck with the ladies. It made him wonder about the whole issue of equality. If women didn't want to be judged anymore by the way they looked then surely they should pay men the same respect?

But still, he wasn't lonely. He had his mates. Like Ahmed, the young Bangladeshi lad down at the curry shop who now started writing his order down as soon as he saw Joe coming down the street. He went to his parents for lunch every Sunday. One of his sisters was usually there with a husband and kids attached and he was close to all his sisters and his nieces and nephews. He had his weekly copy of the Radio Times that he used to plan his evenings around the telly and spending an hour or two in the pub. He went to bed every night and tried to knock one out before the beer sent him off to sleep. But he did have a regular sex life with the married woman down the street whose husband was in a wheelchair and whose desperation saw past Joe being considered as big. Maureen came round a couple of times a month. It was no great romance. She always stayed for a chat afterwards, sometimes a gin and tonic, before getting dressed and going home. It was just a meeting of needs, even though somewhere deep inside Joe's heart he'd like to make it more.

'My God!' Sara exclaimed when a gap in the trees cleared the view, 'I thought the approach to Chatsworth House was exceptional but this is really something else.'

'It is, Sara, but it does make you wonder though.'

'What?'

'Whether all this should be in the hands of one woman,' said Joe.

Sara smiled. 'Well I didn't realise I was going to be working with Arthur Scargill, Joe.'

Joe laughed. 'Oh I'm no Arthur Scargill, Sara. I voted Liberal Democrat last time.'

'And look where that got you.'

They were ushered into a drawing room so large that Joe remarked he could probably fit his entire house into it. It was decorated in heraldry prints and deep, dark colours that looked like they'd cost a fortune and probably had. No sense of warmth though, Sara noted, just a smell of history and privilege.

Eleanor came into the room with the aid of her walking stick and she shook their hands before gesturing for them to sit down. She looked like a reincarnation of the Queen Mother but even Sara wasn't going to be fooled into believing that she was anything other than a pretty devious old bitch. What other kind of geriatric would harbour a Nazi war criminal?

'Now then officers,' said Eleanor who thought of the two police officers in front of her as being impertinent little bastards. 'I presume you're here about my house guest? Well unfortunately for you I have broken no law in inviting Dieter to stay here and neither has he. He told you immediately that he was here, he didn't try and hide from you and all we both want is for this business to be over and done with.'

'We need to interview Mr. Naumann in connection with the extradition request made by the Polish government,' said Sara. 'Could you tell us where he is, please?'

'He's upstairs taking a nap,' said Eleanor. 'And that's where he'll stay.'

'I think you're getting the balance of this situation a little wrong, Lady Eleanor,' said Sara who'd taken an instant dislike to the witch. 'We ask the questions and you provide plausible answers.'

'You are in my house and you will behave according to my rules,' said Eleanor, sharply.

'Er, no I still don't think you're getting it,' said Sara who could see the look of absolute disgust on Lady Eleanor's face. She wasn't used to being challenged. 'This is a police investigation, Lady Eleanor, and nobody is above compliance with that.'

'Dieter is an old man and what you're doing to him is cruel.'

'And what are we doing to him?' asked Joe.

'Pursuing him in this way,' said Eleanor, 'I don't know what it's going to do to his state of health. You're all fools! There was a war on and people had to do what they could.'

'Are you saying there's some truth in the allegations against Mr. Naumann?' said Joe.

'I'm saying nothing of the kind!' snapped Eleanor. 'I was talking about the fools who are messing up the life of a good person like Dieter.'

'Well if he's that good of a person then why has he been living under another name for more than sixty years?' asked Sara. 'What was he so ashamed of from his past?'

'And why have you given him sanctuary, Lady Eleanor?' asked Joe who was also irritated by this relic of the old world. 'How did you know him? And how did you know his true identity?'

This was where Eleanor wasn't sure of what she should say. She and Dieter had made their agreement with the authorities back in 1945, an agreement that had saved them both from being charged with treason. They were told then that their status would never be in jeopardy but even though Dieter's identity had now been revealed, neither of them had been contacted. Perhaps they needed more time. In any case, the impertinence of these two fools in front of her would soon be seen to have been a waste of time.

Nobody was going to pin anything on her or Dieter.

'Lady Eleanor, a European arrest warrant has been issued by Poland for Dieter Naumann,' said Sara. 'So could you please go and wake up Mr. Naumann and fetch him down here so that we can get on with our business?'

When Paul got home he noticed that the lights next door were on. He was very close to his neighbours Kelly and Lydia, they were his best friends. Kelly was an air stewardess who'd got herself a cushy number flying only the shuttle service between Manchester and Heathrow. Lydia was a charge nurse at Hope hospital just down the road. They'd been together for over ten years and though they had their ups and downs like any couple, they were solid. Kelly had shoulder length black curly hair and the brightest of blue eyes. She'd once been a fashion model in the North West and could've gone nationwide but she'd been thwarted by an industry that was overflowing with gay men but which still didn't seem to like the idea of lesbians. Lydia was of Irish stock, red haired and could be temperamental when pushed. They both had short finger nails which Paul had learned were an essential attribute for a lesbian and more especially, for her girlfriend.

He went round and poked his head round their back door.

'Hello!'

There was nobody in the kitchen and when he went through to the living room there was nobody there either. Then Kelly came downstairs, miles away in thought and was initially startled by Paul's presence.

'Aw, Jesus, you gave me a fright!'

'I came in through the back door.'

'No change there then,' said Kelly, giggling. 'Hello, love.'

They kissed cheek-to-cheek.

'You're smoking,' said Kelly, looking at the cigarette burning between Paul's fingers.

'Oh well, ladies and gentlemen, welcome to Mastermind and here is our first contestant, Miss Kelly Eaton and her specialist subject is stating the bleeding obvious.'

'Why have you started smoking again?' she demanded. 'You were doing so well, Paul.'

Paul rubbed his chin and looked up as if he was searching for inspiration.

'Well now, let's see, my Dad is dying, I don't know what the hell is going on with Jake, and my mother still beats me although with words now instead of her fists.'

'You should try some retail therapy.'

'You know I'm not into that,' said Paul who hated shopping. He only did it when he had something specific to get and even then he was in and out of town before any of his friends had been able to reach for their credit cards. A day of wandering around the Trafford Centre would be like torture to him.

'Oh that's right you're a straight man when it comes to shopping,' Kelly teased.

Paul stuck his tongue out at her. 'Go and get me some wine, lesbian!'

Whilst Kelly was in the kitchen Paul took the opportunity to finish off his cigarette and light another one. It felt good to be smoking again. He didn't care what anybody said, it certainly helped bring his stress level down. Kelly brought the wine and two glasses through. She put everything down on the coffee table and then sat down beside him on the sofa. She poured them both a glass and handed him one.

'So how's your Dad?' Kelly asked.

Paul swallowed hard. 'Every movement causes him so much pain and it breaks my heart. It's gone past the point of them being able to do much about it now. I'm sure he'd be better off in hospital than at home but he just won't hear of going back in. I'm going to miss him, Kelly. I am going to miss him so much.'

'You'll always miss him,' said Kelly, squeezing her friend's hand, 'I know. But we'll be by your side when it happens just like we are now.'

Both Kelly and Lydia had lost their fathers to cancer and it still cut Kelly up sometimes even though it had been a dozen years since it happened.

'Just like you have been all the way through,' said Paul, 'I don't know how I would've got through these last few months without you and Lydia'

'That's what friends are for, love,' said Kelly.

'I just wish I could hear something from Jake,' said Paul, 'all this not knowing is driving me crazy. I see all these reports on the news and I pray to God each night that he isn't caught up in it. Then when they say they've found the body of a soldier it just cuts right through me until they read out the name and it isn't Jake.'

Kelly had mixed feelings about Paul's relationship with Jake. She didn't dislike Jake as such and when he and Paul were together he certainly made Paul very happy. But it wasn't what Kelly would call a relationship and she thought that Paul was selling himself way too short.

'I still say he doesn't respect you the way he should,' said Kelly, repeating what she'd said many times before. 'He keeps you apart from the rest of his life because he hasn't come out to his family and I can just about understand that. But it means that everything is on his terms and that's not fair on you, Paul. And deep down you know I'm right.'

'Finished?'

'You should give him his marching orders when he gets back from Afghanistan.'

'Kelly! How can you even talk like that when God knows what he might be going through out there?'

'I know that, love. I watch the news too and believe it or not, I worry about him too, so does Lydia. It's not that we don't like him, it's just that we don't think he treats you right or gives you what you really need.'

'He might do one day,' said Paul. 'That's why I hold on.'

'Paul, for Christ's sake, he's had enough time and opportunity to commit properly to you but he hasn't.'

Paul went quiet for a few minutes then he freshened up their glasses. The trouble was that Kelly was right, like she tended to be right about everything. But he also knew that it was more complicated than she was making it out to be. He knew Jake better than she did.

'You know that song by Sheryl Crow?' Paul asked. 'My Favourite Mistake? It's about being in love with someone when you know it isn't really right but you just can't bring yourself to break away. That's the song of my relationship with Jake. He's my favourite mistake.'

'Yes and he knows that and he plays on it.'

'Alright, so I'm weak,' said Paul, 'I can't help it where Jake is concerned.'

'Isn't that the truth,' said Kelly who wished Paul could meet someone else who'd take his heart away from Jake. 'Why don't you just ring him, Paul? Why don't you just ring his mobile and find out what's going on? You've every right to.'

'He said he'd get in touch with me when he could,' said Paul. 'That's always been the arrangement when he's away.'

'Ring him, Paul. If he can't answer his phone then he won't have it on so either way, you've got nothing to lose.'

★

Tim Norris was putting on his jacket to go home when Sara came out of her office and walked over to him. He ignored her and carried on to the door.

'Tim, please,' said Sara.

'I'm going home to my wife,' said Tim. 'What are you going home to, Sara? A ready meal you put in a microwave and a vibrator?'

'If things were different that might have been funny.'

'Yeah, well, they're not.'

'Now look, Tim, I'm… '

'…no, you look!' said Tim as he angrily pointed his finger at her. 'If I decided to make trouble for you here then you'd end up being the one getting out first.'

'Oh you think so? And what would you do exactly? '

'Look, no man in the station would be on your side after they'd learned what you'd done. Your position would be undermined because nobody would work with you.'

'All the boys sticking together.'

'And you're saying that all the girls never do that?' Tim snorted.

'You want to make this war?'

'That depends on how you treat me,' said Tim. 'If you so much as try to use your position as my superior officer to score any points I will destroy you, Sara.'

Sara was genuinely shocked by the ferocity of Tim's anger even though it was written all over his face. 'Tim, I don't want things to be like this between us.'

'Yeah, well' said Tim. 'I'm not the one who started all this. You haven't once said sorry for keeping your pregnancy secret or for giving my son away. You've never once wasted any time thinking about how I might feel. You're a beautiful woman, Sara, but your character is that of an ugly, selfish bitch. I will support you as my superior officer but we will never have any kind of personal relationship. I won't even crack a joke with you. Those are my terms and you'll just have to deal with it. You gave me no choice and I'm not giving you any choice either. Don't like a taste of your own medicine? Well that's just tough.'

Tim drove home and wondered how he was going to keep the pain he was feeling from his wife Helen. After Sara had dropped her bombshell he'd sunk further and further into a depth of disappointment he'd never known before. Did she think he wouldn't have stood by her and the baby? It wouldn't have been easy explaining things to Helen but he could've got round it somehow. He'd been out with girls who'd not wanted to know anything about his romantic past but Helen was much more grown-up than that. That's not to say that it would've been easy for her to accept that another woman was having his child but she wouldn't have made him cut Sara and the baby out of his life. She wouldn't have been vindictive against a child. Years ago he'd always thought that he loved Sara but that night they'd slept together made him realise that he didn't love her enough. He loved her but he wasn't in love with her. It just wasn't the same as it was with Helen. Sara was a beautiful girl and any heterosexual man would notice that.

But she wasn't Helen and before he'd met Helen he hadn't known what true love was.

He'd been watching Sara interact with the rest of the squad members all day. She was all feminine guile and persuasion, using her sexuality to get what she wanted out of the male members of the squad. Joe Alexander had been walking round with a smile on his face since he'd gone out to Gatley Hall with her. Sara operated in a very subtle way, not throwing her weight and rank around, but using her interpersonal skills to build the respect of her officers. She saved the sharper side of her character for her personal relationships and Tim now knew that better than anyone.

'Hi!' he called after he'd closed the front door behind him.

'Well hello husband!' gushed Helen with open arms. She still got that wonderful butterfly feeling in her stomach about him coming home, even after five years. Her eyes had met with his that night, and from that moment on she knew there'd never be anybody else.

They kissed and embraced and carried on kissing. Tim loved the feel of her body. She wasn't overly tall but her shape was perfect. He especially loved her large breasts and long curly black hair. She owed that to her Portuguese Mum who her father had met on a golfing holiday in the Algarve back in the seventies. It meant that they had to spend every summer holiday in Portugal but that was no problem for Tim. He could think of worse places and her grandparents and the extended family had really taken him to heart. He'd even learned Portuguese.

'You're being particularly amorous tonight,' she whispered. She could feel his hardness, his devouring of her neck with his kisses and his outstretched hands across her back.

'I just want to show my wife how much I love her.'
'Do you want to go upstairs before dinner, detective?'
'I thought you'd never ask.'

CHAPTER FOUR

PAUL WAS SITTING in his office when he took a call from his friend Colleen Price, the Head of Tatton High school.

'Hi gorgeous!' said Paul. 'Are you still making it hard for other women to look good?'

'Why do I always get my best compliments from gay men?'

'Well with all due respect to your shamelessly handsome husband who gets better looking, the older he gets with his greying hair and bright blue eyes, straight men don't know dick unless they want to get it into your knickers.'

'Howard loves it that you fancy him,' said Colleen, laughing. 'He thinks that being fancied by a gay man makes him really cool. He boasts about it to all and bloody sundry.'

'Well it's nice for him to know that he's got options, Colleen.'

Colleen laughed even louder. 'Enough, you! I need to talk to you about something serious.'

'Oh yeah?'

'Sam Cowley? He's with the school nurse. He came in this morning and his teacher could see there was something wrong so he asked him what that might be.'

'And?'

'He started sobbing uncontrollably and he hasn't really stopped since. We've been trying to talk to him but he says he only wants to talk to the man from the social called

Paul. I assume that's you.'

Paul drove straight down to the school and Colleen took him to the room where Sam was. As soon as he walked in Sam ran to him and held on to him for dear life. He was sobbing his little heart out.

'Hey, mate' said Paul, softly. 'What's up?'

'She's burnt all my books!' he cried.

Paul knelt down and placed his hands on Sam's shoulders. 'Who, mate?'

'Me Mum' said Sam between sobs. 'She made a bonfire in the back garden and threw all my Harry Potter books on it.'

I'll swing for her, thought Paul. I'll fucking swing for the pig ignorant bitch.

'Then she said I can't come anymore to the extra reading classes that Mrs. Price has got for me.'

Paul looked up at Colleen who could see the anger in his eyes. Then he turned back to Sam. 'Sam, I want you to stay here with Mrs. Price whilst I go and see your Mum. Okay?'

'I don't want to go home' Sam pleaded. 'She'll hit me if she finds out I've told anybody.'

'Now you listen to me, Sam. Nobody is going to hit you. Do you understand? I'm going to see to that.'

Paul ran out to his car followed by Colleen.

'Paul' she said 'Don't go in like a bull in a china shop. Take some deep breaths and relax. I can see how worked up you are.'

'Leave this to me, Colleen' said Paul. 'I'll have calmed down by the time I get there but she's not getting away with this.'

Lorraine Cowley opened the door and then left it open for Paul to come in.

'What happened to Sam's Harry Potter books, Lorraine?'

'I burned them,' said Lorraine. Sam would do as she told him and that was that. She wasn't going to have the likes of this stupid Paul bastard dictating to her how to bring up her kids. Reading and books and all that shit was for other families, not hers.

'So you don't deny it?'

'Why should I?'

'Well do you want to tell me why you did such a deliberately hurtful thing to him?'

She pointed her finger at him. 'It was your fault not mine.'

'I beg your pardon?'

'You accused me of not taking enough interest in what he was reading and that whatever he was reading might be … what did you call it? … oh yeah, I know, you called it … inappropriate. So I decided to make sure that if anything was inappropriate he wouldn't be able to read it anymore. I was following your advice. If he's upset then it's down to you.'

'Lorraine, you are not twisting this to absolve yourself of the responsibility.'

'Will you speak fucking English?'

'I am not to blame for you burning Sam's books, Lorraine. You are and nobody else. It was a deliberate act of cruelty on your part and you know it.'

'What gives you the right to come in here and talk to me like that?'

'I'm an employee of the state, Lorraine, and this whole household and everyone in it is funded by the state. That's what gives me the right.'

'Big fucking brother!'

'Only those with something to hide use that argument, Lorraine' said Paul. 'What I'm trying to get through to you here is that education should mean everything to a family like you. Your kids may not have had an equal start but they can have the chance of a future if we all work together on their behalf. Don't you want that for your kids? Don't you want them to be able to stand beside kids from more advantaged backgrounds and hold their own? Lorraine, am I getting through at all? You've got too lazy and complacent, too reliant on people like me to tell you it's not your fault and that all you need are more benefits. That's the case, isn't it, Lorraine? Because that's what it looks like from where I'm standing.'

Lorraine shrugged her shoulders indifferently.

'Lorraine, do you want me to take Sam into care?'

'Might be better all round' said Lorraine. 'I can't cope with him.'

Paul scratched his head. He'd probably get into bother with the head of social services at the council, who'd say he'd been too hasty and too quick to judge, but he didn't care. The Children's Act clearly states that the interests of the child should always be the first consideration. Well he'd applied that principle and concluded that Sam would be better off in a foster home than in his own.

'I'll make all the necessary arrangements with regards to Sam,' said Paul after he'd followed Lorraine into the back garden. There wasn't much in the way of garden there. It seemed to be more about another place to dump stuff. 'Lorraine, Sam made it very clear that he didn't want to come home. Your own eight-year-old son pleaded with me not to make him go home. You're his mother, Lorraine. What do you have to say about that?'

'If you take him into care will I lose the benefits I get

for him?'

The squad had been waiting for information on Dieter Naumann to come through from the Polish authorities before they proceeded. Now that it had come through it was Joe Alexander's job to decipher it. He sat at his desk and read the text on his computer screen.

"Dieter Henrick Naumann was born in Munich in 1918 to an upper class staunchly Roman Catholic family who'd lost everything in the depression following the First World War. His father joined the National Socialists and Dieter joined the Hitler Youth movement when he was 15. Dieter rose quickly through the ranks and became part of the Fuhrer's inner circle just before the outbreak of the Second World War. Despite his young age he showed great courage and promise, so much so that he was promoted into the SS and became part of the invasion force that advanced across Poland in September 1939. Ruthless doesn't come close to describing the way he carried out his duties but it was an incident in the early months of the war that had made him infamous and that had soured relations between Poland and Germany ever since. In a small village just inside the border with Germany, Naumann discovered that nearly a hundred men had formed an underground resistance to the German occupation. He rounded them up and they were hung in the town square whilst their wives and children were made to watch. Their wives were then forced to dig a mass grave and after their husbands bodies had been thrown in, the wives were shot, most of them by Naumann himself with his own pistol firing a bullet into the back of their heads. Their bodies were then piled on top. The children were left to fend for themselves except for the blond, blue-eyed ones who were taken away to Germany, never to be seen again."

Joe felt sick. This was some twisted bastard. Joe briefed Sara and she shared his revulsion. Naumann had been arrested as part of the European arrest warrant process and Lady Eleanor had put up the bail that had been set at one hundred thousand pounds. Naumann had then been released on condition that he surrendered his passport, which was in the name of Gerald Edwards, and that he stayed at Gatley Hall. A case had to be made against him within twenty-eight days for the arrest warrant to remain current. The Polish woman who'd recognised him in the shop that day had been a small child back in 1939 when Naumann had murdered her parents, first her father then her mother, in front of her. She'd been taken in by a cousin but she's never forgotten the face or the eyes of that cold blooded killer.

'Mr. Naumann, why did you come to England back in the 1940's?' asked Sara as she started the interview with Naumann at Gatley Hall. 'We know what you're alleged to have done in Poland but we need to find out what happened after then, that led you to being given a British identity. That was quite a journey after all.'

'Very well,' said Dieter who'd decided with Eleanor to give the police enough of the truth to keep them happy. 'Lady Eleanor Harding was always against the war and in favour of making a deal with Hitler. She was very well connected in the higher echelons of British society including the royal family, and when the opportunity presented itself she persuaded Churchill that she could contact a member of Hitler's inner circle who could negotiate a way out of the war that would save the face of both Britain and Germany. I was that person, I was that opportunity. I was married to Lady Eleanor's sister Ruth and we were in close contact.'

'And what was the proposal?'

'That Britain would leave Germany to do whatever it wanted with the continent of Europe in return for Germany's promise never to touch any part of the British empire. It was quite an audacious yet marvellous and sensible plan dreamed up by Eleanor entirely by herself. You see, detectives, much of the British aristocracy supported the idea because much of their wealth was gained from the empire and they had no desire to go to war for anyone across the Channel. Support for the plan went all the way up to the then Queen herself. It was the one thing she had in common with her brother-in-law Edward and his wife Wallis Simpson but it's a fact that's been, shall we say, airbrushed out of history because such a belief would contradict her status in later years as a faultless Grandmother of the nation.'

'You're saying that the Queen Mother was a Nazi?' asked Sara, astonished at Naumann's assertion. 'They'd have had your head for that a couple of centuries ago.'

'No, I'm not saying she was a Nazi. Not in the sense that I was. But she did support moves to make a pact with Hitler. And if all of continental Europe had now been speaking German whilst this untouched sceptred isle of Britain was still lauding it over her empire, she wouldn't have gone to her grave broken hearted.'

'Well now I'm really intrigued, Mr. Naumann,' said Sara who hadn't learned any of this in history lessons at school. 'Go on.'

'I took my instructions from the Fuhrer and secretly flew over to be the guest of Lady Harding here at Gatley

Hall where negotiations with the British government would be held.'

'And if you'd succeeded then the whole course of the war could've been very different?' said Sara.

'That is correct,' said Dieter, 'I suppose you could even suggest that if we had succeeded then Eleanor and myself might've been eligible for the Nobel peace prize.'

Sara and Joe looked at each other and just had to let that one go without comment. 'So why didn't you succeed, especially if the plan had the backing of the British government?' said Sara.

'The Fuhrer sent the Luftwaffe over the English Channel and the Battle of Britain killed off any chance of a deal.'

'But why did he do that if he'd been serious about Lady Eleanor's plan?' asked Joe.

'Because of my wife, Ruth. Not long after I'd arrived in England she was arrested back in Berlin. I knew then why the Fuhrer had apparently torn up our plan to negotiate with the British government. I'd had no idea that Ruth had been a double agent and neither had her sister Eleanor. It came as a terrible shock to us both but it meant that I was no longer trusted by the Fuhrer.'

'What happened to Ruth?'

'She was executed,' Naumann answered coldly. 'I didn't waste any sympathy on her. She'd betrayed the Reich and made it impossible for me to go home. Because of her I would probably have been arrested and executed too if I'd gone back to Germany. They would not have believed that I didn't know about her treachery. So I persuaded the British authorities to let me stay. It was in their interests too, seeing as I was privy to much secret information. They made a deal with me. I would remain under house arrest at

Gatley Hall until the end of the war and then I would be given a new identity and a chance to start again.'

'And at the end of the war they gave you the new identity of Gerald Edwards?' said Joe.

'Yes,' said Naumann. 'When the end of the war came I completed my medical studies and graduated in 1949. Not long after that I met Joan, the woman who would become my wife and the mother of my children and was able to put the past behind me, at least on the outside. On the inside I never stopped being Dieter Naumann and I never stopped loving Eleanor. Our affair has lasted seventy years.'

'And your wife didn't know?'

'No, she didn't,' said Dieter. 'When my wife died I didn't marry Eleanor for the sake of my children. I wanted to protect them from the reality of my existence.'

'But Lady Harding was a widower too by then,' said Sara. 'Why would your children have needed to know the truth? You could've come together as Lady Harding and Gerald Edwards? Why didn't you do that?'

'My children loved their mother very much,' said Dieter, 'I don't think they'd have accepted someone else in my life.'

'And why didn't Lady Eleanor divorce her husband back in the forties and marry you then?'

'Because Eleanor and Ronald had an arrangement that Ronald insisted that she kept to,' said Naumann. 'He was a homosexual who wanted the cover of marriage. You might imagine that he and I were never the best of friends after that.'

'Do you think you should face justice now for your alleged war crimes, Mr. Naumann?' asked Joe.

'Justice?' scoffed Dieter. 'We were at war. I knew that the present Polish government would have to bow under the pressure they'd be under from various Jewish organisations and their sycophants around the world. But I'm not overly concerned. They can do what they like to me now. I'm too old to care.'

'Nearly a hundred men were hung in that Polish village on a bitterly cold winter's day at the end of 1939,' Joe went on.

'What village might that be?'

'The village that you were in charge of,' Said Sara. 'Your presence there is well documented and will form the basis of any war crimes case against you.'

'There was a war on and I played my part in trying to ensure that Germany would be victorious.'

'So you're admitting to your involvement in the murders?' said Sara.

'I'm admitting to nothing, Detective,' said Dieter, 'and you are not a lawyer. You're merely a law enforcement agent.'

'It became known as one of the most infamous massacres of the entire war,' said Joe.

'Many things happened during the war years that couldn't be explained.'

'Would it not be the honourable thing at this stage in your life, Mr. Naumann, to admit your complicity in the massacre?' said Joe. 'Don't you think you owe it to the dead if not the living?'

Naumann smirked, 'I don't owe anything to anybody. As for these so-called charges, well, just you try and prove it.'

'The men were hung in front of their wives and then you made the women dig a mass grave and when they were done burying their own husbands you killed each and every one of them with a bullet in the back of their heads.'

'I say again, detective,' said Naumann who hadn't flinched or even blinked his eye. 'Just try and prove it. Your accusations are fanciful and irrelevant.'

'Irrelevant?' Joe questioned.

'To the life I've lived in this country for all these years, to the contribution I've made to this country for all these years.'

'And you think that will save you?' said Joe. 'Think again, sir.'

'How would it look in the press?' Dieter demanded angrily. 'Me being such an old man with little left of the strength I once had? If there's one thing you can count on the British for it's their sentimentality about their old folk.'

Sara took a deep breath to try and quell her mounting anger. The old bastard was playing them good and proper.

'Not when it comes to matters relating to the war, Mr. Naumann,' said Sara.

'If you say so, detective.'

'We will be back, Mr. Naumann,' said Joe.

'As you wish,' said Dieter.

'You didn't even tell your children about your past, Mr. Naumann,' said Sara. 'How do you think they feel about you having betrayed them? How do you think they feel about you having betrayed their mother for all those years?'

'Leave my wife out of this!'

'I will,' said Sara. 'Pity you didn't.'

'She never knew anything about any of this!'

'Any of what, Mr. Naumann?'

'You'll wait a very long time before you trap me into admitting anything, Detective, no matter how clever you think you are.'

'I don't think I'll need to, Mr. Naumann,' declared Sara confidently. 'Badly disguised admissions of guilt are flying out of you like bats out of hell.'

'An amusing analogy,' said Naumann, 'but it won't get me into court.'

'We'll see about that,' said Sara. 'In the meantime, don't make yourself too comfortable here. If I've got anything to do with it you won't be staying long. I'm sure the Polish authorities have got a very nice cell waiting for you.'

Naumann was livid. 'You won't get through to me unless I allow you to. I've lived this life for seventy years and someone of your clearly limited capabilities isn't going to make the slightest dent in my armour.'

'Oh well, that's where you're wrong, Mr. Naumann' said Sara, 'because you will face justice. I'll see to that.'

The art of deer stalking was one that was lost to most of the Cheshire-set neighbours of Martin Southern. But he was a colonial boy. His father had worked for a mining company and Martin and his siblings had grown up in Zambia when they weren't at boarding school back in the UK. Martin was now an airline pilot, a Captain on Boeing 747 jumbo jets, an upper middle class professional in his early forties with a stay-at-home wife and two teenage kids in local private schools. Life was good on the whole but he needed this time out in the hills between Macclesfield and the Derbyshire spa town of Buxton. His wife let him have one day in each set of time off between working trips to do whatever he wanted to do. The rest of the time she had him fitting a new kitchen, or a new bathroom, or an extension to the extension. Or she'd made plans for them with the Armstrong's or the Hamilton's, or her parents. The only time he got to be in control of anything was when he was at work or when he was out here on his own.

He was lying on the ground, just on the edge of the woods, looking out across the field to where the deer stood underneath a couple of large overhanging trees. This was the area of hills that really were rolling and if he lost the deer over the edge it would take it too close to the farm about three hundred metres ahead. He didn't want some angry farmer coming after him for having scared or even killed one of his livestock by mistake.

The blood was pumping through his veins. He'd spent the last hour and a half stalking his prey. His neighbours didn't understand any of it because they were the usual English hypocrites when it came to eating meat. A cow, a pig, a lamb, a fowl bird were all okay as long as they didn't know how they'd ended up on their plate. But the thought of consuming any other being always spilled over into squeamish territory that made him wish he'd been born French. They didn't bother over there. They just hunted it and then they created great cuisine out of it. They had the right idea. Hunting didn't carry the same class war baggage as it did in Britain either. Everybody did it from the very bottom to the very top. He'd once mooted the idea with his wife of moving to France but she wouldn't hear a bar of it. Not because she had any objection in principle to living there. After all, she believed everything she read in the Daily Mail about Britain going down the pan, even though her own personal position was sound and secure because of Martin's job and the lifestyle it gave her. But the problem was that she wouldn't leave her Mum. She wasn't ill or even that old but Martin's wife never did anything without consulting her Mum first and Martin sometimes wondered which of the two women he'd married. The one who wore the ring he'd bought for her or the one who would never live anywhere 'foreign'. His mother-in-law was always saying that you could never beat anything that was 'English.'

He rolled over to get into the right position with his rifle and aimed at the part of the animal where he would cause it the least pain during the death process. But Martin didn't get the opportunity to close the deal. His right foot fell onto what felt like something's head. By instinct he looked down and received the shock of his life. He sat up and dropped his rifle. He pushed himself away with the palms of his hands and the heels of his boots scraping across the ground. He gasped in horror at what his eyes were telling him. The head was attached to the body of what looked like a young teenage girl, her eyes open, her clothes torn and her skin covered in scratches. She looked as if she was about the same age as his daughter.

CHAPTER FIVE

WHENEVER HELEN NORRIS didn't have to get up for the early shift and switch herself on immediately, she slipped into the other half of her Gemini twin and gradually came to, going through the motions of normal early morning activity. That was the only problem with shift work. Even when you didn't have to get up at some obscene hour your body clock was so used to it that it woke you up anyway. But still, if it was a working day for Tim then she didn't mind because it allowed her to get up and make his breakfast whilst he was in the shower. She knew she was lucky to have a husband like Tim who didn't expect her to iron his shirts or do all the cooking. But there was a part of her that liked to take the opportunity from time to time to play the traditional wife and she would make no apology to any feminist over it. She liked to do it. It was her choice and try as she may her traditional Southern European roots of the woman looking after her man still shone through.

'You smell all fresh and clean,' said Helen as Tim held her, newly dressed in his suit and open-necked shirt. He'd even had a shave today which was a good job because the growth on his face had been starting to turn into a beard.

'I should hope so seeing as I've just come out of the shower,' said Tim.

'Sit down Detective, and eat your breakfast.'

'Yes, ma'am.'

He picked up a piece of toast with one hand and with

the other he brushed Helen's hair away from her face. He loved the way she looked first thing in the morning with all the sleep in her eyes. She was so cute.

'You're still a little sleepy head,' he teased.

Helen rubbed her eyes. 'I'll go back to bed when you've gone,' she said. 'I probably won't sleep anymore but the rest will do me good.'

'We could have some good news this month.'

'You mean I might be pregnant,' said Helen, sipping her glass of orange juice.

'You could be,' he said, 'we've been trying hard enough so if there's any reward from the Gods for effort then you will be.'

'Tim, I'm not going to turn into one of those women whose world caves in if I don't get pregnant,' said Helen. 'I've seen enough of them at work and they completely lose perspective. I'm not going to get like that.'

Tim took hold of her hand. 'I know,' he said, 'I know what you're like. But we haven't really talked about what we'd do if you don't get pregnant.'

'We can adopt,' said Helen, simply. She didn't know if it was her nurses training but she tended to look at these things in a very practical matter-of-fact way. 'There are loads of kids out there in need and we don't need to create our own baby in order to be good parents.'

'Well if that's what you're happy to do, then why do you want us both to go for tests?'

'Because it would be good to know if there is something wrong with either of us.'

'Good?'

'Well you know, not good, I didn't mean that,' said Helen, 'but it's early and I'm tired. It might be useful to know, that's all. Don't you think?'

Tim smiled. It would break her heart if she knew that a test on him would be pointless because he already knew that there was nothing wrong with him. Sara had made that clear.

'Of course,' said Tim as he gathered her into his arms. She was wearing a red and white striped robe over the long t-shirt she wore in bed for sleeping. 'You're the medic in the family. I bow to your better judgement.'

'Just so long as you know your place, Detective,' said Helen. Then she kissed him and ran her hand down the side of his face.

'Oh I know it,' said Tim, kissing her. 'And I like it.'

Their moment was interrupted by Tim's mobile. He picked it up and looked at the caller display. It was Sara.

'It's the boss,' he said.

'Sexy Sara?' said Helen. 'Better see what she wants. And when are you going to invite her over for dinner? I'd like to catch up.'

'One day,' said Tim, 'once she's settled in.' He lifted his phone to his ear. 'Yes?'

'A body has been found, Tim,' said Sara, down the line. 'A young teenage girl who's been identified as Shona Higgins. She lived on the Tatton estate.'

It was Anita Cowley's first morning at the social services centre as 'office assistant' and she'd turned up looking like she'd defy anyone to say a single word to her that she didn't like. Her hair hadn't been washed and was scraped back in a tight ponytail. She wasn't wearing any make-up and her skin was pasty. She had on a black and white track suit and Paul would swear there was a stain of what looked like baby sick on the left shoulder. She hardly looked like she was on her first day in a new job, her first ever job at that. Her face was tripping her up. Her arms and legs were folded as she sat defiantly on a chair behind the main reception desk.

'So what am I actually doing here?' she asked.

'I've given you a job, Anita,' said Paul who'd had the idea after being at Lorraine Cowley's house, the morning he'd called about Anita's brother Sam.

'Why?'

'Because you need one and there was a vacancy here.'

'So why me?'

'Because I think you deserve a chance,' said Paul, who knew this was going to be a long haul but he wasn't going to give up. 'When I came to see your mother about your brother Sam the other day it occurred to me that you'd be perfect for the vacancy we had here.'

Anita then took a call on her mobile at ten past nine.

'Hiya! Oh God, that's mental... I can't believe his parents are going for custody of her when you're the one who's given up school to look after her ... it's just so not fair on you ...'

She went outside to take the rest of the call. When she came back she offered no apology or explanation. Just the same set face as before.

'Where've you been, Anita?' asked Paul.

'What's it got to do with you?'

'I'm your employer, Anita, and you disappeared for half an hour on my time. That's what it's got to do with me.'

'God, this is like being at school!'

'Well if you don't want to be treated like a child then don't act like one.'

'What's that supposed to mean? I'm not a kid.'

Not much, thought Paul. 'I'm still waiting for an explanation, Anita.'

'It was me friend, Belinda Hunter, okay? She's dead upset because the parents of the father of her baby have dared to say that she's not a fit mother and they want to go for custody. I think they've got a bloody cheek if you ask me. I mean, what's it got to do with them or the baby's father? The baby belongs to my friend, end of.'

'How old is your friend?'

'She's fifteen.'

'Well then don't you think that the parents of the father of her child might have a point? They only want the best for their grandchild.'

'And what about the best for my friend, eh? She's in bits because of them!'

'It's not about her, Anita. It's about her child and it's about her being underage when she became pregnant.'

'But it just happens.'

'No it doesn't just happen, Anita,' said Paul. 'You can walk into any chemist shop and get contraception.'

'But I wanted a baby.'

'So it doesn't just happen,' said Paul. 'You make it happen. So why do you do that when you're underage?'

'Because it's my right.'

'No, it isn't your right!' said Paul, angrily. 'It's nobody's right to have a baby, Anita. But it is society's right to expect you to take advantage of the education the taxpayer provides you with. You can't use a baby as an excuse to absolve yourself of personal responsibility and check out of normal life.'

'Why can't I if it's what I want?'

'Because you're not the one who's paying for it,' said Paul. 'You shouldn't have a child unless you can support yourself and it. You can't define yourself just by having a baby but you'll be a better role model for your daughter if you get down to work and do something for yourself. It isn't your right to have that baby but it becomes everyone else's responsibility because you're too young to support it.'

'So?'

'So that isn't fair on everybody else.'

'So?'

'So take advantage of the chance I'm giving you today to repay some of what you've taken.'

Anita's mobile rang again.

'Hiya Mam… Well I've not done anything yet… yeah, I know it's gone ten o'clock… yeah, you're right, it is a complete waste of time… look, I'd better go, I'm getting the evils… no don't worry, Mam, I won't take any shit off anybody… yeah, see ya, ta ra.'

Paul's patience was staring to run out.

'Anita, I'm giving you a real chance here…'

'…Look, my family have had enough of you!'

'Anita, the more educated you are, the more choices you're able to make and the less threatened you are by anything. Don't you see that? Don't you see that being at work and earning a salary is more beneficial to your child than sitting at home all day and claiming off the social?'

'I'm entitled to the social!'

'Really? You haven't paid anything into the system so why should you get anything out of it?'

'Well my Mum…'

' …exactly. Your Mum hasn't paid anything into it either. Benefits should be about a fair system of exchange, Anita. You work, you pay in, you get something out when you need it. Am I making sense?'

Anita sighed. 'Whatever.'

'Anita, your baby is being well taken care of in our day care centre. I'm not even asking you to work full-time. Be here for nine every morning and you can leave at three. Anita, a lot of good teachers, good well-trained dedicated teachers tried to make you see that you do have choices in life but you threw it all back in their face.'

'School was boring,' Anita declared, 'I hated every minute of it. It didn't teach you anything you really needed to know like how to bring up kids and that.'

Paul ran his hands through his hair. She could try the patience of a bloody saint.

'Anita, you've just turned eighteen. Are you happy to wipe away the rest of your life?'

'What do you mean?'

'I mean that if all you want out of life is a string of meaningless relationships, ever more demanding kids and a never ending struggle with money then you've arrived. This is it. But you'll never get to travel, never be able to buy yourself anything nice to wear, never be able to feel really proud of yourself and what you've achieved.'

'Look, I don't care about any of that, right? It's all crap and you're talking rubbish. All I want is my baby and my benefits.'

'But life isn't all about taking everything you can and giving nothing in return,' said Paul. 'Anita, we are all prepared to teach you whatever you need to know to make a go of this job for the sake of yourself and your baby. Now will you at least meet me halfway?'

Anita had run out of answers, 'I don't know how to work the computer.'

'Then we'll teach you,' said Paul, 'so are we going to start again?'

'I suppose I've got no choice now I'm here.'

'And please keep your mobile switched off during working hours.'

'You're my worst nightmare you are.'

'No, Anita, I'm your best friend. You just don't realise it yet.'

★

'The Derbyshire police have sent us their initial report, sir,' said Sara. She was addressing the whole squad but directing her speech at Superintendent Hargreaves. 'According to forensics her body had only been there, they estimate, for less than twenty-four hours and DNA testing was able to identify her as the same Shona Higgins who we did for shop lifting two years ago.'

'And what else does it tell us, DCI Hoyland?' Hargreaves asked.

'Shona Higgins had been the victim of a nasty assault, sir,' said Sara who caught her breath before continuing. 'She'd been strangled. There was also clear evidence of recent sexual activity and the bruises and marks on her backside and the inside of her legs suggests it wasn't consensual. Shona was fifteen years old and now she's never going to see her baby son grow up.'

'Have her parents been informed, Sara?' asked the Superintendent.

'Yes, sir,' said Sara, 'they're inconsolable as you can imagine, but they did admit something very interesting. Apparently, Shona went missing a month ago. She went to school on the morning of the 15th and never came back but her parents didn't call us or inform any of the authorities.'

'Did they say why?' asked Tim.

'No, DI Norris,' answered Sara. 'But it's not that they couldn't say it's that they wouldn't say. Someone has frightened them into silence. I've got uniform conducting house-to-house enquiries and if they come up with anything they've been told to inform me immediately.'

'Good work, DCI Hoyland,' said Hargreaves. 'Does the DNA tell us anything else?'

'There are at least twenty different examples of male contact, sir,' said Sara, quietly. 'But it's going to take a while for them to try and identify it all.'

'Sick bastards!'

'Quite so, sir' said Sara.

'What about the area where she was found?'

'Remote Derbyshire peak land, sir. It was a deer stalker who chanced upon her body. Gave him quite a shock I believe, as I suppose it would. There was a lot of overnight rain in the area which washed away any trace of tyre marks from a vehicle. There's a farm two miles to the west and the nearest village is three miles to the north. The main A6 runs about five miles to the east and there are only narrow lanes and dirt tracks from there to the spot where Shona's body was dumped. Our Derbyshire colleagues are making enquiries in the area.'

'We've got to push harder on the parents,' said DC Steve Osborne.

'Well,' said Sara, 'as soon as it's appropriate, sir, I'm going to visit Shona Higgins' parents myself. See if I can get them to talk or at least to open up enough to give us something to go on.'

'Ma'am, why isn't it appropriate to do that now?' chirped Steve Osborne again.

'It's not the job of the police to twist the knife of

someone's grief, DS Osborne,' said Sara. 'The officers who saw Mr and Mrs Higgins said they were genuinely distraught. This has clearly come as a huge shock to them and I'm only talking about leaving it for twenty-four hours. Any problem with that, DS Osborne?'

Steve was suddenly self-conscious. 'No, ma'am,' he said, looking over at the Superintendent, 'none at all. I was just asking a question.'

'Good,' said Sara, 'well in the meantime, we've got an active investigation to be working on. DS Alexander has uncovered some information that leads me to believe that the extradition case of Dieter Naumann may not turn out to be as straightforward as we first thought. As you all know his bail conditions require him to stay at Gatley Hall as the guest of Lady Eleanor Harding. But we've found that this is not the first time he's lived there and the hall itself has a macabre history that potentially places Dieter Naumann right at the centre of suspicion. Joe?'

'Ma'am,' said Joe who then cleared his throat. 'A man called Peter Jenkins was murdered at the Hall on June 12th, 1940, four days after Dieter Naumann arrived in the country on his secret mission to negotiate a deal between Britain and Germany. Peter Jenkins had been having an affair with Lady Eleanor at the time but according to Naumann he and Lady Eleanor began their affair almost as soon as they'd laid eyes on each other. Wilfred Jenkins, who was then Lady Eleanor's head of household, and Peter Jenkins' father, were hanged for the crime on the sole evidence of her ladyship. Now we know from the transcript of the trial that Wilfred Jenkins said he found Peter in the swimming pool of Gatley Hall lying face down with Lady Eleanor and one other gentleman present but he didn't know who that gentleman was.'

'And you think it was Naumann?' said Tim.

'Yes, we do, sir,' said Joe. 'Lady Eleanor's version of events, given at the trial was that Wilfred Jenkins flew into a rage when he saw his son and her together because he totally disapproved of their affair. In the struggle that followed he killed his son and she categorically denied that anybody else was present.'

'But you think she lied to protect Naumann?'

'Yes,' said Sara. 'We suspect that Dieter Naumann may have been the real killer that night in a sort of crime of passion for Lady Eleanor. But she would've wanted to cover it up to protect Naumann's anonymity and what better way to do that than to use Wilfred Jenkins so that Naumann could escape justice.'

'It would've provided him with the perfect alibi,' said Joe.

'And what's adding to our suspicious,' said Sara, 'is another murder that happened at the Hall in 1974.'

'Christ, it's turning into the house in Psycho,' said Tim. 'No wonder the place is on all those murder websites.'

'Sir,' said Joe. 'On October 19th, 1974, Lady Eleanor's daughter Clarissa allegedly fatally shot her father before disappearing without trace. Lady Eleanor had told the police at the time that, once again, she'd been the sole witness to events.'

'But you think that if she'd lied to protect her lover Dieter Naumann in 1940 then she could've done it again in 1974?'

'Yes sir,' said Sara. 'He was known as Gerald Edwards then but they were still protecting his identity.'

'No point in protecting it now,' said Tim. 'It's all over the press.'

'Yes, and the revealing of his existence could

fundamentally change both cases,' added Sara.

'So what are you proposing to do, Sara?' asked Hargreaves.

'I'm going to re-open the cases, sir,' said Sara. 'I'm convinced that justice has yet to be served on both of them and that a potentially innocent man went to the gallows. I'm also convinced that Dieter Naumann holds the key but first I want to speak to Lady Eleanor. She knows something that will lead us to make the right connections. She strikes me as being a born liar and manipulator.'

'You're taking on a lot here, DCI Hoyland,' said Hargreaves, 'what with this and the Shona Higgins case.'

'I know, sir,' said Sara, 'but we can deal with it.'

It had been a long and pretty gruelling day at the centre and when Paul got home he poured himself a large scotch. He sat down and let his head lean back against the sofa. He closed his eyes. During the day he had so much to distract him from thinking about Jake. It was when he got home that it hit him like a ton of bricks. Every night was the same. He'd make himself something to eat, open some wine, watch some television and if his father wasn't occupying his every thought right up until his head hit the pillow, then Jake was. He couldn't do anything about his father. He couldn't take his pain away or rid him of the disease that was so cruelly savaging such a good man. But he could do something about his worry over Jake. He could do what Kelly had suggested. He could get hold of himself and do something about finding out why Jake had not been in touch for so long and he had to be prepared for any consequences.

He downed his scotch and then poured himself another. Then he picked up the phone and dialled Jake's mobile. His hand was shaking and he told himself not to be so stupid. Then a young sounding woman with a broad Lancashire accent answered.

'Hello?'

'Oh … is that Jake's phone or have I got the wrong number?'

'Yeah it's Jake's phone,' said the woman.

'Sorry, is he still in Afghanistan?'

'Afghanistan? No, he's been back from there for nearly three months now. He's just gone out to collect a pizza for us. Who's calling please?'

Paul swallowed. Three months? He's been back for three fucking months? He felt sick. 'I'm… I'm Paul Foster. I'm a friend of Jake's in Manchester.'

'Ooh sorry, Paul, you must think I'm a bit rude but I just didn't recognise your voice,' she said, adding a touch of nervous laughter. 'I don't think you were at the wedding were you?'

'Wedding?'

'Mine and Jake's. We got married a month ago. I'm Tiffany, his wife. Shall I tell him you called? I didn't know he had a friend called Paul in Manchester. Have you known him long?'

CHAPTER SIX

KELLY FOUND A LEMON in her fridge so she did the only thing she could do in the circumstances and went out and bought a bottle of gin and some tonic water.

As she passed Paul's place on her way back from the corner shop she noticed that the lights weren't on but she could see him sitting there in the front room. She had a key so she let herself in.

'What are you doing sitting here in the dark?' She reached for the light switch on the wall but Paul held his hand up.

'No please don't, Kelly.'

She could see that he'd had a few. 'What on earth has happened? Is it your Dad?'

'No,' said Paul, 'it isn't my Dad.'

She sat down beside him. 'Then what is it?'

'I rang Jake's mobile.'

Kelly held her breath. 'And?'

'And his wife Tiffany answered.'

'Oh no!' Kelly exclaimed before putting her arms round him. 'Oh, Paul.'

'I've been such a bloody fool, Kelly!'

'So he's back from Afghanistan?'

'He's been back for the last twelve weeks apparently.'

Kelly was furious. 'When I think of how you've worried yourself sick all this time!'

'I know.'

'So what did this Tiffany sound like?'

'A young woman in her early twenties head over heels in love with her handsome soldier boy. I wish to God I was in her place.'

'Has Jake tried to call you?'

'No.'

'Bastard!'

'You know what really pisses me off is that he didn't even care enough about me to dump me by flaming text! At least that would have been something. I gave him everything, Kelly, all my heart, all my soul, all my devotion. And in the end he acts like none of it ever mattered to him.'

'Well what will you say if he does contact you?'

'Ask him if there's a wedding list...'

'I know what I'd like to give him for a wedding present,' said Kelly, 'but it's not something you can buy in a shop. I'll bloody kill him if I see him.'

'No you won't because I'll have got there first.'

'Well I think it's good that you're angry as well as hurt,' said Kelly.

'I can't tell you how angry I am, Kelly.'

'But look, think what this means,' said Kelly. 'You're free again now, Paul.'

Paul was aghast at Kelly's apparent insensitivity. 'Oh yeah, it's all so easy to pick myself up, dust myself off and start all over again!' he retorted. 'If you and Lydia finished tomorrow could you do that as easily as you expect me to?'

'No, I was...'

'... and look, I know I never lived with him and that I didn't see him as often as I would've liked. But that doesn't give you the right to play down the value of what we had together.'

'Which was what exactly?'

'As close as we could've made it,' said Paul, suddenly distraught all over again.

'And you're still in love with him.'

'I always will be,' said Paul. 'That won't ever change.'

Kelly sat back and paused after receiving Paul's onslaught. She knew that his heart had been beating for Jake since the day he met him. Of course it wasn't going to be easy to just wipe all the hurt away and she hadn't meant to say what she'd said in the way that she'd said it. It had just come out all wrong.

'I'm sorry,' she said.

'It's okay,' said Paul. 'I'm just a bit raw tonight, you know.'

'I know,' said Kelly, rubbing his shoulder. 'I just don't want you to think of it as the end of the world.'

'Yeah, well sorry to disappoint, but that's just how it does feel.'

'I can't seem to say anything right tonight, can I.'

Paul took hold of her hand and squeezed it. 'I'm sorry too, Kell. I shouldn't take it out on you.'

'You're in pain, Paul,' said Kelly. 'I understand.'

'I think I'm going to stick to wine from now on,' said Paul. 'At least if you get a bad bottle of wine you can just open another one.'

Kelly laughed. 'Look, why don't you come round to ours and get seriously pissed?'

'What, and have Lydia put Shirley Bassey on at full blast like she always does when she's had one too many? No thanks. I think I'd lose the will to live if I had to watch her miming to Goldfinger tonight.'

'Well at least you're holding on to your sense of

humour,' said Kelly.

'Oh Kelly, why can't you have a cock?'

'Hey listen love, if I had a cock I'd be dangerous.'

'Do you ever wish Lydia had one?'

'Sometimes,' said Kelly, thoughtfully. 'But we've got a…'

'…yes, okay,' said Paul, holding up his hand, 'too much information even for a gay best friend thank you very much.'

'Well anyway, she makes up for it in other ways and at least I don't have to put up with man smells in the bathroom which is what you get when you invite cock into your life.'

'Jake used to leave the most wonderful man smells in my bathroom,' said Paul, wistfully. 'Real masculinity; sweat, strength. Just the sort of smells that really turn me on.'

'Don't,' she warned, waving her finger at him, 'you'll have those man smells in your bathroom again. They just won't come from that spineless bastard.'

'But why are you so determined to implicate my poor Dieter in cases that were all over and done with years ago?' Eleanor demanded as she sat in front of Sara and Joe Alexander in the drawing room of Gatley Hall. She was being interviewed under caution.

'Well not quite, Lady Eleanor,' said Joe, 'your daughter is still missing.'

'Is there no end to your vindictiveness against a defenceless old man?'

Sara could've laughed. Defenceless was one thing that Dieter Naumann wasn't. She'd met some hardened criminals in her time but Naumann sent a shiver down her spine like no other.

'As part of the extradition process we have to take a thorough look at Dieter Naumann's life. Surely you can see that? Especially when two murders occurred at which Naumann could've been present. We're not trying to implicate him, Lady Eleanor, we just want to find out the truth.'

Eleanor didn't bother to reply. She was sick of it all. It was such a waste of time. No charges would ever be allowed to be made against her or Dieter. She knew that even though they didn't.

'Tell us about when you first met Dieter Naumann, Lady Eleanor?' said Sara.

'He landed his plane at an RAF base in Yorkshire that night in June 1940 and I went to meet him. I hadn't been able to go to my sister's wedding in Berlin and with the build-up to the war it meant that she and Dieter weren't able to come over here. Everything was covered in great secrecy that night and the atmosphere was rather tense but we fell instantly in love with each other. I'd never known passion like it, nor had Dieter. When the deal he'd come to negotiate was scrapped and he was placed under house arrest here at the Hall, I suppose you could say it meant that he and I had the most glorious war. We were together day and night and it was like that until the end of the war when a different kind of reality stabbed us both straight through the heart. You see, my husband wouldn't give me the divorce I wanted in order to marry Dieter, or Gerald Edwards as he'd then become. I wanted so badly for us to be together but my husband Ronald wouldn't grant me a divorce under any circumstances.'

'And how did you feel about that?' Sara asked.

'Well how do you think? It broke my bloody heart.'

'And why wouldn't your husband grant you a divorce?' Sara asked. 'He was the Conservative Member of Parliament for the area for many years, right up until his death. Was he afraid of a scandal?'

'No, he simply insisted that I keep to my side of the agreement we'd made,' said Eleanor. 'He was a closet homosexual and in those days they had no choice but to stay hidden and keep their proclivity secret. Nowadays of course if a Conservative politician wants to do the same as Ronald did then, the multi-millionaire can claim he was saving money when he had his handsome researcher share his hotel room. That is rather pathetic given today's more, shall we say, enlightened times, but for Ronald that kind of subterfuge was an absolute necessity. We'd grown up together and were great friends and the arrangement had suited us both when we first got together. Ronald had cover for his sexual activities and I could never see myself settling down with just one man and wanted to carry on playing the field.'

'With men like Peter Jenkins?'

'Oh Peter was such a deliciously handsome boy,' said Eleanor, recalling every inch of him. 'Like some Hollywood matinee idol. God only knows how his dull, ugly parents could've produced him but they did.'

'Did you end your affair with Peter Jenkins when you met Dieter Naumann?'

'Yes'

'Immediately?'

'Give or take a day.'

'And how did Jenkins feel about that?'

'Well I couldn't have cared less then, so don't ask me to care now.'

'Was he angry, Lady Eleanor?'

'Well he wasn't pleased but, look, where is this leading exactly?'

'Did Peter Jenkins get so angry about the way you'd treated him that he sought Naumann out and they fought? A fight that led to Jenkins' death?'

Eleanor narrowed her eyes. 'You really are full of fanciful notions,' she spat.

'But not even your head of household, Wilfred Jenkins, knew about the presence of Dieter Naumann,' said Joe. 'That kind of atmosphere must've led to a lot of game playing.'

'He was here in secret!' Eleanor raged, exasperated at all these ridiculous questions. 'Nobody knew except for the government officials who he was negotiating with. My staff at the time knew someone was here but they didn't know who or why. Then, when we weren't able to make the agreement that Naumann came over for and he stayed, we were able to let go in the presence of the staff.'

'Wilfred Jenkins said at his trial that there was a man he'd never seen before with you on the night his son died,' said Joe. 'That was Dieter Naumann, wasn't it?'

'I'll tell you this once and I won't tell you again,' said Eleanor. 'Wilfred Jenkins found his son and I together and it was his reaction and his anger that led to him killing his son. There was no-one else present. I don't know what Wilfred Jenkins was talking about when he mentioned another man being there.'

'But you'd finished with Peter Jenkins,' said Joe. 'So why did his father find you together?'

'Dieter was busy negotiating and I was bored,' said Eleanor simply. 'I needed amusement and Peter was glad to provide it one last time.'

She really is something else, thought Sara. She really couldn't care less. And she didn't believe her story. She was clever, Sara would give her that, but Sara also knew a liar when she saw one.

'Let's move on,' said Sara. 'After the war you continued your affair with Naumann?'

'Yes,' said Eleanor, her face breaking into a mischievous grin like a little girl. 'We got together once a month without fail. We called it his afternoon surgery. If I hadn't have been able to carry on seeing him I'd have probably ended my life.'

'You adored him that much,' said Sara.

'I'd have done anything for him.'

'Even lie for him?'

Eleanor sucked in air through her teeth. 'Yes, but I didn't have to.'

'Was Naumann the father of your daughter, Lady Eleanor?'

Eleanor stiffened. 'She was blond with blue eyes, the perfect Aryan child.'

'But was Dieter Naumann her father?'

'Yes he was,' said Eleanor, 'of course he was.'

'Your daughter disappeared, didn't she?' said Sara. 'October 19th, 1974. She was twenty-five years old'

'I see you've done your research, Detective,' said Eleanor. 'What do you want to make that mean?'

'She disappeared straight after you allege she killed Ronald?'

'That is correct.'

'Where do you think she went?'

'Detective, if I knew that she wouldn't have remained disappeared.'

'Did you get on with your daughter?'

'No,' said Eleanor, 'I didn't.'

'Why was that?' asked Sara.

'I never tried,' said Eleanor, shrugging her shoulders as if she was stating the obvious. 'That's the truth.'

'But she was your love child.'

Eleanor laughed, 'What a ridiculous cliché.'

'But what about your husband Ronald? Did he get on with her?'

'Oh yes,' said Eleanor, 'they were great friends.'

'And yet you allege in your evidence given to our colleagues back in 1974 that she shot your husband because she was angry with him? What was she angry about?'

'She grew up and fell in love with someone who was rather less than suitable. She and Ronald had always been close, a lot closer than my daughter and I had been, and I suppose she felt a greater sense of betrayal from him because he was more dead against her choice than I was.'

'Why?'

'Because neither Ronald nor myself believed in marriage across the social classes,' said Eleanor. 'It's unfair to place someone in a world they don't understand.'

'But your daughter disagreed with that?'

'Oh vehemently,' Eleanor declared. 'My relationship with my daughter had been nothing until then but it was even less after that.'

'And what happened to this... unsuitable boyfriend of your daughter's?'

Eleanor shrugged her shoulders, 'I don't know' she claimed. 'I never met him. I didn't even know his name and I wasn't in the least bit interested.'

'Are you really expecting us to believe that, Lady Eleanor?' said Sara.

'Believe what you like,' said Eleanor. '

Sara thought this bitch was in a class of her own. She felt sorry for her daughter. She must've had a horrible time of it.

'But what did her father have to say about it? I mean, Dieter Naumann?'

'Well she was there when he came to visit me here at the Hall of course but he made no effort to get close to her. There was no point. He had his children with Joan and to protect his identity as Gerald Edwards he had to cultivate his relationships with them.'

'Could you look at things any colder, Lady Eleanor?'

'I deal with facts, Detective,' said Eleanor. 'I've no time for useless emotions and neither has Dieter.'

'And I take it your daughter didn't know that Dieter Naumann was her father?'

'She knew nothing,' said Eleanor.

'There's been no trace of her since that night in 1974 when you reported her missing.'

'I know,' said Eleanor.

'So where do you think she went?'

'I have absolutely no idea,' said Eleanor.

'Was Dieter Naumann here that night?' asked Sara.

Eleanor looked up at the Heavens. 'Yes.'

'So he was here on both nights that murder was committed at this Hall.'

'Meaning?'

'Did you lie to protect Dieter, Lady Eleanor?' said Joe.

'Protect him? From what?'

'From being accused of the murder of your husband?'

'How dare you?!'

'You've got to admit, it all fits,' said Joe. 'He was your lover and the only other witness, your daughter, conveniently disappeared and therefore has never been given the opportunity to defend herself.'

'You are going completely down the wrong road here, Detective.'

'Are we? Dieter Naumann was the mystery man that Wilfred Jenkins spoke about at his trial and he was here the night your husband was killed. You're protecting him with lies, Lady Eleanor, you know it and so do we. And we're going to prove it.'

'Really?' Eleanor sneered. 'Then I wish you the very best of luck.'

Paul got up and showered, trying to wash away the hangover that Kelly and Lydia had inflicted on him after the evening he'd spent with them. He wasn't going to think about much until he'd managed to get a couple of Nurofen and a slice of toast down him. That's after the smell of coffee had stopped making him feel sick. He'd kill those two lesbian bitches for pouring all that wine down his throat and all that scotch afterwards. They'd pay for it. They were probably still snugly tucked up in bed like two bloody fish fingers in a box.

He was going to spend the whole day with his Dad and he hoped that if he drove with the window open he might be able to feel halfway decent by the time he got there. He was sitting at the kitchen table massaging his temples with his fingers and he cursed when his doorbell rang. He went to answer it and was shocked to see Jake standing there.

'What the hell are you doing here?'

'Tiffany is working so I thought I'd drive over on the off chance,' said Jake. 'I need to talk to you, Paul.'

Jake was the last person Paul wanted to see. None of his ruggedness or stocky build would work on Paul now. Why couldn't he have just phoned? This wasn't fair. Jake was standing there looking all vulnerable and unsure of himself but still every inch the man Paul had fallen in love with.

'You'd better come in,' said Paul who led Jake through to the kitchen.

'How's your Dad doing?' Jake asked.

'Not good,' said Paul. 'I'm going over there today.'

'Give him my best,' said Jake 'I often think about him.'

'Jake, he's a dying man and for all these weeks you've let him think you were in mortal danger. I don't think I can forgive you for that.'

'I'm sorry. What more can I say? I like your Dad, I always have.'

'Oh, well that makes it all alright then.'

'Paul, don't be like that. I've missed you.'

'Don't say that, Jake.'

'Why not? It's true.'

'For God's sake! I have been going out of my mind with worry about you. I even got down on my knees and prayed for you some nights. Every time Afghanistan came on the news my heart was in my mouth in case your name was read out as the latest dead soldier. You stuck me in a dark hole for weeks on end and yet all the time you were cutting wedding cake and building your love nest with Tiffany. That was cruel, Jake. That was so bloody cruel and you have no idea what it did to me. You didn't even pay me the respect of telling me it was all over. How do you think that made me feel?'

Jake buried his head in his hands and began to weep. Paul immediately wrapped his arms round him and held him tight. He had no other option. He couldn't watch him wallowing in that state.

'I've missed you so much,' said Jake, his face buried in Paul's neck which was now wet with Jake's tears. He gripped the sleeve of Paul's shirt as if he'd fall down into the centre of the earth if he let go. 'You don't know what it was like out there.'

'What happened out there, Jake?'

'Something was happening all the time,' said Jake who was thinking about his mates who were blown up by the Taliban right in front of him. He was lucky to escape with his own life and it had affected him in a way that he still couldn't put into words even for Paul. 'It was bad, man. You don't know how bad it was. Every time we went out on patrol… we didn't know if somebody was going to be there waiting to execute us for their cause. Hold me, Paul. I know I shouldn't ask but please just hold me.'

Paul tightened his grip around his former lover. 'Why don't you tell me what happened, Jake? '

'I can't,' Jake wailed, 'I want to tell you but I just can't.'

'Did you talk to anybody about whatever it was?' Paul went on.

'I didn't want to talk to anybody.'

'You can't bottle it up, Jake,' said Paul. 'It won't do you any good.'

'I only wanted to talk to you and I couldn't even do that,' said Jake. He'd lost it back in Afghanistan. He'd lost it when his mates had been killed. It had driven him down a path that he would never have chosen before and there was no way he could tell Paul about that.

'So what can you talk to me about, Jake?'

'I came here to tell you about Tiffany.'

'How long have you been married to her?' Paul asked.

'Three months.'

'And how long had you been seeing her?'

'About a year,' said Jake as he gently pulled away from Paul's embrace. 'I thought I could keep you both happy but it was destroying me and I couldn't go on much longer without making a choice.'

Paul swallowed hard. To know that Jake had betrayed him for all that time was hard to take. He must've gone straight from his bed to hers sometimes and vice versa.

'Does she know about me now, Jake?'

'No.'

'Well what did you tell her about me when she told you I'd called?'

'I said that you were an old army buddy from way back and that we'd lost touch.'

'I see,' said Paul who didn't know what else to say to that.

Jake sat up and wiped his face clean with his hands. 'I never tried to hide the fact from you that I'm bisexual, Paul.'

'I know, but I could understand if we'd just had a one-night stand or a brief fling but we had something going for four years, Jake.'

'Paul, I'm not completely straight but I'm not gay either. You knew my eye used to wander sometimes if a pretty girl came in the room.'

'I tried not to notice.'

'But you knew it happened. You knew I hadn't given up on girls.'

'Yes, but I thought you were happy with me.'

'I was but I can't lead a fully gay life, Paul. It's just not who I am. I couldn't set up home with you and for the two of us to live together as a couple. I knew that's what you wanted but I just couldn't give it to you. I couldn't cross that line.'

'But you still needed me when the going was tough.'

'Because you know me better than anybody.'

'That's right, Jake. I know you better than your wife does.'

Jake stood up and walked over to the window. He placed his hands round the back of his head and pulled his elbows forward. He had wanted to get over to see Paul for weeks but hadn't been able to find the courage. If he could just try and make him understand that hurting him was the last thing in the world he'd ever have wanted to do. But he wasn't being entirely truthful with himself or Paul. He did love him. He loved him very much. It just wasn't as easy as that for him. Gay equality was a good thing. The rest of society not batting an eyelid anymore was a good thing. But it didn't make any difference to men like Jake who still could never have faced their family with it. They were working class and proud and that meant men got married to women and never laughed at the likes of Julian Clary.

'I don't regret one minute of the time we spent together, Paul, not one minute. I just couldn't see a future for me with you. I'd have ended up hurting you sooner or later. Please try and understand that.'

'I can understand that you can fuck me but you can't introduce me to your friends, Jake. That's what I understand.'

'Paul, I love you, I always will,' said Jake. 'I just can't be with you in the way you need me to.'

'Well that'll be a great comfort to me tonight when I'm alone in bed and you're with Tiffany.'

'I don't know what else to say.'

'Say you love me.'

'I do love you.'

'But not enough,' said Paul. 'You don't love me enough to even try sharing your life with me.'

'I wouldn't put it like that.'

'I would.'

'It's not as simple as that.'

'Look Jake, what I can't understand is why you let me worry all this time? Why couldn't you have just come and told me it was all over?'

'Because I was scared of facing you with it,' Jake admitted. 'I knew you'd have been able to tempt me into changing my mind'

'I'd never have done that, Jake. I have some pride and self-respect. I'd never have tried to make you stay if you didn't want to.'

'But you're so much stronger than me, Paul. I'm happy with Tiffany and I'm looking forward to us being a family but...'

'...You mean she's pregnant?'

'Yes,' said Jake, 'yes, she's pregnant.'

Paul paused. It was the ultimate slap in the face. A man could wash another man's clothes, cook his meals, make sure he was well looked after in the bedroom. But he couldn't have babies for him. In the battle for a man's love, that's where women play their ace card.

'That picture of you in your desert kit you sent me? It's in a silver frame by my bed. I used to kiss that photo every night. Some nights I even went to sleep clutching it.'

'Oh Paul, Jesus, I'm sorry.'

Paul couldn't take much more of this. 'What's happening to your regiment?'

'Oh, I've left the army now,' said Jake.

'What? You loved being in the army, Jake. It was your life.'

'I know but I thought it would be better for Tiffany and the baby, you know.'

'So what are you doing now?'

'I'm in security,' Jake told him which was the truth but not the whole truth. 'It pays better and we need the money. We've bought a little house on the edge of Burnley, a modern type place, you know, three bedrooms, a garden. We didn't have much money left over after we'd paid for the wedding. Tiffany's family don't have any money and you know mine don't so we had to sort it ourselves.'

'What kind of security? I mean, tell me about it. Is it a big firm, small firm, group 4? What?'

'There's not much to say about it,' Jake lied. 'It's just a security job.'

'What are you hiding from me, Jake?' asked Paul.

'Nothing, man, nothing,' Jake lied again.

'Really nothing at all.'

CHAPTER SEVEN

LORRAINE COWLEY HAD a visit from her nephew Tyrone. He was twenty-four and had never worked since leaving school with no qualifications at the age of sixteen. It was a badge of honour amongst Lorraine and her friends while there were always immigrants to blame.

'There's nobody standing up for the likes of us, Tyrone,' Lorraine asserted. We want money in our pockets and all they do is throw flaming courses at us and tell us we've got to prepare for work, whatever the fuck that means.'

'It's disgusting,' Tyrone agreed. 'They're trying to tell me Dad that they might take his benefits away if he doesn't turn up for some stupid interview at the job centre.'

'I should hope he told them where to bloody go?'

'Too right, Aunty Lorraine,' said Tyrone, laughing. 'You should've seen him. He gave them what for alright. He told them there was no point going to work for the crap wages they pay these days and he wasn't going to pay Cameron's taxes.'

'Unless you're foreign,' said Lorraine.

'Oh aye' said Tyrone. 'You can get what you like if you're Polish.'

'Or one of them Muslims.'

'And they're all terrorists who should be kicked out of the country,' said Tyrone.

'And what I want to know is, how come they can carry on as they like whilst I get my benefits for Sam taken off me? Work that one out if you can.'

'I can't,' said Tyrone. 'No decent white English person could.'

'And that's it,' said Lorraine, 'decent white English people like us don't get anything these days. We should be fighting back.'

'Some of us have already started,' said Tyrone. 'Me and some of the lads started throwing stones at some of the Muslim kids who were walking home from school the other day. It wasn't anything they're not used to. I mean, they go in for stoning and all that out there. It was a right laugh.'

'I'll bet it was,' said Lorraine, laughing along with her nephew. 'And I say you did the right thing. They should be made to feel so unwelcome that they piss off out of it. Somebody should tell the same to that Paul fucking Foster as well. I'm forced to look after my granddaughter whilst her mother is at school. It's all wrong. Our Anita thinks she can do some stupid job and get her own flat and everything. I've never heard anything like it in my life. Everything she needs is here with me. I'll knock all these stupid ideas out of her if I have to, you mark my bloody word.'

'Is our Sam at the same school now he's in care?'

'Search me,' said Lorraine.

'The reason I ask is that the Headmistress, that Price woman, says she's clamping down on truancy and she's threatening to take loads of parents to court if they don't get their kids to school and that.'

'Have you ever heard anything like it!' Lorraine exclaimed. 'She's got no bloody right. She's another one who fills our kids heads with ideas above their fucking station. Learning? What fucking good is that? Do you want another coffee?'

'Yeah, please, Aunt Lorraine,' said Tyrone, handing her his mug. 'Neighbours and Home and Away are on soon.'

'Are you going to stay here and watch them with me?'

'Yeah, sound,' said Tyrone.

'Tyrone?'

'Yeah?'

'Can you lend me thirty quid?'

'Thirty quid? No, I can't. Thanks to all the immigrants taking all the jobs proper English people like me are broke.'

'I don't suppose your Dad could help me out either?'

'No,' said Tyrone. 'He's never got any cash, you know that.'

Lorraine had bitten almost all of her nails off, but she just kept on going. At this rate she'd have none left but she didn't care. Her daughter Anita was being leaned on by that arsehole of a social worker, Paul Foster, who'd virtually forced her into taking a job at the centre he ran. It was so bloody typical of that sort to want to take a young mother away from her baby, but he even had an answer for that. There was a so-called children's centre at this place where women from the estate could leave their kids whilst they went to work. He said it would do her and the baby good if she could take some steps towards supporting herself. He should be strung up for even suggesting it.

It was Paul Foster's fault that she was now on the bus going to her mate Martha's house on the Livermore estate just this side of Bolton. Foster was trying to set up a credit union on the Tatton and in the meantime had asked the police to patrol the streets for loan sharks. He had no flaming right! A credit union? More swanky rubbish he wanted to force on them but Lorraine wasn't going to give him the satisfaction of doing what he wanted her to do. She couldn't go back to Glenn Barber for anymore money. She was too scared to even talk to him. That's why she was going to get some money off another loan shark on another estate.

It was possible to buy a one-day pass for the local buses but Lorraine couldn't be arsed. The driver had said that it would save her money especially as she'd told him she was going to go shopping in Manchester afterwards before going home to the Tatton. But she'd just told him to give her a single ticket to Harrison Road. She didn't like to shell out all her money in one go even if it would end up saving her. She didn't like to think that far ahead and she didn't like anybody telling her what to do.

When she got there Martha made them both a coffee and the two of them sat in the living room drinking the coffee and smoking a cigarette each.

'Have you heard anything from your Jim?' Lorraine asked.

'No,' said Martha. 'It's been six months now.'

'Bastard.'

'I wouldn't mind but the social say that now our little Jim is at school I've got to think about getting a job,' said Martha, all affronted. 'Can you believe that? How can I get a job when my nerves are like they are?'

When the loan man arrived Lorraine got the shock of her life. It was Glenn Barber. He told Martha to leave them and she did as she was told, noting the look of terror on her friend's face as she walked out of the room. There was another bloke with Barber whom she hadn't seen before but who Barber kept referring to as Jake. Barber was in his usual long black leather coat with gloves to match. This Jake character was in a zipped up bomber jacket and jeans. He too was wearing black leather gloves.

'Please, sir, I'm desperate!' Lorraine begged, 'I've lost all the benefits I got for my son and I didn't know what else to do, sir, please! Please don't hurt me, sir, please don't hurt me!'

'My network stretches far and wide, Lorraine,' said Glenn in a quiet voice that terrified Lorraine even more. 'Did you think you'd escape me by coming over here?'

'I didn't want to escape you, sir, I just needed some money!' she wailed. Barber and the other bloke who answered to the name of Jake, towered above her making her feel the most vulnerable and petrified she'd ever felt. What were they going to do to her?

'Well if you'd needed some money then why didn't you just come to me?' Barber wanted to know. 'Do you really want to have to satisfy two paymasters? How stupid would that be, Lorraine? But then, you weren't in the front of the queue when brains were handed out, were you. You've always known that a condition of your loan is that you don't go anywhere else if you need any further funding. Now you've broken that condition, Lorraine, and you need to be punished. And that grieves my heart, Lorraine, because it means I've got to hurt you.'

Jake held Lorraine down whilst Martha came in with a steam iron that she plugged in and handed to Barber. She looked at Lorraine and for a moment their eyes met before Martha quickly looked away again.

Barber placed his hand over Lorraine's mouth before lifting up the front of her sweater to expose the naked flesh of her stomach.

Lorraine was so frightened she couldn't move or even make the most basic of protests over her predicament. All she'd come here for was a few quid to help her through. That's all she needed. Just a few quid to help get her back on her feet after the benefits she'd received for Sam had been taken away now that he was in care. The rotten little bastard. He'd be alright now. He'd be with some do-good middle class family who'd never known what it is to suffer.

'You can't have any more money, Lorraine,' said Barber, holding the iron in the air whilst it heated up. 'Your existing debt is already sky high. You've no idea. You've no idea how to manage your money but you see, the thing is, Lorraine, I should applaud that. I should thank you for being so fucking stupid. But there are limits, Lorraine. There are limits to what even I can tolerate and I've reached the level of my tolerance. You thought you'd give your business to some other loan man. Well let me show you what I mean by the word disloyalty.'

Glenn Barber pressed the button which made the steam blast through the small holes on the iron's stainless steel surface. Then he placed it down onto the skin of Lorraine's stomach, branding her like some piece of cattle. She struggled, she cried, she looked like it had really hurt. Barber was pleased.

'So don't try and go behind my back again, Lorraine,' said Barber after he'd put the iron down and watched as Lorraine bent over double in pain. 'Otherwise, it might not be so easy for you next time. Now, you can have some money, Lorraine.'

Lorraine lifted her head and looked at him in tear-stained bewilderment. 'I can?'

'Yeah, five hundred do you?'

'But how can I ever pay that much back?'

'You don't have to,' said Barber. 'Your daughter Michaela will pay it all back for you.'

'What do you mean? How can she?'

Barber gripped her chin firmly. 'That's my business. But she won't be home for her tea tonight and not again for some time. And if you open up your ugly little mouth to about it to anyone then I really will hurt you. Understand?'

Paul was woken up by a creaking sound coming from the stairs. He swallowed hard. He'd always dreaded a burglar getting in. He could've sworn he'd locked the doors. He went cold. He looked at the clock on his bedside table. It was just after half one. He picked up the phone and was about to call the police when his bedroom door opened and Jake came in. Paul sat bolt upright and exclaimed. 'Fuck's sake, you gave me a fright!'

'I remembered I still had this,' said Jake, holding up his key to Paul's front door. He threw it gently at him. 'I guess you want it back now.'

'I guess, yeah.'

'I'm sorry,' said Jake who slumped down on the edge of Paul's bed. 'I just wanted to talk to you, be with you. I'm sorry.'

'Why do you need to be with me, Jake?' Paul asked wearily.

'Because there's no-one else like you.'

'Don't mess with my head like this, Jake.'

'I'm not,' said Jake, 'but I can't talk to Tiffany about any of it. Please, Paul, let me in tonight. Let me talk to you.'

Paul had never seen Jake in this state before. His eyes were full of trouble and pain and his whole demeanour spoke loudly of being in need. Paul still loved him. What choice did he have?

'Okay,' said Paul. He punched the pillows in the space next to him and Jake lay himself down. 'I'll sleep some other time.'

'I didn't tell you everything the other day when I came round.'

Paul rubbed his eyes, 'yeah, well I thought as much.'

'I did a really bad thing out there, Paul.'

Paul held his breath. This wasn't going to be easy. He turned onto his side and propped his head up by bending his elbow. 'So tell me.'

'We were out on patrol,' Jake began as he went all the way back to that day, in a land so many thousands of miles away but which had come right back into his head making him understand that he could never escape, no matter how far he travelled from the reality of what had happened. 'We were on our way back to base at the time. A bomb had been placed at the roadside which was detonated by remote control as we passed. I watched my two mates, Richie and Errol get literally blown up in front of my eyes. I watched as bits of their bodies scattered across the ground.'

'Oh Christ, Jake,' said Paul as he squeezed his arm.

'I got out with a few minor burns, just some fucking cuts and bruises.'

'But that wasn't your fault, Jake,' said Paul, sensing that Jake was feeling guilty over the loss of his mates. 'It could easily have been you instead of your mates.'

Jake pressed a finger into his chest and spoke with an emotion that shook Paul a little. 'Easy to say but not easy to feel in here.'

'I know, I know,' said Paul, wanting to calm him down.

'It wasn't me, Paul,' said Jake.

'What do you mean it wasn't you?'

'It wasn't me who got blown up,' said Jake. 'The vehicle was a fireball but everything around was quiet. I was lying on the ground and there were people just stood there staring, saying nothing, not doing anything to help me.'

'They were probably as terrified as you, Jake.'

'I don't know how but I still had my rifle in my hand. This local guy stepped forward with something in his hand and I opened fire. He must've had half a dozen bullets in him by the time I'd finished. His wife and kids started screaming. They would've had me, Paul. The crowd would've had me. I saw the hatred in their eyes. And do you know what? All he wanted was to offer me some bread. He sold bread at the roadside and he saw me lying there and wanted to offer me some of it. And I killed him for it. I killed him in cold blood because he tried to show me a bit of humanity with the only thing he had. His wife is a widow and his kids are without their father because of me.'

'It was war, Jake.'

'And they were innocents,' said Jake. 'I shouldn't have been there. I shouldn't have been in their country, none of us should've.'

'You were an innocent too, Jake.'

'Don't make excuses for me, Paul.'

'I'm not,' said Paul, 'but I am trying to help you make sense of it.'

'How can I make sense of it? I killed a man for no reason. You don't have to live with that so please don't even try and tell me that you can make sense of it.'

'Okay,' said Paul, 'but it was just by chance that it wasn't you, Jake.'

'I know but I still feel the guilt.'

'Well look, tell me how you got out?'

'The patrol that had been following us picked me up. The crowd was shouting and jeering. To them I was evil.'

'You were under pressure, you were scared, and you reacted,' said Paul, who never imagined that the war in Afghanistan would come right into his bedroom in such a vivid and personal way. 'And so did the crowd.'

'You don't think I'm evil then?'

'No I don't think you're evil, Jake,' said Paul. He'd always supported the country's involvement in Afghanistan. But it had been ten years since the 9/11 attacks and still there was no sign of defeating either the Taliban or al-Qaeda. And young men like Jake were paying the price. He used to think that Britain was far too sentimental about 'our boys'. They weren't a conscript army after all. They'd joined up of their own free will. But now he was having his doubts. Were men like Jake out there so that the streets of Britain could be safer? He didn't know anymore. What he had seen as evidence that it may be worth it, were the millions of Afghanis lining up to vote in the elections there despite the Taliban's death threats. It had annoyed Paul to compare that with the voting record of those who lived on the Tatton estate. Hardly any of them had bothered to vote in the last general election. The sacrifices of heroic soldiers like Jake were lost on those lazy bastards.

But he was also quickly realising that it wasn't just the dead bodies being brought home that symbolised the shadow of death. It was the ones who'd come home and who'd gone through a death inside that should be added to the list of fatalities. And they were the hardest kind to deal with.

'Tiffany thinks I'm working all night,' said Jake. 'I thought I was too but it turns out I'm not needed anymore tonight. My boss has stood me down.'

'Do you want me to make you something to drink before you go home?'

'I don't want to go home,' said Jake.

'No, Jake,' said Paul, sitting up and folding his arms across his bended knees.

'You're the only one I could've talked to about what happened over there,' Jake pleaded as he raised himself up beside Paul. 'Paul, I really need to be with you tonight.'

'No, don't do this to me, Jake! It's not fair. It's not fair that you come round here and pour your heart out and then come on to me like this.'

'Please, Paul,' Jake pleaded, tears filing his eyes. 'It's not about that. That makes it sound so dirty.'

'Jake, you've made your choice,' said Paul who was starting to cry himself.

'What if it's the wrong choice?'

'You've got a baby on the way.'

'You can't send me away, Paul. We both know that.'

Paul didn't answer. Then Jake leaned forward and kissed him.

'I've missed you so much,' said Jake as he caressed Paul's face with his hand and looked straight into his eyes. 'Let me stay. Please.'

'This isn't fair, Jake,' said Paul who wanted Jake so badly at that moment. He breathed in the smell of him, the taste of him, his touch and the strength of his body.

'I need you, Paul,' said Jake as he softly kissed Paul's neck. 'I can't do it without you.'

'Jake, I…'

'... I do love you enough, Paul. I just didn't know how I could do it.'

Paul gripped Jake's shoulders and pushed him back slightly so he could stare into his tear-stained eyes for a moment. He felt himself fall deeper and deeper into somewhere he wanted to go but knew that he shouldn't. Then he began to undo the buttons on Jake's shirt and switched off the light.

Sara and Joe decided to bring Naumann into the station for his latest interview under caution. It was time to up the stakes on both him and Lady Eleanor.

'Mr. Naumann, were you at Lady Eleanor's estate the night Peter Jenkins died?' Sara began.

'Yes, I was,' said Dieter.

'Lady Eleanor said that you weren't there,' said Sara who was surprised by Naumann's answer. She'd expected him to deny it.

'I'm afraid she got it all a little wrong,' said Naumann who'd agreed with Eleanor that he would now admit to being there when Peter Jenkins died. They concluded that the more they tied these buffoons up the less likely his extradition deadline would be met and the more time they'd give the relevant authorities to rescue them both from this nightmare.

'You mean she lied.'

'I mean she got it wrong because it was a long time ago.'

'She's a liar.'

'Don't you talk about her in such disgraceful tones! A pathetic imbecile like you isn't worthy of licking Eleanor's damn boots!'

'Now that's enough, Mr. Naumann,' said Joe who noted that Naumann's face was still full of disgust. 'Just answer DCI Hoyland's question, please. Tell us what happened that night, Mr. Naumann, now that you've admitted to having witnessed Peter Jenkins death.'

Naumann paused whilst he calmed down.

'In your own time, sir,' said Sara.

Naumann glared at Sara before continuing. 'Well now, as I recall, Eleanor and I were in the swimming pool. We were being desperately intimate. Well we were young and had just fallen madly in love…'

…Oh spare us, thought Sara. She didn't want to bring her breakfast back up. She'd thoroughly enjoyed every mouthful of that sausage and bacon barm. It's not often she treated herself to something as deliciously bad as that these days and she wanted to savour the memory until she treated herself again…

'…and we wanted to spend as much time as possible together. But as far as Peter Jenkins was concerned my presence had created a love triangle. He was as madly in love with Eleanor as I was but the difference was that in my case it was returned. In Peter's case it was just sex for Eleanor. That's how she looked at it. Peter came in, he was very drunk, he saw Eleanor and I together and he went berserk. He threw himself into the pool and attacked me. He had me by the throat when his father came rushing in, jumped into the pool and pulled him off me. In the struggle that followed Wilfred Jenkins threw his son against the side of the pool and both Eleanor and I heard the neck crack. Blood then started to pour out of his mouth and his ears. He slid down under the water. He was clearly dead. Wilfred Jenkins had killed his own son and because of my status in this country poor Eleanor had to carry the burden on her own.'

'Lady Eleanor categorically denied that you were present when Peter Jenkins died,' said Joe.

'Yes but I reminded her that I was.'

'Now why would you do that, sir?' asked Joe.

'To give you an accurate account of events,' said Naumann, 'isn't that what you want?'

This was very interesting, thought Sara. Naumann and Lady Eleanor had obviously talked about getting their stories right but why had they changed their minds about admitting that Naumann was there when Peter Jenkins died? Presumably it was to make it look like Naumann was a witness to a murder and not the murderer himself.

'Wilfred Jenkins protested his innocence right up until the end, Mr. Naumann,' said Joe.

'Oh Detectives,' said Naumann in a voice as if he was having to chastise recalcitrant children. 'Every condemned prisoner protests their innocence and in my experience, they all beg like little babies crying out for their mother when faced with an execution.'

'You'd know about that, Mr. Naumann,' said Sara, gravely. She'd like to slice that appalling look right off his face with a blunt carving knife.

'I had some experience some years ago,' said Naumann, 'in the war.'

'Well being such an invisible person at the time gave you the perfect alibi for the murder of Peter Jenkins.'

Dieter laughed. 'Oh you're so good! But so wrong.'

'Wilfred Jenkins was sent to the gallows solely on the word of Lady Eleanor,' said Sara, 'she would've done anything to protect you, wouldn't she.'

'Are you two on some sort of crusade to kick me when

I'm down?'

Sara noted the touch of anger coming into the self-controlled tone. She was confident that they were finally beginning to crack the veneer that had sustained Dieter Naumann for the best part of a lifetime.

'No,' said Sara, 'but you're just another war criminal who may have also committed other crimes since. We're just doing our job, sir, and being as thorough as I'm sure you were when you were serving in the German army.'

'You drag me all the way down here to play your little games,' said Naumann, his voice dripping with a chill that made both Sara and Joe shiver, 'but you won't succeed in re-writing my history to suit your purposes.'

Paul changed the sheets on his father's bed and settled him back down. His Dad's condition was deteriorating rapidly and he no longer had the strength to make any kind of movement without help.

'I'll make you comfortable for the night, Dad,' said Paul. 'Then Mum won't have to do it. Wouldn't you be better off in hospital, Dad?'

'I'm not ending my days in hospital, son,' said Ed. 'You do understand that, don't you?'

'Of course I do. I just worry about how comfortable you are.'

'When do you have to head off?'

'I'll head off when Mum gets back,' said Paul.

'The two of you can't bear to be in the same place at the same time, can you?'

'Dad, I wish I could make it better for you before… but I don't think I can, Dad. I just don't think I can.' He wiped his father's face with a wet flannel. 'I am sorry, Dad'

'It's not your fault, son.'

'Perhaps I could try a bit harder?'

'It wouldn't do any good, son. I know that.'

Paul wasn't often short of something to say but he couldn't find the words to give his father some small glimmer of hope that his relationship with his mother might one day heal. His father looked so drawn and lost, battling with every ounce of strength he had against the pain. But it wasn't a fair fight.

'But you've always tried, our Paul,' said Ed. 'I know that too.'

'It's how you brought me up, Dad, to have respect and an open mind. I'm not always good at it but not everybody was that lucky.'

'I did something right then.'

'You did a lot right, Dad,' said Paul, 'and I have got some good news.'

'What's that, son?'

'I've heard from Jake. He's alright. He's okay.'

'Thank God for that. You must be relieved.'

'I am, Dad. I am.'

Paul wasn't going to tell his father the full story about Jake. It wouldn't be fair to burden him with all that now.

'Sit down, son,' said Ed. 'I know it isn't easy but we really do need to talk about your mother.'

Paul sat on the edge of his father's bed. 'Dad, I know I've never been her favourite.'

'It goes much deeper than that, son.'

'What do you mean, Dad?'

The front door opened and Paul's mother returned.

'I don't know why they bother putting up a timetable for the trams,' moaned Mary as she stomped through the house. 'I waited nearly half an hour at Bispham after I'd had a bit of dinner with Eileen.' She looked up and saw Paul standing by his father's bed. 'Oh, you're still here.'

'Yes, Mum,' said Paul. 'Are you okay?'

'I'm alright, there's nothing wrong with me,' said Mary. 'Nothing wrong at all.'

'Well I'll go now, Mum,' said Paul who was wondering what on earth his father had been talking about and why he didn't want to say anything in front of his mother. 'Unless you need anything doing?'

'I'm fine,' she said. 'Just fine.'

Paul turned back to his Dad. 'I'd best be off, Dad.'

'Come here, son,' said Ed who raised his hand as high as he could to beckon Paul over.

'What is it, Dad?' Paul asked as he went up close to his father.

'We need to talk, son,' said Ed.

'I'll be back tomorrow, Dad,' said Paul. He kissed his father's forehead. 'We can talk then. In the meantime, you need to rest.'

CHAPTER EIGHT

JOE ALEXANDER WAS DRIVING onto the Tatton estate with Detective Sergeant Steve Osborne in the passenger seat.

'What's in the bag?' asked Joe with a sideways glance at the paper bag on Steve's lap.

'What?' said Steve, looking down. 'Oh I forgot, I got you a pie.' He held it up in Joe's direction.

'What kind of pie?'

'Meat and potato,' said Steve. 'I didn't manage any breakfast this morning and I was starving so I got one from the shop on the corner. I thought you'd want one too.'

'Well that's very kind, Steve, and I'm very touched.'

'Fuck off and eat it.'

'I have to think of my waistline, Steve.'

'Is it a fond memory?'

'You cheeky bastard.'

'I'll keep it for you for later.'

'Good man.'

Joe and Steve often worked on cases together. Joe didn't mind Steve. He had a good sense of humour, although he thought he could be a little callous at times, a little too ready to come up with simple solutions to cases. He always seemed to be in a rush to get them tied up and then onto the next one without farting time. Joe thought of himself as the sensitive, thoughtful type compared to Steve's more blusterous approach but what he hated Steve for, was his apparent ability to eat whatever he damn well liked without seeming to put on weight. Joe got mightily frustrated about that.

'God, this is the arse end of hell,' said Steve. 'These people deserve everything they get.'

'That's a bit tough, Steve,' said Joe. 'It's not always someone's own fault that they're dependent on the state.'

'I'd forgotten I was working with our resident boy scout.'

'You know what I'm saying, Steve.'

'Yes, I do, but it pisses me off.'

'Yeah, yeah, yeah,' said Joe who was tired and wasn't in the mood for Steve's thinking on the order of society. 'But can we leave all the social commentary to the leader writers of the bigger papers? I've got a headache.'

'It must be due to working with the new DCI,' said Steve.

'Sara Hoyland?'

'That's the one,' said Steve.

'She's alright, Steve.'

'Is she fuck? Everybody knows she only got the job because she's got a front bottom and they seem to be nurturing those girls who seem exceptional.'

'Jesus, you were so born in the wrong century!'

'It was my due,' said Steve.

'You're not even a DI yet, Steve.'

'I've been in this squad a lifetime compared to her.'

'I don't believe I'm hearing this from a supposedly grown-up man,' said Joe. 'She was in another squad doing the same as you only in their opinion she was doing it better and from what I've seen of her so far, Steve, they were right.'

'I'm glad I can always count on my mates for a vote of confidence,' said Steve, folding his arms.

'It's because I'm a mate that I can tell you the truth, Steve,' said Joe, looking sideways at him. 'Maybe it's because I grew up with four older sisters. I've got more respect for women than you have and Steve, from where I'm sitting…' He started laughing. '…I wish I had a camera.'

'Why?'

'Because you look like my nephew when he can't get his own way and he's only bloody seven years old.'

Steve started smiling despite himself. 'She'll be spending a lot of the time with Norris anyway. I probably won't have to deal too much with her.'

'And you don't like Norris because he's younger than you and a DI.'

'The only thing I like about Tim Norris is his wife Helen.'

'Who is happily married to her husband.'

'That reminds me, are you still dicking that married bit from down your street?'

Joe had always regretted telling Steve about his regular liaison. He tended to bring it up whenever he was on approach to wanting to appear superior.

'I've always admired your delicate touch, Steve.'

'Hey, I'll never win first prize for diplomacy, I know that. So anyway, are you?'

'Yes.'

'Just don't like to think of you not getting your end away.'

'And are you still refusing to make an honest woman out of Amanda?'

'Marry Amanda? Isn't having me enough without a license and a ring?'

'A little thing called commitment?'

'Aww, now you're talking like a bloody woman,' said

Steve. 'Get yourself a blond wig and a short skirt. Mind you, with your body shape, maybe not.'

Steve knew he was regarded within the squad as being a little truculent. A lot of the time it was a valid judgement. He was truculent. His partner Amanda, with whom he'd lived for several years, would say that. But he was also someone who, by his own admission after several glasses of wine, had grown up with a massive chip on his shoulder. His parents divorce when he was thirteen meant that he'd had to be lifted out of his private school where he'd been doing exceptionally well and into an east Manchester state school where he'd been picked on for being clever. His two half-siblings, born of his solicitor father's second marriage, had both gone to private school and were now at university. Steve hadn't been able to go to university. His mother couldn't afford it and his father, under pressure form his second wife, had in the end, after a lot of negotiation, refused to finance it. So Steve had joined the Greater Manchester police force as an ordinary recruit when, in his mind, he should've been on a fast track promotion scheme and if it hadn't have been for his father betraying his mother then he would've been. Tim Norris had taken the promotion that Steve had considered to be his and Sara Hoyland had jumped over them both. That was enough for Steve to hate her guts.

'But anyway,' said Steve, 'consider myself put back in my box.'

'Oh, behave, you stupid bastard,' said Joe, 'and give Sara Hoyland the chance she deserves.'

'Yes, sir,' said Steve who despite everything still retained a sense of humour and liked to banter with Joe. 'As you say, sir.'

'Fuck off and keep an eye out for Kendal Rise.'

'Are you going for a pint tonight? Amanda's having to work late so I'm off the leash!'

'Well if you insist.'

By the time they got to Lorraine Cowley's house, Steve had already made his judgements about the area and the people who lived there. Trees lined the street and some houses even had a front garden, though most of them had been turned over for car parking or for the storage of valuable household items such as discarded bath tubs, bikes without wheels, old kitchen units that were in the process of being chopped up for God knows what, and various sizes of vehicle tyres.

Joe introduced them but it was all lost on Lorraine. She tried to shut the door in their faces but Joe managed to wedge his well proportioned foot in her door.

'It will do you more favours to talk to us, Lorraine,' said Joe who was waiting for support from Steve but it didn't seem to be forthcoming. 'Your daughter Michaela has been missing now for nearly a week.'

'I've got nothing to say to you!' Lorraine protested.

'Oh but we think you have,' said Joe. 'Now let us in and we can get on with things.'

Lorraine had to let them in but once they were across the threshold she was anxious to get the door closed behind them.

'What are you worried about, Lorraine?' asked Joe. 'First you don't want us here and then you can't get us in quick enough. You wouldn't be scared of someone?'

'I'm scared of nobody.'

Both Joe and Steve almost laughed. Her big bravado act was looking so bloody ridiculous. Steve looked round but didn't want to take a seat in case he caught something. The place was filthy. Why didn't these people ever take care of the houses that were provided for them by his taxes?

'When did you last see you daughter Michaela?' asked Joe.

'It's none of your business!'

'But that's not your choice to make, Lorraine,' said Joe, still with a sideways glance at Steve. 'Your daughter is underage and alarm buttons have been pressed because she's not been at school. Lorraine, do you know what happened to Shona Higgins?'

Lorraine sat down at the kitchen table and began to weep.

'What is it, Lorraine?' asked Steve, finally breaking his silence much to Joe's relief. 'Come on now. What do you know about what's happened to these girls?'

Neither of them made any move to comfort Lorraine. Joe placed a hand on her shoulder but that was the only concession to whatever predicament she was in. Steve especially didn't have much sympathy with her.

'I don't know,' Lorraine wailed, between sobs.

'But what do you know?' Joe asked.

'That she left for school that morning and she didn't come home.'

Joe sat down beside her. 'But you know more than that, don't you, Lorraine? You know why she didn't come back?'

Lorraine began to weep again and then said 'No, I don't know.'

'So who else was involved, Lorraine?' Steve asked with noticeably more impatience than Joe.

'I don't know,' she cried.

'Aww, come on, Lorraine! You're obviously hiding something which means that the lives of these girls are at stake. Are you happy if any of them die because you didn't have the guts to tell the truth?'

'Don't,' she pleaded, 'please, don't.'

'Why not, Lorraine?' Steve went on, ignoring Joe's signals to back off and take it easy. 'What do you know that we need to know about?'

'I don't know anything.'

'Rubbish! You know something.'

'I don't!' she cried. 'My daughter disappeared, just like all the others.'

Steve scoffed. 'Then you're okay about whatever happens to your daughter?'

'Just leave me alone!' she begged. 'I can't tell you anything because I don't know, now how many more fucking times!'

Paul was just getting into his car before driving to work when he saw Jake pulling up on the other side of the street. He wound his window down as Jake walked over to him.

'Jake, I'm already late for work,' said Paul. 'It's not that I don't want to talk to you but I've got a lot on and…'

'… Please, Paul. I haven't told you everything and I know I shouldn't put on you like this but… Christ, man, who else would understand?'

'You'd better come in,' said Paul.

Paul got out of his car and led Jake into his house. He took him through to the kitchen and put the kettle on. They stood in silence whilst Paul made the tea and handed Jake a mug. Then they sat down at Paul's kitchen table.

'Jake, what the hell is happening to you?'

'Everything that would scare the fucking life out of you.'

Paul sat back and let out a long sigh. 'You don't give me easy answers.'

'What do you think it's like inside my head?'

'Well that's what you can tell me about now.'

Jake rubbed his chin. 'After my mates were killed in front of me and I was nearly taken by a mob who'd have ripped my limbs apart, I kind of lost it a bit. In fact, I lost it altogether.'

'I can understand that, Jake.'

'I couldn't make sense of anything,' said Jake, rubbing the palms of his hands together. 'My mates were dead and I wasn't. I couldn't get my head round anything and I was in the darkest place I've ever known.'

'Again, that's hardly surprising.'

'The audits that the unit did on all the guns and ammunition wasn't always as tight as it should've been,' he admitted finally, 'I helped myself to some of it.'

'You stole guns and ammunition from your unit?'

'Twice.'

'You fucking idiot! What would they have done if they'd have caught you?'

'I didn't care,' said Jake.

'What?' said Paul.

'I sold the weaponry.'

'Who to?'

'To some bad people! What the fuck does it matter?' I was desperate for cash, Paul. I've got a bad credit history, so has Tiffany. We're a right pair.'

'Why didn't you ask me for help, Jake? I'd have given you my last penny piece, you know that.'

'I didn't think I had the right,' said Jake as he wiped his mouth with the back of his hand. 'And this security job I've got. I don't exactly sit watching a load of CCTV cameras.'

'Christ, Jake, you're scaring the shit out of me! You need help.'

Jake slammed the palms of his hands down on the table causing Paul to jump back.

'No, I don't! Help is the last fucking thing I need.'

Jake then stood up and made for the front door.

'Wait!' said Paul, his anxiety growing at Jake's oscillating behaviour. 'Jake, I'm worried… where the hell are you going?

'Home to my wife,' said Jake. 'Isn't that where I should go?'

'Jake, for God's sake let me help you.'

'This is what you wanted, isn't it?'

'What do you mean?' Paul asked.

'You wanted us to be sat here, drinking tea, perhaps having breakfast, being part of the brave new world of civil partnerships. This is how you wanted us to be.'

'Jake, what's that got to do with…'

'…who am I, Paul?'

Paul reached out and touched Jake's arm. 'I say again, Jake, let me help you.'

Jake stood looking into Paul's pleading eyes. Then without saying another word, he opened the door and left.

★

Anita Cowley had never taken very kindly to being told what to do. Her mother had always instilled in her the value of shouting first before getting shouted at and that way people wouldn't dare to try anything on with you. It had worked. All the way through school she'd approached each day as if it were a battle zone. Her mother had never seen any point in school but had greeted her first ovulation as a sign that money was soon to be made.

Every teacher had been the enemy and depending on how insistent the teacher had been about wanting her to pay attention, Anita had developed a way of dealing with them. She'd twice accused male teachers of making sexual advances towards her and she'd accused three women teachers of having slapped her. She always gave such a good performance of being the wronged against that it was hard for the authorities not to believe her initially. But during the investigations that followed, she could never keep up the victim act and her accusations were always thrown out. But the teaching staff had lost their patience after the fifth occasion. With the backing of their trade union they united in refusing to teach someone who'd made five false allegations against members of the teaching staff. She'd just turned fifteen and it was about this same time that she 'fell' pregnant with her daughter Candice. After that nobody made her think about school again. Her social workers had only been concerned about her getting the right kind of 'support' for her and her baby and finishing her education had not come into it at all. And she'd been happy with that. It had got her off the hook.

But something was now shifting inside her.

Up until now nothing had ever happened at home unless her mother approved of it. But now the two of them were locked in a battle and she was beginning to feel a desperate need to get away from her mother and the example of life her mother had shown her. If her mother had really loved her then she would've insisted that she got down to her schoolwork instead of going off in search of some feckless lad who could father her a child for her. Even when the deed had been done she should've advised her to have an abortion or to give the baby up for adoption, Anita realised all that now. She wouldn't be without Candice but it might've been better for her daughter if she'd been given to a family looking to adopt. It was a mother's job to put her child first. But she hadn't learned that from her own mother.

Anita had known nothing about bringing up a child when the whole process began. She'd known enough to stick a dummy in its mouth to shut it up. She'd known enough to believe that a bag of crisps in one hand and a can of pop in the other could stand as a proper meal. But now she worked with other women who were mothers and she was learning just where she'd got it all so wrong.

She was starting to feel shame at her old ways. Everybody who worked at the centre was really nice and they'd talked to her, got to know her, asked her opinion on things. Not even Paul had tried to play the big 'I am' and some of the folks who came into the centre had made her feel that perhaps she wasn't quite at the bottom of the pile. Some of the cases were so sad that they even broke her heart and nobody had been able to do that before. And her mother was wrong. The people she worked with weren't laughing at her behind her back. They were doing for her what her mother should've always done.

It was the end of her first week of working at the centre and she was happy. But she knew that this happiness would be ripped out of her when she got home. She wasn't in favour with her mother. It was going to be a very long weekend.

'Remembered you've got a kid then?' Lorraine snarled, her face turned sideways towards her daughter who was tucking into beans on toast. Candice had the same and Lorraine had cut it all up for her in bite size pieces suitable for a small person.

'What's the matter, Mum?' asked Anita, impatiently. 'Can't stand it because I'm happy on terms that aren't yours?'

Lorraine swung her arm round and walloped Anita across the face. It was so hard and so dramatic that little Candice burst into tears. Anita picked her up and cuddled her. She then turned her eyes to her mother.

'You bitch!' she screamed.

'You're the bitch in this house, lady!' her mother roared back. 'Going out to work when you know I've got enough on my plate worrying myself sick about our Michaela! You should be here with me.'

'Doing what exactly?'

'Helping me!'

'With what, Mum?'

'With living.'

'Why do you need me to stay at home all day to do that?'

'My God,' Lorraine scoffed. 'Two weeks at work and she's coming out with all the clever rubbish they all talk.'

'Oh Mum, please,' said Anita, who could've just burst into tears but was determined not to. 'Why can't you just be proud of me?'

'Because a mother who dumps her child at a so-called children's centre whilst she swans it about in some stupid job is a rotten, selfish little bitch! She's nobody to be proud of.'

'Oh yeah? And if a mother knows more about her daughter's disappearance than she'll let on to the police then what does that make her?'

'Do you want another slap?'

'Go on, if it makes you happy! If that's all you can do!

Well I'll tell you something. If my sister ends up the same way as Shona Higgins then I'll never speak to you again.'

Sara ran into the station and was given a message that Superintendent Hargreaves wanted to see her. She straightened her hair with her fingers and made sure her dress was tidy by wiping it down with her hands. Then she knocked on the Super's door and he called her in.

'Sit down, Sara,' said Hargreaves as he gestured to the chair in front of his desk.

'Is something wrong, sir?' Sara asked.

'Why do you ask that?'

'The look on your face, sir,' said Sara. 'It says you're desperate to get something off your chest.'

'You're known for being very direct, DCI Hoyland.'

'It's the way I am, sir,' said Sara, noting that he'd switched to DCI Hoyland instead of using just Sara, 'and I'll never be any different.'

'And that's to your credit,' said Hargreaves, 'but rumours have got back to me, Sara. They say that you and DI Norris are not getting on. Want to comment on that?'

'Tim and I have some personal history, sir, yes,' said Sara, 'but we're both professional officers. It doesn't need to affect our working relationship and I for one won't let it. You don't need to worry, sir.'

'Good,' said Hargreaves, 'but if it does, despite your best efforts, get out of control, you will let me know?'

'Of course, sir, but like I said, it is under control.'

'I know what you're thinking, Sara.'

'Sir?'

'That I'm a fine one to talk about personal lives

considering the rumours that go around about me?'

Sara blushed and smiled nervously, 'oh I wouldn't know, sir.'

'Yes, you would,' said Hargreaves, 'I know what's being said about me and a certain WPC. And the reason I'm saying all this to you is that you're a bloody good officer and I don't want anything to spoil the career path ahead of you.'

'I won't let that happen, sir.'

'Good, right answer.'

'So if there's nothing else, sir?'

'No, I think we're done for now,' said Hargreaves. 'Just remember what I've said.'

Sara stood up and made for the door but before she opened it she turned round to face him again.

'Sir? I think you deserve to know this. The rumours you talked about concerning you and a certain WPC? They mainly come from her. She can't help boasting about her relationship with you and she seems to be under the impression that if she was simply to click her fingers you'd leave your wife for her.'

Hargreaves felt rather uncomfortable about what Sara was telling him. He knew that Sharon Howells had not been altogether discreet about their relationship but he hadn't known that she was the source of much of the gossip. The sex with Sharon was good but it wasn't that good to risk the rest of his life on it. As for him leaving his wife? There was no way that was going to happen.

'Thanks, Sara,' said Hargreaves. 'I appreciate that.'

'If I hear anything else, sir, I'll let you know.'

CHAPTER NINE

PAUL HELPED HIS DAD eat some of the fish and mashed potatoes he'd cooked for him. Then he took the dishes out to the kitchen and loaded them into the dishwasher. He'd battled with his mother for years to get one and had considered it something of a victory when she'd finally relented. When he came back into his father's bedroom he stopped for a moment. He'd have to admit that his father looked ghastly. His eyes seemed to have sunken even further back into his head and he was so painfully thin.

His mind swept through memories of his father as a younger man, when Paul was a child, when his father was physically strong and free of the disease that was now slowly taking him away. He smiled. These were the memories he'd need to hold onto, especially in the days after his father had gone and his grief would be at its sharpest.

'How are you doing, son?'

'I'm doing alright, Dad.'

'Paul?'

'Yes, Dad?'

'In the top of the chest of drawers, buried right at the bottom, you'll find a small box. I want you to get it and bring it over.'

Paul went over to the chest of drawers and followed his father's instructions. He then brought the small box over to him.

'Open it,' Ed commanded.

Paul opened the box and his eyes widened at what was inside. It was a man's wrist watch encrusted with small diamonds.

'Bloody hell!' Paul exclaimed. 'Is this yours?'

'It's solid gold,' smiled Ed.

'I never knew you had this.'

'Nobody knows I've got it, not even your mother,' said Ed. 'It was given to me many years ago by someone I loved very much.'

'It's beautiful.'

'I want you to have it.'

'Me?'

'She was the love of my life, Paul.'

Paul sat down on the edge of his father's bed. 'Is this where you tell me you were a bit of a one with the ladies, Dad?'

'I had my moments,' said Ed, smiling as best he could. 'You youngsters weren't the inventors of fun, you know.'

'You dark horse,' said Paul, 'I can see the memories are making you smile. Whoever this woman was I like her for that at least.'

'I loved the absolute bones of her,' said Ed. 'There was nothing I wouldn't have done for her.'

'What happened to her?'

'She died, son,' said Ed. 'It was tragic, really, really tragic. She was so young.'

Kathy Jenkins had never been part of a media circus before. She hadn't known what it was until one of her neighbours had explained. She'd led a very quiet sort of life until her father's execution back in 1940 had been brought back into the spotlight in the last few days. The witch of Gatley Hall, as Kathy had always referred to Lady Eleanor Harding, by giving sanctuary to that evil Nazi, had shone a light on the recent history of the Hall, beginning with her brother's murder and her father's conviction for it. It had also taken Kathy back to a time when she'd been surrounded by pitch darkness as big as the universe and like the universe, seemed to know no end.

'Thank you for this, Kathy,' said Marius Van Urk, Manchester correspondent for 'theuktoday' online news website, as he tucked into the cake she'd baked for his visit. His charm over the phone had been what had led Kathy to giving him her 'exclusive' deal on her life story despite the fact that she'd never heard of something called the internet. But they were going to pay her a grand sum. She didn't know what on earth she was going to do with it.

'Is your tea alright, love?'

'It's fine, thanks, Kathy,' said Marius, his South African accent still as strong as when he'd arrived in the UK five years ago. 'I'm not used to being spoilt like this.'

'Well I'm not used to getting any visitors,' said Kathy. 'So I have to make you welcome.'

Marius was sitting in the living room of Kathy's council flat, fourteen storeys up in a block about four miles north of Manchester's city centre. She'd made it as pleasant as she could but Marius could sense the decay. Carpets were frayed, furniture was old and worn, it was spotlessly clean but he could see that Kathy didn't like to get rid of anything. There were boxes of old ornaments and glassware, newspapers and magazines, all neatly stacked, covering a quarter of the floor space, and the storage cupboard against the wall seemed full to the brim with goodness knows what. This was Kathy's life, conducted within these few small rooms.

'You've got a cracking view, Kathy,' said Marius looking up at the window. 'You could almost reach out and touch the city skyline.'

'Yes,' said Kathy, 'I see the trains, the trams, the traffic all making their way in and out. But I like to look out at the view at night especially. All the lights make it look like Christmas, you know. It makes me think that life must be going on for some lucky souls out there.'

'Who would you call a lucky soul, Kathy?'

'Someone of my age who's got a husband, a family, children and grandchildren. Oh I know you can be surrounded by people and still feel alone but I'd have liked the opportunity to find that out for myself. Anyway, I mustn't get maudlin.'

'How old are you, Kathy? If I can ask a lady that?'

'I'm eighty-three, love,' said Kathy, 'and I feel it, believe me. My brother was murdered and my father was hanged. Have you any idea what it was like to never have the money or the know how to clear my father's name? To never have people who could help you? I've lived with it for seventy years.'

'Didn't you ever marry, Kathy?'

'I was engaged back in 1953,' she declared as she poured them both some more tea, 'the year of the coronation. His name was Harold Mortimer and he had a butcher's shop over on the Stockport Road. But when he found out what had happened to my Dad he dropped me. It was a Thursday night and I was waiting for him outside the pictures. But he sent his mate to say that he wouldn't be turning up and why. I ran home crying and I never bothered with blokes again after that. I didn't see there was much point. I've never been to the pictures since then either.'

Even Marius, with his hardened journalist's heart, couldn't help but feel sad for her. This woman had let her life stop in 1953. What a waste. What a stupid bastard that Harold Mortimer had been.

'I thought Harold was a good man,' said Kathy, her eyes recalling every inch of the man she thought she was going to spend the rest of her life with, her heart breaking at what might've been. 'I never heard from him again. I suppose he got married to someone else and had a family and whatnot and probably never thought about me again. But as far as he and I were concerned, the family curse had struck and that was that.'

'The family curse?'

'We were cursed, Marius. Harold Mortimer was like all the others who backed off from us when they found out about my father. Nobody was ever prepared to believe that my father was innocent. They thought we were a bad lot. My father was hanged. Those of us that were left got a life sentence.'

'What happened to you after he was hanged?'

'The Witch of Gatley Hall threw my Mum and I out of our tied cottage the day before my father's execution.'

'Serious?'

'Oh yes,' said Kathy, 'she said that she needed to clear the place for the man she'd given my father's job to.'

'Well did you go to any family?'

'Our families, on both my mother and my father's side, all disowned us because of the scandal we'd been involved in.'

'So what did you do?'

'We slept rough for a couple of nights, me and Mum,' said Kathy. 'We couldn't believe that life had just turned on us the way it had. We had no hope. My brother Peter had gone, my other brother Colin was away at the war, and my father had been taken from us in the most horrible way. We were alone.'

'But it was the war, bombs were going off. The city must've been a frightening place to be in your situation. How the hell did you manage?'

'We ended up finding a place in a hostel run by nuns until the war ended and then the council housed us. Colin came back from the war but he wasn't right. He'd seen things, done things, and then there was what had happened to our Peter and my Dad for him to have to deal with. He took to the drink and he met a right drunken tart called Brenda. I never had any time for her right from the start but Colin wouldn't hear a word against her. After a few weeks she was pregnant, he married her and nine months later their daughter was born…'

Paul watched her face brighten.

'…Susan brought such light and hope into the family. We thought we'd turned a corner. She was such a beautiful little thing but of course it didn't take long for things to go wrong. Brenda couldn't cope and she just walked out one day and we never saw her again. Colin turned back to the drink and carried on until he dropped into an early grave. Susan was six. She and her father had been living with us since Brenda left so she just stayed with us and we brought her up. It was just mother, me, and Susan. It was hard, we never had any money, we never went on holidays, but Susan always knew that she was loved and wanted.'

'You must be so bitter, Kathy? I mean, the life you've led compared to that of Lady Eleanor'

'Bitter isn't the word,' said Kathy, 'I think I'm more angry rather than bitter Marius, love.'

'I don't blame you,' said Marius, 'I don't see how

anybody couldn't be.'

'We went to see my father the day before they did it. I'll never forget the look on his face. He couldn't say anything to us and we didn't know what to say to him.'

'I can't even begin to imagine what that must've been like, Kathy,' said Paul, 'but tell me what happened to your niece Susan?'

'Susan was a bright girl and despite everything she did well at school. She went to work as a typist over at Hope hospital here in Salford and we really thought the curse had been broken. She was popular. She had a lot of friends and a good social life. She brought so much joy into the lives of me and her grandmother. Then she met Miles. He was a doctor at the hospital, he spoke nicely, God knows what he must've thought of this place. He was so handsome and we thought he really cared for our Susan.'

'Thought he did?'

'Susan found she was pregnant and that's when Miles told her he was married and that what she did about the pregnancy was her business and had nothing to do with him.'

Marius rubbed his hand across his face, 'I knew you were going to say that.'

'He got himself a transfer to a hospital down south somewhere. It turned out that's where his wife and children were.'

'So what happened to Susan after that?'

Kathy breathed in deep. 'During the pregnancy it was hard for her because none of her friends knew what to say and she couldn't really go out with them anymore. These days of course nobody would bat an eye lid, but back then it was still a bit frowned upon. But when the baby was born, a little boy, Susan was overjoyed. She ran around the place looking after him and again we thought that the curse had been broken. But then she went out one day to do some shopping and she got knocked down crossing the road. She died at the scene.'

Marius held Kathy's hand. 'Oh Kathy, Kathy,' he shook his head. 'I just don't know what to say about so much pain. What you've told me is extraordinary.'

'I managed to contact Miles but he didn't want to know,' said Kathy, 'the baby was three months old…' she started to cry.

'Hey, hey, it's alright, Kathy.'

'I had to give the baby a chance, you see. I couldn't let another life be destroyed. The curse would've got him in the end and I couldn't let that happen. So I decided to give the baby up for adoption. I remember the day they came for him. My mother and I cried our hearts out for days afterwards. We'd lost him. We'd lost everyone. It was back to being just the two of us.'

'Oh, Kathy,' said Marius.

'My mother died ten years ago,' said Kathy. 'We didn't go out much and nobody ever came to see us but we were okay in our own little world I suppose. We didn't really know any different. We knew that life could be better and was better for some other people but… well we just got on with what we had.'

'Which didn't add up to a whole lot.'

'No it didn't,' said Kathy, 'not really.'

'So what have done since your Mum died?'

'The same as I did when she was alive,' said Kathy, 'I do the main shop once a week and I go down and get some fresh bits and pieces a couple of days later. That all lasts me till the next main shop. I've got good neighbours thankfully. Cyril is on one side and Norma and Ted are on the other.

I am lucky in that respect. We keep an eye on each other and have a glass of sherry at Christmas, you know.'

'Kathy,' said Marius, getting down to the real point of why he was there. 'Your father protested his innocence throughout his trial and right up to his execution.'

'That's because he was innocent, Marius,' said Kathy.

'Tell me what he said happened that night when your brother was murdered?'

'Well, he said that he ran into where the swimming pool was because he'd heard a lot of noise and a lot of shouting. But the sight that greeted him made him stop literally in his tracks. Lady Eleanor and my brother were in the pool but there was also another man there.' She started to cry. 'Sorry, I was so close to Peter when I was a kid. He took care of me and that, you know. Anyway, he said that she, Lady Eleanor, and this other man were standing over Peter's dead body.'

'So you're saying that Peter was dead when your father got there?'

'Yes,' said Kathy.

'And he didn't know who this other man was?'

'No, he didn't,' said Kathy, 'but what if it was this Nazi who's hiding there now? I'm bitter, Marius, because my father was a decent, honest man but he was made out to be a liar by a system that would rather believe someone with a title. And it led to him dying in the most horrific way. Somebody has got to pay, Marius. Someone has got to finally get justice for my father.'

Paul was having dinner with Kelly and Lydia at the Rice Bowl, his favourite Chinese restaurant in Manchester, down on Cross Street. They often came here after having a few early drinks in town. They liked the largely white walls with their framed pieces of Chinese artefacts and the friendly way with which the staff always greeted them. Lydia particularly liked a Buddha's face in wood that was hanging on the far wall and often stated a desire to steal it for her living room.

Their starters had already been cleared away. Paul had gone for Won Ton soup and the girls had each ordered a selection of Dim Sum. Paul poured some more of the Chilean red wine they were drinking into each of the girl's glasses before replenishing his own and then their main courses arrived, laid out on the table by two waiters dressed in the traditional Chinese black shirts and baggy trousers. Paul had ordered beef in a black bean sauce with crispy fried noodles, Kelly had ordered a large bowl of noodle soup with prawns, and Lydia had satisfied her sweet tooth with a sweet and sour chicken. The first bottle of wine had almost gone so they ordered another. None of them had brought their cars. They were going to get the metrolink home.

'You see, the thing about it is that people didn't expect Labour politicians to be doing it,' said Lydia as a contribution to the discussion they were having about the MP's expenses scandal and how it was taking a long time for the public to trust politicians again. 'They expected it from the Tories. They expected them to be cleaning up whatever they can, claiming for gardening and dog food when they're a multi-millionaire and all that. But they didn't expect politicians from the party of the working class to be claiming two hundred quid for a bathroom towel and to flip their designated homes to avoid paying capital gains tax.'

'Dead on,' said Kelly.

'They've not all been at it though,' said Paul. 'Some of them have done wrong and they need to account for it, fair enough. But there are other more powerful people in society who've done much more damage. Like the bankers who brought the entire financial system of the world to the brink but still expect their million pound bonuses. Captains of industry expecting the same even after the companies they ran lost millions. Multi-national companies dumping toxic waste on African coasts and nobody gives a shit about local people dying because they're only poor Africans and they don't rate in the world pecking order, which is why those multi-nationals go there in the first place. Our politicians, no matter how much they've swindled out of the system, are practically saints compared to all that lot.'

'That's all true enough,' said Kelly.

The waiting staff returned and cleared away the remnants of their main courses and replaced them on the table with some orange segments, slices of melon and a hot towel each.

'The wine is looking pretty low again,' said Lydia, picking up the bottle and turning it one way and then the other. 'Shall we order another?'

'Why not,' said Paul, 'I don't care that it's a school night and I can tell neither of you are on an early shift.'

'Anyway, enough of all this politics,' said Kelly. 'Show us that watch again.'

Paul had said that for one night only he'd wear the watch his father had given him. He'd have to admit that he was bloody proud of it but it would be only coming out on very special occasions. He'd never seen anything like it and neither had either of the girls.

'It's like something out of another world,' said Kelly as

she held Paul's wrist admiring it. 'Be careful wearing it though. It looks pretty valuable.'

'It's probably very old,' said Paul as his eyes followed the line of encrusted diamonds around the watch face. He'd never have bought anything like it but he'd keep it forever now that his father had given it to him.

'It looks like something from another world,' said Lydia. 'It's almost magical.'

'I wonder how much it is worth,' said Kelly.

'Do you think I should find out?'

'It wouldn't do any harm, would it,' said Kelly. 'I mean I'm sure your Dad didn't give it to you for that reason but it might be an idea.'

Paul took the watch off and held it up. 'I wonder what it could tell me if it could talk.'

'How do you mean?' asked Kelly.

'I don't know,' said Paul. 'It's just a feeling I get. Dad didn't tell me much about the lady who gave it to him. Perhaps he was some rich bitch's bit of rough.'

'I'll bet your Dad was a looker in his day,' said Lydia.

'Where did it go wrong with you then, Paul?' laughed Kelly.

'Oh ha fucking ha!'

'Which brings me neatly on to asking how you're feeling?' asked Kelly.

'With my hands as usual,' said Paul.

'No, you idiot, about Jake?'

'Like a hammer came down on my head,' said Paul.

'You've still let him back in though, haven't you,' said Lydia.

'Is that an accusation?'

'No, it's a statement of truth,' said Lydia. 'We know you've let him back into your life.'

'And your bed' said Kelly.

'Christ, have you been checking my sheets for stains?'

'We didn't have to,' said Kelly. 'We saw his car outside your place the other morning.'

'He's different,' stated Paul. 'His experiences in Afghanistan have damaged him. He went through absolute hell out there and I want to help him.'

'But you don't have to anymore, Paul,' said Lydia. 'That's all we're saying. Now that he's made his choice you can wash your hands of him and move on with your life.'

'No, I can't, Lydia,' said Paul, firmly, 'and if you two can't deal with that then it's your problem, but I've never turned my back on anybody when they needed me and I'm not going to start with Jake.'

'You're really playing with fire Paul,' said Kelly, 'you know that. If he's as damaged as you say then he needs professional help.'

'Yeah, I do know,' said Paul, 'but whilst there's a part of him that needs me I'll be there for him. If I end up looking like a twat, well then it won't be the first time that love has done that to me. Look, I just know that you have to follow your heart sometimes and damn the consequences. Otherwise, you may as well be dead.'

CHAPTER TEN

PAUL TOOK THE WATCH his father had given him into a jewellers shop on St. Peter's Square in Manchester to have it valued. Kelly was right about it being a good idea. In any case he probably needed to get it insured.

The man behind the counter was middle-aged and dressed in a rather formal three piece grey pin-striped suit. He'd lost the hair on the top of his head and there was growing evidence that perhaps he needed to think about getting bigger trousers. Paul was in a light brown suede jacket and blue jeans and the man's face lit up when he saw him. Great, thought Paul. I always pull the Adonis types.

'Can I help you, sir?' The man asked with a smile so sweet it was like being greeted by a slice of strawberry cheesecake.

'I'd like to get a valuation on this watch, please,' said Paul as he handed over the watch in the box his father had presented it in to him. He watched the man's expression suddenly change into a mixture of shock and bewilderment.

'Could you wait here a moment, please? I'm the son in Rubinstein and Son. My father started the business and he's the real expert.'

'Is this a problem?' Paul asked.

'Oh no problem,' said the man, all conciliatory smiles and rather camp appeasing gestures. 'No problem at all. I'll just be a few minutes.' He then disappeared into the back of the shop.

When the man came back he brought with him a rather elderly looking gentleman in the same kind of grey pin-striped three-piece suit, but he also wore a hat with a large rim and he had a short beard. He extended his hand to Paul. 'I'm Saul Rubinstein,' he said before turning to his son, 'and this is my son Lionel. Now where did you get this watch?'

The man's tone was accusatory and slightly aggressive. It annoyed Paul.

'Well if it's any of your business, my father gave it to me,' said Paul.

'And where did he get it?'

'He was given it as a present,' said Paul. 'But I don't know why I'm answering your questions. I want the watch to be valued and if you can't do that then I'll take it somewhere else.'

'Yes, alright, alright,' said Saul, 'I didn't mean to offend.'

'Well I'd hate to be on the receiving end when you did mean to.'

'Let's start again.'

'I think we'd better,' said Paul. 'So, can you value this for me?'

'No, I can't.'

'Then give it me back and I'll take it somewhere else.'

'Wherever you take it they won't be able to value it for you,' said Saul. 'It is beyond the normal values of a wrist watch.'

'I'm sorry but I don't understand,' said Paul, slightly confused.

Lionel Rubinstein went over to the other counter on the other side of the shop where a young couple were looking for an engagement ring. Paul glanced at them enviously. They looked so carefree and in love, holding hands, touching, kissing, thinking about the future and never expecting anything to go wrong. He smiled and silently wished them every blessing.

'You've heard of the Holocaust, Mr. Foster?'

'It's Paul and yes, of course I've heard of the Holocaust, Mr. Rubinstein.'

'Then you will know of its origins in the Germany of the 1930's? You will know that the lives of many Jewish people were snatched away from them and they were left with nothing but the yellow triangle the Nazi's forced them to wear?'

'Yes?' said Paul.

'Their livelihoods, their homes, all of their possessions were taken in raids where many suffered and some died. I was six years old. We were driven out of our family home, me, my parents, my four brothers and sisters. My father was in the jewellery business and even though I was young, I learned many things. At the end of the war I was the only member of my family left. The rest had all perished in Auschwitz. I made my way to England and married a Manchester lass. I've been here ever since. We have seven children, nineteen grandchildren and two great-grandchildren. Lionel is our youngest and the only one who isn't married. He has his own flat in the Northern Quarter but comes home every Friday evening for the start of the Sabbath.'

'Mr. Rubinstein, I sympathise with your story, I really do,' said Paul who didn't think it was any surprise that the little Jewish princess Lionel was the only one of Saul's children who hadn't contributed to the continuation of the Jewish line, 'but I just don't understand the connection with me and this watch?'

Saul Rubinstein held up the watch in the space between them. 'Paul, only ten of these watches were made. They were all hand made by my father and my older brothers at our workshop which was above the retail shop in Berlin. The jewels came from our cousins who were in the diamond trade in Antwerp, Belgium.'

'You're saying this watch was hand made by your family?'

'Yes,' said Saul, 'we never intended making anymore than ten. They were meant to be an exclusive line. Paul, we were the most prominent Jewish family in the jewellery trade in Berlin at that time and these watches would've sealed our place and the future financial security of our family. But then the Nazi's happened. I've never set eyes on one of them since everything was taken from us. That is until now.'

'My God,' said Paul, looking at the watch. He'd been quite shaken by what Saul Rubinstein had told him. 'That's quite a story.'

'And it's all true,' said Saul. 'I can assure you of that.'

'Oh I believe you, Mr. Rubinstein, I really do,' said Paul, 'I'm really not doubting you.'

'Who gave it to your father?'

'As far as I know it was an old girlfriend' said Paul.

'As far as you know?'

'Well he only gave it to me the other day and… you see, Mr. Rubinstein, my Dad is dying. He has cancer.'

'I'm sorry to hear that.'

'He wanted me to have the watch before he passed away,' said Paul. 'He's an ordinary working-class man, Mr. Rubinstein. He drove buses all his working life. Considering the history of it I just can't imagine how he would get involved with somebody who had something like this watch.'

'Is your mother still alive?'

'Yes, she is.'

'But as far as you know the watch was given to him by an old girlfriend?'

'That's right,' said Paul, 'my mother doesn't know anything about it. I know that much.'

'Well then if you think your father could bear to tell you,' said Saul. 'You should ask him who she was and if he knows how this watch came into her possession. As I'm sure you can imagine, I'd be very interested to know.'

Dieter was having grave doubts about what Eleanor was about to do.

'Are you sure you should be doing this, liebling? I mean, if it means telling more lies? The police are already highly suspicious'

'I think it's a bit late to worry about that,' said Eleanor. 'About seventy years too late.'

The Kathy Jenkins interview had been published on the news website and had been picked up by all of the national dailies and had made Eleanor's blood boil with rage. All of these matters had been left alone for so many years and throughout that time all the demons had been under her control. Now it was as if they were flying out of her castle windows without her being able to do anything about it. Well she was going to see about that. A few wings needed to be clipped.

'Well I'm flattered by the invitation, Lady Eleanor,' said Marius van Urk. 'Even though more and more people are taking their news coverage from the net, it's still been hard to get ourselves established as a leading news source.'

'I'm not here to flatter anyone, Mr. Van Urk,' said Eleanor. She'd rather taken to this fresh faced young man. He reminded her of some of the ones she'd met in her youth, 'although that would be easy in your case.'

Marius felt himself blush. He'd never been hit on before by a ninety-year old filthy rich woman before. Like all good colonials Marius was drooling about sitting in this massive 200-room house in the old country with all its traditions and history and this woman from another world. Lady Eleanor was physically a little frail, she had a walking stick at her side, but she was immaculately turned out in a Chanel style two piece and her hair was perfectly set in the brushed back style of elderly ladies of a certain age. There were more lines across her face than a Manchester A to Z but her eyes looked like they could freeze hell.

'Your accent is quite fascinating,' said Eleanor. 'Your name suggests you may be from Holland? Or perhaps the Flemish speaking part of Belgium? I have so many friends in Antwerp and Bruges.'

'You're way off, I'm afraid,' laughed Marius. 'My mother is English, from Nottingham, where my grandparents and the rest of my mother's family live, but my father is South African which is where I was born and brought up. My mother moved out there when she married my father.'

'And she's still out there?'

'Oh yes, my folks are still going strong,' said Marius. 'They've been married for almost thirty years now.'

'They must mourn the passing of the old days?'

'The old days?'

'When the right people were in charge,' said Eleanor.

Marius knew exactly what she meant. Since apartheid

ended his family had lost their privileged access to the reins of society. But they were still rich. His father's business was a vineyard in the Eastern Cape that had been raking in the cash since the end of apartheid had led to the world looking more favourably on importing South African goods. In the 'old days' it had just been Israel and a few fascist states that had comprehensively traded with South Africa. Now the whole world drank the country's wine. But he would have to concede that wealth had not been re-distributed throughout the 'new' South Africa. Most blacks had stayed poor whilst some of their 'comrades' had got themselves very wealthy on the backs of the 'cause' they continued to profess to be fighting for. It sometimes left Marius to wonder what had really changed for the majority of his black compatriots. Unlike his Afrikaner father however, Marius had never been a fan of apartheid. He loved the spirit of what his country had become but the reality of it was what had made him leave for the UK. That and splitting up from his fiancée Yvette which had made him want to make a fresh start somewhere else.

'Well I go back home once a year,' said Marius. 'They're about a hundred miles east of Cape Town.'

'Yes, I've been there. But that was back in…'

'…the old days?'

'Precisely.'

Marius looked up at one of the pictures on the wall. It was of a slightly chubby man in the kind of shirt and tie that spoke so wildly of sixties Britain. 'Who's that, your Ladyship?'

'It's Ronald Kray,' said Eleanor, who'd hidden her pictures of the Kray twins when the police had been there. 'He was a great friend and a frequent visitor to my home here.'

'Really? How so?'

'Marius, people of my class have always got on famously with men from less savoury backgrounds. Look at my dear late friend and confidant Lord Boothby and his friendship with the Kray twins as an example. The aristocracy and the working classes have always held each other in mutual respect and each have always known their respective place in the order of things. It's those dreadful middle classes who think they're more important than they are.'

Marius thought it was almost laughable how the British titled classes had such an affinity with the criminal world. He'd heard it a lot from his mother's side of the family and it sounded like this stupid old bitch was no different.

'I'm a very angry woman at this time, Marius,' Eleanor went on. 'I am one of the 91 hereditary peers they let remain in our rightful place in the House of Lords but I know that our days are numbered thanks to the sell-out out to the Liberals by our so-called Conservative Prime Minister.'

'Isn't that part of what being a coalition is about, Lady Eleanor? The two parties involved have to compromise?'

'Coalition?' she scoffed. 'Compromise? They say they want the Lords to be a fully elected chamber but the masses don't use the democracy they've got let alone what this coalition is set to impose on them. My blood is boiling, Marius. We must save England and restore the libertarian values of our Anglo-Saxon culture. They'd rather give equal rights to homosexuals than lower my taxes, so-called human rights have replaced tradition and all our power as a nation is being lost to Brussels.'

'So you feel betrayed by the Conservative party on Europe?'

'Utterly betrayed, Marius!' said Eleanor. 'Utterly

betrayed! It's another example of the Liberals punching above their weight and holding the Prime Minister to political ransom. My family and the rest of my class built the empire Marius, but now this country is being lost to cultures that are alien to it. There are too many mosques and temples being built. There has to be a stop to it.'

'I'm an immigrant to this country myself, Lady Eleanor.'

'And people like you are more than welcome here, Marius,' said Eleanor. 'It's not people like you I'm talking about. I'm glad your paper contacted me because this could be my last ever chance to put my side across. People like me have been wronged against. We need justice, Marius. The white race in this country needs justice.'

'That's all very interesting, Lady Eleanor, but of course you invited us here to respond to the comments on our website made by Kathy Jenkins during her interview with me.'

'And that's what I'm coming to, Marius,' said Eleanor. 'I say again that people of my class are under attack from liberalism. The lies of Kathy Jenkins are part of that. Her father murdered her brother, Marius. Her father murdered her brother but she wants to put the blame on me because of something called class envy. Well she's wrong, Marius. She's wrong about it and she's wrong about her claims. I saw what happened. Her father came rushing into the pool when he saw his son Peter and I in an embrace and in the struggle of pulling Peter off me he threw him against the side of the pool and he died. His father had killed him. He was tried. He was convicted. He was executed. If his daughter Kathy still can't come to terms with that then I feel truly sorry for her. But she's wrong, Marius. Her father murdered her brother and I was a witness to it.'

When Jake turned up on Paul's doorstep out of the blue again, Paul had just got in from work and he was knackered. He hadn't slept well since he found out the history of the watch his father had given him and was trying to work out how he could ask his father about it in his dying days. He needed to know who the woman was who gave it to him. That was the real mystery of it all as far as Paul could see. Whoever she was, where had she got it from?

'You look miles away,' said Jake.

'I've got a lot on my mind, Jake.'

'Got any room for some more?'

Paul smiled resignedly. 'What do you think the answer to that question is? Come on in.'

Something about the way Jake looked at him filled Paul with all the lustful hunger that had always been so much a part of their relationship. And no matter how tired he was, just at that moment sex was all Paul wanted.

'You want to talk?' Paul asked.

'I do, yes,' said Jake.

'Well I want something else first and for once in my life, I'm going to be selfish.'

They didn't need to say anything else. They just ripped each other's clothes off and got down to the business of making love right there in the middle of Paul's living room floor. Paul rode Jake like a horse, arching his back and keeping his hands gripped firmly on Jake's firm, wide shoulders. It was raw. It was sensual. It didn't matter about anything or anyone else except the pleasure they were giving each other. Jake was used to Paul having a lot of sexual energy but he was really going for it this time and Jake was happy to respond in kind.

'That was just what I needed,' said Paul when they'd finished. They leaned against the wall in a post-coital embrace. Paul grabbed one of the throw-over's from his sofa and wrapped it round them. 'And now we're cosy.'

Jake squeezed him. 'I wish we could stay like this forever.'

'That would be nice,' said Paul.

'I was nearly dead, Paul.'

'In the explosion that killed your friends?'

'No,' said Jake, his mind flooding with all the images that fuel his rage. 'It was another day, another patrol, another reminder that we shouldn't be there. I somehow got separated from the others. I was a sitting duck.'

'You mean you were captured?'

'Yes,' said Jake, 'by our friends the Taliban.'

'Jesus, Jake,' said Paul. 'What happened?'

'They took me to some shack somewhere,' said Jake. 'They set me up for execution. There was a whole load of plastic sheeting on the floor ready to capture the blood. About ten of them held me. I was on my knees, they pulled me head back and had one of the biggest knives I've ever seen ready to do the job. They had a video camera set up. They were going to post the whole drama on the internet.'

'God, I feel sick,' said Paul.

'I thought I was in my final moments,' said Jake. 'All I could think about was you. The memory of it still traps me inside my head, you know. Those shackles are still on. Those tight hands with the desire to kill me in every pore of every finger are still in position. The gentle whirling sound of the video camera as it prepared to make me a worldwide hit. I can still hear the voices that ripped through me like tiny daggers until I heard a different kind of voice. A voice that spoke a language I still didn't understand but that I knew was friendly.'

'And who the hell was that?'

'We had a French group working under our command. They stormed the shack and luckily the first one they killed was the one who'd been holding the knife. You see, the Taliban had planned to grab one of the coalition soldiers for weeks. That's why they took me straight to the little studio they'd set up. But it was only a mile from where the French had been on patrol and they received some intelligence on the location. I'll never bad mouth France or the French ever again, not even in jest.'

Paul sat up and cradled Jake's face in his hands. 'Jake, you've got to get some help to sort all of this out in your head.'

'No, I don't!' Jake insisted, 'all I need is to come here and talk to you.'

'Jake, I'm not a professional.'

'You are! You do this all the time at work.'

'Jake, I'm a social worker, not a therapist. I can't deal with all you've got going through your head.'

'You don't know everything that's going through my head.'

'And that's the point!'

'Paul, please, don't close me down.'

'Close you down?'

'Take away the only place I can go.'

Paul couldn't get over the look in Jake's eyes. They were full of pain. They'd witnessed his imminent death and his lucky escape. What was the country doing for these guys? The country sends them out and makes a big show of driving their dead bodies through villages where people turn out to show their respect. But what happens to men like Jake who come back alive but without everything in their soul that they'd taken out with them? Are they just left to deal with it on their own? Would those who publicly display their support for the dead look the other way when the living show their problems? Is it too uncomfortable for them? It's easy to applaud dead bodies. Anybody can do that. Reaching out and helping the living was more difficult.

Paul held Jake's hand. 'I'll do what I can, Jake.'

'I know you will,' said Jake who had tears running down his cheeks.

'Do you want to stay for dinner?'

'Yes, I do.'

Paul stood up. 'I'll go and see what I've got. I haven't done much shopping this week so we might have to send out for something.'

Jake reached out for Paul's hand and held it. 'Paul?'

'Yeah?'

'Thanks.'

Paul smiled. 'What are we going to do, Jake?'

'About us?'

'And Tiffany and the baby.'

'I don't know. I want to be here with you more than anything but I can't leave her. I don't know what I'm going to do.'

CHAPTER ELEVEN

IT HAD QUITE MADE SARA'S DAY when she got to work that morning and a very cute PC called Kieran Quinn, who'd caught her eye a few days ago and who was manning the reception desk downstairs, had noticed that she'd had her hair trimmed the night before. The comment had made her blush. Either he's into older women or he doesn't realise how much older than him she is. But then she thought, so what? He'd look very nice inside her. It had been a while since she'd been taken down and dusted and three weeks without sex for a woman as physically inclined as Sara was like an eternity.

Her friends all said she had a man's attitude when it came to sex. If she wanted it she went looking for it or she welcomed it if it came to find her and she didn't see any wrong in that. Samantha, her great heroine from Sex and the City had shown all the women of the world the way and that it was okay for women to chase cock as much as men chase fanny. She liked sex. There was nothing like the feeling you get from it when it's good and as far as she was concerned people who said they didn't need it were only making up for the fact that they couldn't find it. She wondered how experienced young Kieran was. Sometimes younger men could surprise a girl with their knowledge. Her vibrator had been seeing a lot of her lately and that was all very fine but she couldn't talk to it about the football. Kieran looked like he'd be into football. He was well over six feet tall with dark blond hair and green eyes.

He'd tan well in the sun and he had the sexiest dimple in his chin. He clearly had an eye for her and she couldn't wait to get his pants off, so by the end of the day she'd have exchanged numbers with him and made arrangements for him to come round and check out where she slept. Although he won't be doing much sleeping once she'd got him under her duvet.

But first there was work to do. Yesterday she'd had the most blazing row with Steve Osborne. He'd accused her of trying to undermine him because she wouldn't accept his theory that the social worker Paul Foster might be involved in the disappearance of the missing girls. His argument was that Foster was the only common link they knew about so far between all the girls. They and their families had all been clients of his. He was only offering it as part of a discussion but one thing led to another and before they knew it voices were being raised and doors were being slammed shut. The first thing she intended to do today was build some kind of bridge with the sexist prick and she was glad when she caught up with him in the corridor.

'DS Osborne.'

'Ma'am,' said Steve, he carried on walking but she called him back.

'DS Osborne?'

Steve sighed and turned around, 'Yes, ma'am?'

'I think we need to talk, don't you?'

'I've consulted my federation rep, ma'am.'

'About what?'

'About the guidelines on workplace bullying.'

Sara was absolutely incensed. 'Are you seriously suggesting that I was bullying you?'

'That's what it felt like to me, ma'am, yes.'

'DS Osborne, I completely reject the idea that I was

bullying you and I can assure you that I will fight any complaint vigorously, but if there was any bullying going on then I think it was going both ways. Ever since I set foot in this building you've done nothing but take any step you can to confront me. Now I know you're sore because I took the box of toys you thought were yours but you've got to deal with it, Steve. Or else you'll never get to play with them. Now, underneath all this pointless attitude you treat me to I truly believe there's a bloody good copper just screaming to get out. Your assessment is due in a couple of weeks' time. Let's not make it war and peace without the peace.' She held out her hand. 'Let's grow up and get on.'

For once in his life Steve knew he had to bow to the intellectual superiority of a woman. Sara was tough. And he'd have to admit that he didn't think he'd have been able to confront the bad blood between them like she just had. So he would give her a chance. But only one.

'Okay,' he said, shaking her hand. 'This is day one.'

'Good.'

'I must say I'm impressed, ma'am.'

'With what exactly?'

'In our argument you didn't bring in the whole man-woman thing,' said Steve, feeling he was being clumsy with his words although he knew exactly what he was trying to say. 'You didn't try to say that it was due to you being a woman and me being a man.'

'That's because I've got balls, Steve.'

Steve smiled. 'Yes, I think you have.'

'But do me a favour?'

'I'm spoken for, ma'am, sorry.'

Now it was Sara's turn to smile. She wouldn't take her clothes off for Steve if someone offered to pay her, however much she liked the physical side of life.

'That's a shame, I'm really gutted,' she said, 'but what I meant was don't wear that tie again.'

Steve looked down at his red, white, and blue stripped tie.

'What's wrong with it?'

'What's right with it?'

'My mother bought me this last Christmas.'

'Then as an act of revenge I would accuse her of having abused you when you were a child.'

Sara went into the ladies and couldn't help laughing but was also relieved that she and Steve had settled things. She used her usual mix of firmness, honesty, and humour and it seemed to have worked. She did believe that Steve was a good copper. It just needed to be wrestled past his attitude.

She then went into a meeting with Tim, Joe, and Steve. Joe briefed them that as a result of intense house to house enquiries made by uniform and the checking of school attendance records, it was now certain that fifteen teenage girls had gone missing from the Tatton estate and other estates across Greater Manchester and in all cases none of the parents had reported anything to the police. None of the parents would talk. Sara hadn't even been able to prize anything out of Shona Higgins parents. Whoever had frightened these people into silence had done a bloody good job.

'So what do we think?' Sara asked.

'That there is a connection between them all, ma'am,' said Steve. 'All the girls have been declared missing and their details fed through all the national channels. We have checked out all the paedophiles on the watch list who are living in the area and managed to eliminate them all from our enquiries and in any case, to put it bluntly all of these girls would be too old for them.'

'The youngest is thirteen and the oldest is fifteen, right?' Tim wanted to confirm.

'Yes, boss,' said Joe. 'There are two offenders who have previous for having sex with underage teenage girls that live on the estate but we've been able to rule both of them out too.'

'And didn't anybody notice anything on the days these girls disappeared?' Sara wanted to know.

'Ma'am, no witnesses have come forward and no incidents have been recorded,' said Steve.

'But I can't believe that nobody saw anything,' said Sara, 'I mean, nobody from the schools they were supposed to be attending? The local shops? Bus drivers?'

'On the face of it, it's baffling to tell you the truth, ma'am,' said Steve. 'These girls just seemed to have walked off into nowhere.'

'So where do we go from here?' asked Tim.

'Yes, sir,' said Joe, 'the only thing we can do at this stage is to look through that lot.' He pointed at the mountain of tapes taken from CCTV cameras on the various estates and outside the schools the girls were supposed to have attended. 'It'll take a while but it might bring something up.'

'Okay then, Joe,' said Sara. 'Thanks for everything so far. Let's see if you get something positive from the tapes.'

'We can try, ma'am,' said Joe. 'I'll keep you informed.'

'But who could be frightening them?' Sara asked. 'That's what I want to find out.'

Later that morning Sara met with Superintendent Hargreaves to bring him up to date on both the missing girls and the Naumann extradition case.

'They've both changed their story, sir,' said Sara. 'First, Lady Eleanor insisted that nobody else had been there at the time of Peter Jenkins' murder and had dismissed Wilfred Jenkins assertion at his trial that there had been. Then Naumann tells us that he was the said mystery man who was there when Peter Jenkins died.'

'So what are we saying has happened here?' asked Hargreaves who'd always had a more modern attitude to female officers than some of his contemporaries. As far as he was concerned if an officer could bring in the results then he didn't care whether they were male, female, black, white, brown, yellow, gay, straight, or indifferent.

'I think that Naumann may have killed Jenkins and Lady Eleanor is protecting him like she's always done,' said Sara. 'Naumann also had a motive to kill Ronald Harding, Lady Eleanor's husband who was a closet homosexual who'd refused to give Lady Eleanor the divorce she'd asked for when the war ended and she wanted to marry Naumann. For decades they'd carried on an affair and Naumann was the biological father of Lady Eleanor's daughter who she blamed for the killing.'

'Even though Naumann waited until 1974?'

'Opportunity, inclination, there could've been several reasons why Naumann waited that long.'

'And Lady Eleanor's daughter disappeared straight after?'

'Exactly, sir,' Sara went on, 'Naumann had been married to another woman but he'd always remained in love with Lady Eleanor. He had motive and the need to protect his anonymity provided the perfect alibi.'

'So where the hell did the daughter go?'

'Who knows? But we know that people can just disappear if they really want to.'

'The evidence is flimsy to say the least though, Sara,' said Hargreaves.

'It is at the moment, sir, I agree,' said Sara. 'But what we need to do is to trace people who worked at the Hall back in 1974 and find Clarissa Harding's boyfriend.'

'Alright,' said Hargreaves as he leaned back in his chair and rubbed a finger over his chin. 'But let's stay aware of the timescale we have on Naumann. Don't let it start running out on us.'

Lorraine was pegging her washing out when two strong arms grabbed her from behind and one of the hands went up to cover her mouth. It was a fairly secluded back garden and nobody would've been able to witness the scene unless they happened to be peering out of their window at the time. And even if anybody had seen they wouldn't risk talking to the coppers or anyone else for that matter.

Jake threw her down into the armchair in her living room. The curtains had all been drawn closed. He didn't like what he was doing but he didn't feel like he had any choice. He'd been dishonourably discharged from the army after they'd discovered he'd taken the handguns and ammunition. His previous exemplary service coupled with his two brushes with death at the hands of the Taliban had proved to be enough in the way of mitigating circumstances for him to escape a much harsher judgement. But still he felt like there was unfinished business to attend to with regard to the army. He didn't want to take anything out on the army itself. Nobody amongst their ranks would ever be the target of his hunger for revenge. But what he did want to do was to show whoever would listen enough to make sense that the troops shouldn't be out there. But that was for another day. That was what he was saving up for. Other people who have never had a knife held at their throat, save up their money for a new dining room suite. Jake was saving up to buy something that money couldn't.

'No, please, not again!' Lorraine pleaded, her face covered in the tears. 'Sir, please, I didn't tell them anything.'

'Tell who?' asked Glenn Barber who was sat opposite her on the sofa.

'The police! They came round here but I didn't tell them anything, I swear I didn't.'

Glenn sat with his legs folded over each other and a cigarette on the go. He nodded to Jake who hoisted Lorraine up and dragged her down at Glenn's feet. He was holding her by her hair and once more she was almost passing out with fear. Glenn leaned forward.

'Now, Lorraine,' said Glenn. 'Who raised all these suspicions in the first place? Who was it that let the cat out of the bag? Was it you?'

Lorraine shook her head as vigorously as she could in the grip of Jake's firm hands. 'No, sir, no, it was that social worker.'

'Who? A bleeding heart social worker?'

'He was the one who called in the police to investigate what had happened to the girls. He's the one who's made you have to watch yourself, sir.'

'And what's his name, Lorraine?'

'Paul Foster, sir,' said Lorraine, using her hatred for Paul Foster to get herself off the hook with Barber. He needed to be taught a lesson anyway and Barber was the one to do it. She didn't know why she hadn't thought of it before. 'He works down at the centre in Broughton. He lives round here somewhere but I don't know where.'

Jake heard Paul's name and it felt like a knife going

through his heart. Jesus Christ, could things get anymore complicated?

'Paul Foster,' said Glenn Barber as he rolled his cigarette in his fingers. 'So he's the one who thinks he can interfere in my business? Well he'll have to learn like you all do.' He stabbed the still burning cigarette into Lorraine's chin. She let out a scream but Jake held her steady. He was doing his job well despite being knocked way off centre by the mentioning of Paul's name. He knew what Glenn Barber would intend to do about Paul and it sent a chill through his soul.

'Don't keep me waiting for information again, Lorraine,' said Barber after he'd stood up. Lorraine was crouched down on the floor holding her chin. 'Let me know as soon as you do. Then we wouldn't have to make these little visits.'

'One thing puzzles me about you, Lady Eleanor,' said Marius Van Urk as he began his second interview with her Ladyship in the cavernous drawing room of Gatley Hall.

'Then I suppose you could say you were very lucky,' said Eleanor, chuckling at her own humour. 'Many have been puzzled about me over the years and for all sorts of reasons. I'll be interested to hear yours.'

'Well without being too delicate about it, your Ladyship, what's going to happen to all of this when you're no longer here? Surely you don't want it all to pass to the Treasury?'

Eleanor smirked at her questioner. 'That's for me to know about, Mr. Van Urk.'

'So are you saying there is someone to hand your title onto?'

'Please don't try and read between my lines, Mr. Van Urk...'

'...but surely I don't need to, Lady Eleanor? You just said that there was someone you could hand it all onto?'

'I said no such thing, Mr. Van Urk,' said Eleanor, firmly. 'I merely implied that there may be more to my story than you'll be able to print.'

'So you're teasing me again?'

'I love doing it.'

'That's clear from our previous conversation.'

'It's such good sport.'

'So why aren't you giving me the whole story?'

'What do you mean, Mr. Van Urk?'

'That throughout our two conversations I've been left with the strong feeling that there's something else on the table that I can't see,' said Marius.

'You're a journalist, Mr. Van Urk,' said Eleanor. 'Your nose is trained in such a way that you sniff around.'

'I'd have put it a little more delicately than that, Lady Eleanor.'

'I'm sure but I have nothing to prove and I'm in my own house,' said Eleanor. 'So on both counts I can speak freely.'

'I wish you would, Lady Eleanor.'

'You wish I would what, Mr. Van Urk?'

'I wish you would speak freely, Lady Eleanor,' said Marius. 'Instead of exercising such control over what you say.'

'You will have to deal with your frustrations in your own way, Mr. Van Urk,' said Eleanor. 'I cannot help you any further with that I'm afraid.'

Marius sat back and pondered. His article on Lady Eleanor was more or less complete as far as what he could get out of her. But he knew there was more to be had from this old bitch from the discreet conversations he'd held with some of her staff. Her head of household, Colin Bradley, had been particularly candid about the comings and goings with her Ladyship. He was seriously buried in personal debt so when Marius came along with his journalist's cheque book, Colin had virtually bitten his hand off.

'Tell me about Glenn Barber, Lady Eleanor?'

Marius watched the colour drain from her Ladyship's face that was well in need of being ironed.

'I don't know anyone of that name, Mr. Van Urk,' said Eleanor who was furious. Who the hell had been talking? She wanted to know and when she found out they'd be very sorry.

'Yes you do,' said Marius. 'He comes to see you here at the Hall at least once a month and I'm wondering what a woman of your standing would have in common with one of Manchester's most successful and most feared loan sharks?'

'Get out of my house!' said Eleanor who was so full of rage she didn't know what to do. Somebody in her household must've talked and when she found out who it was she'd cut their bloody tongue out herself.

'Well would it be impertinent to ask you again what's going to happen to all of this when you're gone?'

'Get out, Mr. Van Urk,' Eleanor repeated, 'get out or I'll have my security people throw you out!'

'Very well,' said Marius, collecting his things together. 'It's your funeral. The ones who come after me won't be as friendly, especially after what I plan to write up on the website. The vultures really will be after you then.'

Fall From Grace

Paul couldn't understand why Jake kept calling him on his mobile but hung up before Paul had the chance to speak. It had happened seven times just in the last hour. Paul had tried to ring him back but it kept going straight to voicemail. He didn't know what was going on. He just hoped Jake was okay.

He left work and on the way home he listened on his car radio to the PM show on Radio Four talking about the issues of the day. It was part of his Radio Four routine. The 'Today' show on the way to work and PM on the way home.

By the time he got home the show was featuring a piece about people who kept free range chickens battling against the supermarkets for, allegedly, not stocking enough of them. Now, Paul had a problem with all this. Many of the families he dealt with could make a cheaper, battery reared chicken stretch to three meals and couldn't care less whether or not the chicken had been able to run around a farm yard and quite frankly, nor could he. It seemed to him that only those in a position of economic choice made a fuss about the source of their food. Those who didn't have an economic choice just bought whatever they could within their budget to feed their kids. That's why he'd refused several invitations to join the Labour party. He'd been to a couple of meetings where he'd met too many middle class socialists, who he found were too pre-occupied with stuff that showed how they had completely lost touch with those who were too poor to worry about climate change or whether or not something was organically produced.

When he got home he went into the kitchen and got

a packet of chicken kievs out of the freezer. He had some rocket leaves and avocado with which he'd make a salad. He didn't care about the source of the chicken. He switched the oven to 200 degrees and waited for it to heat up whilst he poured himself a glass of wine. Then his mobile went again.

'...Paul? It's me. Get out of there, just fucking get out of there...!'

The line went dead and Paul stood there staring at the phone. What the fuck did all that mean? Get out of there? It was Jake but what the fuck was he on about?

He looked down at the chicken kievs and decided to put them both in the oven. He didn't have much time to worry about Jake's very garbled message when the back door burst open and tape was stuck across his mouth. A bag was placed over his head. His hands were cuffed behind his back and he was dragged out into the alleyway at the back and thrown into the back of a van. He was told to lie still if he knew what was good for him. But it was Jake's voice. What the fuck was going on?

His feet were tied together but there was no other violence shown other than his body being thrown across the floor of the van as it sped towards wherever it was going. He was terrified and utterly bewildered that Jake could be involved in doing this to him. He could feel his heart beating in his chest and his body begin to sweat.

When they got to wherever it was, he was pulled out of the back of the van and dragged along what felt like a concrete floor. After a few seconds they came to a stop and someone began kicking him. They kicked him in his back, in his kidneys, in his stomach, underneath his chin, finishing up in his groin. The pain lashed through him like fire through a house and he thought he was going to pass out.

That's when somebody pushed their hand under the bag over his head and ripped the tape from his mouth.

'If you think I'm going to let you interfere in my business then you'll end up dead my friend!'

'Who are you?'

That brought him another sharp kick in his lower back. He felt his back arch like it had never done before and he was able to cry out with agony for the first time since the attack had started. His mouth was dry. He was overwhelmed with pain and fear.

'I loan money to people who can't get it anywhere else,' said Barber. 'I provide a public service and I don't tolerate competition. You've been offering them the idea of some crap called a credit union, well let me tell you, Foster, keep your nose out of my affairs and keep your mouth shut. Otherwise, I won't be so gentle next time.'

Barber replaced the gag over Paul's mouth and then nodded at Jake for him to pick up where Barber had left off before. Barber turned to light a cigarette and waited to hear the action commence but there was only silence. He turned back and saw that Jake was just standing there staring down at their victim.

'What's the matter with you?' Barber demanded. 'Get on with it!'

Jake looked at him but said nothing.

'I said get on with it! Jake? I'm telling you!'

Paul had never known terror like it. Lying there helpless at the mercy of his attackers was bad enough but to hear Jake's name being mentioned made him feel like all the blood in his body had turned to ice. But now it was all starting to make the most deadly but perfect sense. That's why Jake had been making all those calls to him. He was trying to warn him. Telling him to get out of there was his way of saying that they were on their way and he didn't want to find Paul when he got there. This was the bloody security job he'd been so cagey about. He was minder for a fucking low life loan shark. Paul had never been more scared in his life and all he could think about was his poor old Dad. If Paul died here tonight then how would his Dad cope with that?

'Jake, I told you to get on with it! Now do as I say!'

Jake still made no motion towards Paul's twisted body.

'Alright, I'll fucking do it myself,' said Barber who braced himself to start kicking the shit out of Paul but he was stopped when Jake pushed him back.

'What the fuck has got into you?'

'You!' said Jake who could see that Barber didn't know what to make of his behaviour. 'Scum like you have got into me and twisted their way into my soul. I gave everything for Queen and country, and it nearly cost me my fucking life, twice. But what happens? I come back here and have to work for scum like you.'

'Nobody else would give you a job after you'd stolen those weapons, Jake,' said Barber. 'You should be grateful to me.'

Jake laughed. 'Grateful? Grateful that I now get to go around terrorising fat, stupid women who've never known any better? Grateful that I should be here now beating up one of the most decent human beings I've ever known?'

'What? You know this guy?'

'Yes, I know this guy,' said Jake, 'and that's why I'm going to do this'

Barber coiled back at the gun Jake had pulled on him.

'Now take it easy, Jake,' said Barber. 'I've got no quarrel with you. You know that. You lads shouldn't have been out there.'

'And what did you do about it? Yeah, you might've got annoyed at some news item on the TV but that's as far as it went.'

'Jake, I don't take it all for myself. You know I've got a boss who creams it all off. She never gets her privileged hands dirty but she's got as much dirt on them as I've got on mine.'

'Is this how you plead for your life, Barber?'

'Look, Jake, I don't know what it is you want from me.'

'Don't you? Well let me put you out of your little misery.'

Jake shot Barber at point blank range, ripping his head apart with half a dozen bullets. Each shot made Paul wince. He tried to speak but he couldn't get the words out through the gag. He wanted to beg Jake to stop.

After the final shot was fired an unbearable silence fell onto the scene. Then Paul started struggling against his restraints and made as much noise through the gag as he could. He was appealing to Jake to free him but he didn't hear any movement from Jake at all.

Paul then heard Jake running off, his footsteps fading the further he got and all Paul could do then was cry.

CHAPTER TWELVE

WHEN THE HOOD was taken off his head, the sun had come up, Paul had to squint his eyes several times to focus.

'Have you been there all night?' asked the security guard after he'd taken the gag off Paul's mouth.

'Yeah,' said Paul, weakly. His body felt like it was never going to feel normal again. The cuffs on his hands and feet had been cutting into his skin for the many hours of the long night. The pain was shooting through his body like the blows were being struck over and over again. 'What time is it now?'

'Just coming up to seven,' said the guard, 'lucky I found you.'

'How did you?'

'I look after the car dealership across the way there,' he said. 'I looked across and saw you.'

'Where am I for God's sake?'

'At a disused factory just off Bury New Road,' said the guard. 'Jesus, from the look of you someone gave you a good going over.'

'You're not kidding,' said Paul. He could taste dry blood on his lips and smell it all over his body. But it was the memory of who'd been there that was causing him the greatest pain. He felt himself breaking up again inside but managed to keep it under control. He didn't want to start crying in front of the security guard and he remembered the dead body that was rotting only a few metres away.

'Can you do anything about these cuffs? Christ, they really hurt.'

'Well I've no key but I have got something that will break them open,' said the guard. 'I'll go back and get it. Look, I don't know what it is you've got yourself into, mate, but I had to call the police. They're on their way along with an ambulance.'

Paul looked across to Glenn Barber's body. It looked like the picture on the front cover of a horror film DVD. Paul swallowed hard. This just couldn't have happened.

'It's okay,' said Paul, 'they'll want to speak to me but I had nothing to do with him over there.'

'Do you know who did?'

Paul just looked at him, unable to work out what to say.

'It's okay, mate,' said the guard, 'I understand. You probably don't want to say. I'll go and fetch those cutters. The police and the ambulance shouldn't be long.'

The security guard was true to his word and came back minutes later with a giant pair of cutters that released Paul from the cuffs. Before he paid any attention to the broken skin around his wrists and ankles he took his mobile out of his pocket and checked for calls. If there'd been any he would've heard them but he wanted to make sure. There were no missed calls which meant that he hadn't missed anything to do with his father, thank God.

But where the hell was Jake?

The police followed Paul to the hospital and once the medical staff had cleaned him up, the uniformed officers took a basic statement from him and passed it on to Joe Alexander and Steve Osborne when they turned up soon after to question him more thoroughly.

'How are you feeling, Mr. Foster?' asked Joe.

'Like I've been hit by the Piccadilly to Euston train at full speed,' said Paul as he struggled to pull himself up in the bed. He had a broken rib but the rest was down to some painful cuts and bruising; the damage usually associated with being kicked about and beaten up.

'You're okay, sir,' said Joe, holding up a consoling hand. 'We won't keep you long. If you're more comfortable lying down that's fine.'

If Steve didn't know better he'd say that Joe would be better off training as a priest and giving up life as a police officer. But he'd worked with Joe long enough to realise that although their styles clashed he didn't doubt Joe's ability as a police officer.

'Thanks,' said Paul. He gave up the fight to sit himself up straight. That could wait until the painkillers they'd given him had really kicked in. He flinched as his injuries reminded him why he was there.

'Looks like you had a lucky escape, sir,' said Steve.

'I think I did,' said Paul. 'It only hurts when I laugh as they say.'

'So why don't you tell us what happened?' asked Steve.

Paul took them through all the events that made last night the longest of his entire life and how it had all scared him half to death. But he left one important detail out. He said he didn't know who'd shot Glenn Barber. All he'd heard was a voice.

'And you didn't recognise the voice?' asked Joe.

'No, detective,' said Paul. He'd never taken to lying. He was the sort who wore his heart on his sleeve and he found it difficult to hide his feelings. It had got him into no end of trouble in the past. But he couldn't drop Jake in it. He didn't know where the hell Jake was and it worried him senseless but he just couldn't drop him in it. He'd been over and over it again and again in his mind. And he just couldn't, even though he couldn't get his head around what Jake had done. 'I'm afraid I didn't.'

'Are you sure about that, sir?' asked Steve.

'Yes, detective,' said Paul, 'I'm sure.'

'Why did Glenn Barber have any argument with you, Mr. Foster?' asked Joe.

'You know he was a loan shark, detective?'

'Of course,' said Joe, 'were you a customer of his?'

Paul was horrified at the thought. 'No,' he said emphatically, 'I was not. I've been trying to organise a credit union for the residents on the Tatton estate and naturally, Glenn Barber didn't like it because it would've taken some of his trade away.'

'I see,' said Steve, 'so trying to help people led to you lying here.'

'I wouldn't make such a direct connection, detective,' said Paul.

'Well what kind of connection would you make? I mean, it seems fairly direct to me. You tried to muscle in on his trade and you paid for it by ending up here.'

'You could've easily been killed yourself, Mr. Foster,' said Joe.

No, thought Paul. He knew one thing for certain. Jake would never have killed him. But then again, how could he be so sure? He never thought he'd ever kill anyone else unless it was on the battlefield of war.

'I suppose I could've been,' said Paul, 'but thankfully, I wasn't.'

'However, Mr. Foster,' said Steve, 'a man was murdered in your presence last night even though you say you couldn't see anything. That is right, isn't it? You didn't see anything?'

'As I said to your uniformed colleagues, Detective, the bag was kept over my head the entire time. I saw nothing. I didn't even know where the hell I was.'

'But are you sure you didn't recognise the voice of the third man there?'

'Yes, detective,' said Paul. 'I'm quite sure I didn't recognise it. I'm sorry.'

'Mr. Foster, we only know of one man who worked for Glenn Barber on a regular basis,' said Steve, who got the feeling that Paul Foster knew a lot more than he was letting on, 'his name is Jake Thornton.'

'Is that name familiar to you, Mr. Foster?' Joe asked.

'No, detective,' said Paul, feeling very uncomfortable about the lies he was telling. He hated himself. He hated Jake too at that moment. 'I'm afraid there's nothing else I can add to what I've already told you.'

Lady Eleanor had some decisions to make following the news of Glenn Barber's death that had come to her on that morning's Granada Reports.

'New arrangements will have to be made,' she said as Dieter sat beside her holding her hand, 'I'm putting you in charge of things now, Colin.'

Colin Bradley shifted uncomfortably in his seat. In the past he had run errands for her that would've put him in a court of law if he'd been found out and he'd even beaten people up for her when her usual associates were busy. But this was moving things up quite a notch and he didn't think he could do it.

'Hey now, wait a minute…'

'...Colin, there simply is nobody else,' Eleanor insisted. 'You know the addresses, you know all the clients and you know all about the financial side of things. I'd say you were perfect to step into Barber's shoes.'

'Lady Eleanor, I've got a wife and two children, I'm trained as a butler and now as head of your household I think I do a good job. I know I've done some things for you in the past but I didn't sign on to become involved in murder.'

'Colin, you're up to your neck in it already,' said Eleanor. 'All it would take is one phone call and I'd be able to summon up a team of gentlemen who would be anything but gentle in their methods of persuasion. Now I don't want to have to do that to you, Colin. You've been a loyal servant. But I will resort to those tactics if I'm pushed.'

'You wouldn't dare.'

'Or maybe I could have something happen to your wife or one of your children?'

'You leave them out of it!'

'That's it, Colin,' said Eleanor, 'some well placed anger is such a good thing. We bottle too much up.'

Colin Bradley wished he was anyone but himself at that moment. He had no doubt that this twisted old bitch would carry out her threat if he didn't comply with what she wanted. Anybody who'd ever crossed her had paid the price for it, usually with their life. He couldn't risk anything happening to Monica or the boys. He'd never be able to live with himself. He wished he had enough money for him to take them off somewhere Lady Eleanor couldn't find them but he didn't. And she knew that. How the hell did he get in this state? One too many credit cards, repayments on a loan on top of two others that stretched the finances so much every month that he was nervous all the bills would be paid. Now he was going to end up in hock to this evil witch and her Nazi. There had to be some way out but he was damned if he could find it.

'I will give you all the necessary details with regard to who you need to collect the payments off,' said Eleanor. 'I'll arrange for you to have some muscle with you when you do. But to reduce the risk of anyone finding out about our other operation, I'm going to have to ask you to consider murder a solitary act.'

'It's really not that difficult, Colin,' said Dieter. 'Once you've done it once you can do it time and again without any thought at all.'

You might've been able to, thought Colin. But I'm not you. He felt sick.

'Now Colin, you'll be making a lot of cold, hard cash by agreeing to what I ask and you could be spending it on that wife and family of yours. Can I take it you're in, Colin?'

'I don't think I have much of a choice, Lady Eleanor.'

'I'm glad you've been sensible,' said Eleanor. 'Now if you go to the property you'll find a girl called Michaela Cowley. She earned us a lot of money in the short time she's been with us but now she's outlived her usefulness and needs to be dealt with. She'll be your first, Colin and seeing as it's your first time, I'll give you a week to get the job done.'

'Or else?'

'I think I've already spelt out my terms in as clear a way as I can.'

'Come and see me when you've finished your shift here, Colin,' said Dieter. 'I'll show you a particularly effective strangulation technique. It's been a while since I practised it but it's like riding a bike. You never lose the touch.'

It must've been the look on Colin's face that provoked a reaction from Lady Eleanor.

'Colin, I'm inviting you to sit at the top table.'

'You're inviting me to commit murder,' said Colin, 'and you're not even inviting me.'

'Oh well of course you could say no and there'd be no hard feelings.'

Colin knew this must be some kind of trap. 'That's not what you hinted at before.'

'Well if you do agree to work with us then I'll have no need to tell your wife about your affair with the barmaid of your local pub,' said Eleanor. 'What's her name? Cheryl, isn't it? We've got pictures and I think she looks rather common compared to your wife Monica, but who am I to judge?'

'Alright!' Colin snapped. 'I'll do it. Just don't tell Monica about me and Cheryl. Please, don't ever do that.'

'Then listen to instructions and listen good,' said Eleanor. 'I'm not good at repetition.'

Tim and Sara had settled into a kind of suspended animosity of late. They weren't exactly bosom buddies but they weren't barely concealing their mutual contempt whenever they were together either. Both of them knew that the rest of the squad had noticed and that was the point when they'd had to get a grip on the situation, doing whatever they could to put their personal feelings aside.

They'd been through the employee records of Gatley Hall going back to the early 1970's. Out of the many names they could've started with they decided the most obvious choice was the man who'd been head of household for

Lady Eleanor at the time of her husband's murder and her daughter's disappearance. He lived in Stockport and they drove over to see if he'd be able to shed some light on the identity of Clarissa Harding's mysterious boyfriend.

'I could've taken Joe with me on this,' said Sara who was driving, 'but I thought it would be good for us to do it.'

'Why?'

'Tim, it's been like there's the Atlantic Ocean between us,' said Sara.

'Do you really think I'd have turned my back on you and our child?'

'Oh here we go, you see this is why we should've given it longer.'

'Well forgive me for not being able to let go of the fact that you didn't tell me you were expecting my baby.'

Sara took a deep breath. 'Okay,' I'm sorry. But I did explain my reasons.'

'You did,' said Tim, 'I'm just struggling to come to terms with them. I was the father. I should've had a say. It wasn't all down to you.'

'And I'm sorry for that now, Tim,' said Sara. 'I truly am.'

'And I'm sorry for the things I said to you the other day,' said Tim. 'I was pretty harsh.'

'It was a bit much, Tim,' said Sara, 'but I didn't consider how you'd feel about the baby and perhaps I deserved it.'

'Can we try and move on?'

'I'm willing to give it a go,' said Sara, relieved that the conversation was going this way.

'I suppose it hit me harder because Helen and I have been trying for a baby for the last two years,' said Tim, 'she wants us to go for tests.'

'And now you know there's nothing wrong with you?'

'Yeah,' said Tim, 'and I don't know if I should front up or go through with the tests and wait for the results to give her the answers. I'm between a rock and a hard place, you see. Either way she's going to be hurt.'

'I'm sorry, Tim,' said Sara.

'Yeah, me too.'

They waited almost a minute after they'd rung the doorbell before the door was opened. The man standing in front of them was tall, well over six foot and he had a mop of neatly combed white hair parted on his left hand side. He was neatly dressed in a shirt and tie, sharply pressed trousers and shiny black shoes. He was from another generation that believed in always looking your best and he reminded Sara of her dear old Granddad who she still missed even five years after he'd passed away.

'Leonid Sulkov?' Tim asked as he and Sara held up their warrant cards.

'Who is it who wants to know?' asked Leonid.

'I'm DCI Norris and this is DI Hoyland, sir,' said Tim, noting Leonid's soft but unmistakable East European accent. 'Greater Manchester Police. We're re-opening an investigation into the death of Ronald Harding at Gatley Hall and the disappearance of Clarissa Harding, Lady Eleanor's daughter. You were Lady Eleanor's head of household at the time and we wondered if you could help us?'

'It was a long time ago,' said Leonid, 'but there's a lot I can tell you. Please come in.'

Tim and Sara looked at each other before following Leonid into his council semi and through to the living room. He gestured for them to sit down.

'Can I make you some tea?' Leonid offered.

'No, we're okay,' said Sara, 'but thank you.'

The first thing Sara noticed was that there were no photographs on display anywhere. Usually, even people who'd had a fairly lonely time of it had a photograph of someone to show off. Her parents used to have a neighbour called Elsie. She was a widow and she hadn't seen her only son Trevor and his family for years since they'd emigrated to Australia. But she still had a photo of them in a nice frame. Shame they didn't get to see how proud she was of them. They hadn't been home in the twelve years since they left but when she died they came over to 'sort out the house' and claim their inheritance. Of course they'd never been able to afford to come over whilst she was alive. But as soon as she'd gone they somehow found the money for the airfare. Funny that Sara had thought. But Leonid had nobody to keep their beady eyes on him and Sara wondered why that was. The room was functional. It had furniture, a TV set in the corner. But it was all cold. Everything was in dark colours except for the walls which were painted a plain off-white.

'So Mr. Sulkov,' Sara began, 'can you just confirm to us when you worked at Gatley Hall for Lady Eleanor?'

'Yes, I started there in late 1945, shortly after I arrived in England.'

'Where did you come from?' asked Sara.

'The war,' said Leonid, simply 'but originally from Ukraine.'

'And you left Lady Eleanor's employment in 1974?' asked Tim.

'That is correct,' said Leonid, 'right after the unfortunate incidents involving Lady Eleanor's husband and daughter.'

'But you'd been with Lady Eleanor a very long time,

sir,' said Tim. 'Something pretty drastic must've happened to question your loyalty to that extent?'

'Did you witness the death of Ronald and disappearance of Clarissa Harding, sir?' said Sara.

'Yes.'

'But you told detectives at the time that you didn't,' said Sara. 'You told them that you'd been in a different part of the house and that the only thing you were aware of, was that a row had been going on and you heard a gunshot.'

'I lied,' said Leonid.

'Why?'

'To protect my friend.'

'Who was your friend, Mr. Sulkov?' asked Tim.

'His name was Ed Foster' said Leonid.

'And why did you need to protect him?'

'Because he shot Ronald Harding.'

'But Lady Eleanor said that her daughter Clarissa shot him?'

'Well she lied,' said Leonid. 'Ed Foster shot Ronald Harding. I watched him do it. He was a fool but he was in love and nothing could've stopped him.'

On the way back to the station, Sara received a call telling her that DNA found on the body of Shona Higgins pointed to Glenn Barber having murdered her.

Kelly and Lydia drove over to Blackpool to see Paul's Dad and were both shocked to see the deterioration in him since the last time they'd been.

'Hello,' smiled Ed, 'it's lovely to see you two.'

The girls went either side of Ed and each took one of

his hands in theirs. 'How are you feeling?' asked Kelly.

'Better for seeing you two.'

'We bet you say that to all the girls,' said Lydia.

'No,' said Ed, attempting a smile. 'Only to my special ones.'

'We're special, then?'

'Always have been'

Paul's mother always made herself scarce when any of Paul's friends came to see his father. They always looked at her as if she was guilty of the most heinous of crimes and of course, as far as Paul was concerned, she was. Kelly and Lydia especially gave her the evils and so she made tea for them and then said she was heading for the shops.

'How's our Paul doing?' asked Ed.

'He's alright, Ed,' said Kelly. They'd decided to abide by Paul's wishes and not tell his father about how he'd been beaten up and by whom. The bruises on his face wouldn't be visible in a day or so and then he'd be back to see his Dad. But the girls were worried. Kelly especially was furious with Paul for not telling the police that it was Jake who'd beaten him up and shot Barber. She didn't mourn the loss of a lowlife like Barber. But she feared what Jake might do on the run and the danger that could put Paul in.

'He's worried about everybody just like he always is, Ed,' said Lydia.

'He showed us that watch you gave him,' said Kelly. 'It's stunning.'

'Yes,' said Ed. 'It always was.'

'So come on then, Ed?' said Lydia, teasingly. 'Tell us about the girl who gave it to you.'

'She was Paul's mother.'

Kelly and Lydia's jaws dropped.

'His what?' asked Kelly.

'Two years into my marriage to Mary I had an affair with a woman called Clarissa,' said Ed who was so glad to be relieving himself of this terrible burden he'd been carrying around all these years. 'We had Paul but Clarissa died and I came back to Mary with Paul who was only a tiny baby at the time.'

'I take it Paul knows nothing of this?' said Lydia, shocked at what she was hearing.

'No,' said Ed who then asked Kelly to take an envelope out of his bedside drawer.

'It's got Paul's name on it,' said Kelly.

'Yes,' said Ed, 'when I first became ill I wrote the whole story down in a letter to Paul and I want the two of you to keep it until after I've gone. Then you can give it to him.'

'Oh Ed, sweetheart,' said Lydia. 'Paul's our friend. I don't know if we can do this.'

'I'm a dying man, Lydia,' said Ed. 'Surely you can't deny me a dying wish?'

'Well when you put it like that, Ed,' said Kelly, squeezing his hand affectionately.

'I haven't got the strength to deal with it all now, Kelly,' said Ed. 'It's all explained in the letter. When the time comes just tell him that I love him and that I never meant for there to be any trouble.'

The girls watched a tear run down Ed's face.

'And tell him that, despite what he might think after he's read the letter, I did what I thought was best. His mother meant life itself to me and I've never forgotten her.'

CHAPTER THIRTEEN

'NOW,' SAID LEONID, 'I will need to put the events of that night into context for you or else you will not be able to comprehend.'

Sara always wondered why it was that foreigners could often sound so much more eloquent in English than many of her fellow countrymen and women.

'Please do, sir,' said Tim.

'Ed Foster was a prominent member of the British fascist movement right throughout the sixties and into the seventies,' said Leonid. 'Oh he never did anything violent but like the political wings of various paramilitary groups today, he knew who the perpetrators of violence on behalf of the cause were, and on some occasions he provided the okay for such actions. But he was always there when the movement demonstrated in the streets, usually to protest against a coloured family moving into a street or a neighbourhood becoming overrun with such types of people. The movement went into the white community that were afraid of such influxes and stirred up trouble. They gave them the bullets to fire, Detectives, figuratively speaking of course. They put fire into the will of all the local white thugs.'

'So you were also a member of this movement?' said Sara.

'No, I never joined,' said Leonid. 'I went to some meetings which is how I met Ed Foster but I never joined. I sympathised to a certain extent but I think that was more to do with my own experiences in the Ukraine, you know, sides had to be taken and the side that I took led me away from my homeland for the rest of my life. I had nothing against anyone from India or Jamaica. I just wanted to protect my own kind, the white man, the Ukrainian whose country had been snatched away by the Soviets. And you see, lying low these past decades meant that I didn't really want to join anything that might draw attention to myself.'

'You didn't marry, Mr. Sulkov?' Sara enquired.

'No,' said Leonid. 'Oh there were ladies here and there, I was even engaged once. But I just couldn't get the family I'd left behind in the Ukraine out of my mind.'

'You must've been very lonely,' said Sara.

'Well in the intimate sense, yes, I was,' said Leonid, 'but I always had good friends around me.'

'They're no substitute,' said Sara.

Something in the way Sara said it made Tim turn and exchange a look with her that spoke of an unspoken tenderness from long ago.

'What were the experiences that led you away from the Ukraine, Mr. Sulkov?' asked Tim.

'Well now,' said Leonid. 'You see, everybody talks about the Holocaust as being the event of the Second World War that we're not allowed to forget. But there were other Holocaust's, detectives. During the 1930's Stalin's actions in the Ukraine led to the deaths of ten million people. Yes, ten million people. The Ukraine was the bread basket of the entire Soviet Union but because we had the courage to want our independence, Stalin punished us. All the wheat we grew was forcibly sent to other parts of the Soviet Union and we were left, literally, to starve. It was known as the Holodomor.'

'I had no idea,' said Tim.

'Me neither,' said Sara.

'Not many people do,' said Leonid. 'There's no official recognition internationally and it isn't taught in schools. But I lost my parents and my older brother and countless members of my extended family. Then when war came I knew that I was on the side of anyone who was fighting Stalin. I ran away and joined the German army. I wasn't the only one. Many of my compatriots did and none of us were ashamed. We were fighting a system that had wreaked such an evil catastrophe on our brethren. It was an opportunity to fight back and we didn't care that they were Nazis. They were fighting Stalin and that's all that mattered to us.'

'So what happened at the end of the war, sir?' asked Tim.

'I couldn't go back to the Ukraine because my family would all have been murdered by Stalin for my collaboration with the Germans if his secret police had found out,' Leonid explained. 'So to protect them I had to stay here and they would assume that I'd been killed in action fighting for the Red army because you see, that's who I told them I was running away to fight for. However painful it was, it meant that they would be safe, or as safe as they could be living under Stalin.'

'So,' said Sara who couldn't help but have sympathy for Leonid. War was such a fucking complicated business, more complicated than she'd ever thought before and more complicated than any case she'd had to deal with. She was grateful for having been born where she had been and when she had been. She'd known nothing of the struggles Leonid had known. She couldn't begin to comprehend how lonely life had made him to not be able to go back to his own country. 'You went to work for Lady Eleanor.'

'Yes,' said Leonid. 'I knew she was sympathetic to the Nazis and naturally, I knew that if I'd made my immediate past well known to most people then I wouldn't have been too popular. There was a network of fascist thinking people even back then and yet it was so dangerous just after the war.'

'Understandable, don't you think?' said Tim.

'Yes,' said Leonid.

'Sir, bring us up to that night in October 1974 when you lied to police officers about the murder of Ronald Harding,' said Tim.

'When Ed and I became friends I was at his house regularly, I knew his wife Mary and when their daughter Denise came along I was honoured when they asked me to be her godfather. Then one night, in a pub near Gatley Hall, Ed and I were drinking when Clarissa Harding came in. They hit it off and fell in love.'

'How come they hadn't met before?' Sara asked. 'If Lady Eleanor was a member then why hadn't Ed Foster, who you say was prominent in the organisation, why hadn't he met Clarissa Harding before?'

'Because Clarissa was not a fascist,' said Leonid in a voice like he was the impatient teacher of young dense children. 'She never had been and so wouldn't have anything to do with her mother's activity. Ronald Harding was a right-wing member of the 1922 committee Tory but he wasn't a fascist and she took after him. She detested fascism. I tended to think that her hatred for her mother was tied up with her abhorrence for fascism but that would've been a job for a psychologist. Anyway, what was genuine was the love Clarissa and Ed had for each other. Ed left his wife Mary for her and they set up home in a little flat in

Urmston. Because of Clarissa's distaste for fascism Ed resigned from the movement. He'd have done anything to please her.'

'Did he ever go back to it?' asked Tim.

'No,' said Leonid. 'He hasn't been part of it since then.'

'Sir?' said Sara. 'Why did Ed Foster shoot Ronald Harding?'

'Because he'd upset Clarissa so much.'

'Enough to shoot him?'

'Well by then it wasn't just about their love for each other,' said Leonid, 'which Clarissa's parents wouldn't entertain at any price. Both Clarissa and Ed really saw red when Clarissa's parents wouldn't accept their grandchild.'

'You mean Clarissa and Ed Foster had a baby?' asked Sara, incredulously. This investigation was turning into something like one of those Russian dolls. As soon as you lift one there's another underneath. She could usually get a feel for investigations but this one was losing her. She had no idea where the hell it was going to go.

'Oh yes,' said Leonid, 'he was a great little chap but the Harding's just would not accept him. Clarissa flew into a rage as I remember. She was dreadfully upset. Ronald Harding was particularly adamant that they would never accept what he called her 'bastard' child. That's when Ed, I'm afraid, lost it. He took one of the Harding's guns from the cupboard and shot Ronald. The baby was there and drops of Ronald's blood were spilt over him.'

'So what did you do then?' asked Tim.

'I dragged Ed out of the room,' said Leonid. 'He was in a state of utter shock and bewilderment at what he'd done but somehow he was in a trance-like state. It was as if something else had taken him over. He loved Clarissa more than life itself and he so desperately wanted to make her happy. But he had no defence against her family. He went back into the room. I followed him. Clarissa and her mother were fighting to get control of the gun Ed had used to shoot Ronald. There was a lot of shouting and screaming. Ed rushed over to help Clarissa but in the struggle that followed the gun went off and Clarissa was dead. Ed was beside himself. He'd shot the woman he loved and even though it was an accident he was inconsolable. I had to negotiate with Lady Eleanor on his behalf. We agreed that she would not tell the police that Ed had been there if he agreed to take the child and never have anything to do with them again. Ed had all the power, you see, because he knew that Wilfred Jenkins was not the murderer of his own son, Peter Jenkins, in 1940.'

'But who was the murderer of Peter Jenkins?' asked Sara.

'It was Lady Eleanor herself,' said Leonid, 'he let it slip one night to both Ed and myself and we didn't know then that it would give us a bargaining chip so many years later. That's the knowledge we used to keep Ed out of trouble.'

'A case of mutually assured destruction,' said Tim.

'You can put it that way, yes.'

'So you and Ed took the baby and went where?'

'We took him back to the house he'd shared with Mary and he begged her to take him back and to bring up his son as her own and she agreed.'

'Does the son know anything about this?' said Tim.

'Paul?' said Leonid. 'No, he doesn't. Ed has written him a letter to be opened once he's dead. Ed Foster had always wanted to make peace with it all before he passed on and when Gerald Edwards real identity as Dieter Naumann was revealed, he saw it as a sign that the time had come.

He'd been wondering how he could do it. He hasn't much time left.'

'Mr. Sulkov?' said Sara. 'Are you prepared to make a statement about all of this?'

'Yes, I am,' said Leonid.

'So you've remained friends with Ed Foster for all these years?' said Tim.

'Oh yes,' said Leonid, 'very good friends.'

'Even though he did things as a member of the fascist movement that you might not have approved of?'

'I think it would be very boring if we concurred with everything our friends did,' said Leonid.

'And your friend Ed Foster is willing to take the consequences now?' said Sara.

'Yes, he is,' said Leonid, 'but don't forget he's bedridden and in terrible pain. We're talking days, not even weeks.'

'And what about his son? How do you think he'll react to all this?'

'Paul loves his father very much,' said Leonid. 'He idolises him, always has done. I worry about his reaction to tell you the truth. I worry about what he'll think when he sees his father fall from grace.'

'What does his son Paul do for a living?' asked Sara after a penny had dropped inside her head.

'He's a social worker,' said Leonid. 'He manages the centre over at Broughton.'

Anita looked up at the two men standing in front of her at the social services centre reception desk and knew instantly that they were coppers. She's seen so many of that sort on the Tatton estate but something had changed about her reaction to them that went with her general change in her attitude to life.

'So what can I help you with?' she asked.

'We want to see Paul Foster,' said Steve Osborne. 'Is he here?'

'Yes.'

'Well then we'd like to see him, sweetheart,' said Steve who liked the look of this Anita. True, she was young but she was so pretty and for some reason he got the feeling that she'd know what to do to please a man. She might appreciate having an experienced man in her bed rather the boys she's no doubt used to. 'Can you show us the way?'

All that Paul had been able to think about these past few days was where Jake had fled to. He'd tried to call him but each time it had gone to voicemail and despite leaving eight messages that had grown more frantic in tone, Jake hadn't called him back. He didn't know what else he could do. He'd lied to the police about what had happened. What else could he do to protect him?

'Paul?' said Anita after she'd knocked on the door of his office and then opened it. 'There are two police officers here to see you.'

When Steve Osborne and Joe Alexander marched themselves in it was clear to Paul that they weren't there on exactly friendly business.

'Thanks, Anita,' said Paul.

They waited until the door had closed and then they launched their attack.

'Why didn't you tell us that you and Jake Thornton had been lovers for the last four years?' Steve demanded.

'Because it wasn't any of your business,' Paul retorted.

'None of our business? This is a murder investigation,

Mr. Foster. Every detail is our business like the fact that Jake Thornton called you a dozen times on the day of your disappearance and physical assault. Care to enlighten us there?'

'I think he was trying to warn me,' said Paul who'd love to know who'd dropped him in it.

'Oh you do?' said Steve, 'so you lied to us, Mr. Foster.'

'Alright!' said Paul as he stood up. 'I admit it. I lied to you. No point in denying it if someone has tipped you off, which I suspect they have?'

'We received a tip-off, yes,' said Joe, 'but we'd also pulled your mobile phone records by then which told us that you'd been less than honest.'

'Do you know the penalties for deliberately withholding information from police in a murder inquiry?' Steve demanded.

'Yes, I do,' said Paul who was struggling to hide his shame. 'I'm sorry, detectives.'

'So was it Jake Thornton whose voice you heard the night you were held?' asked Joe.

Paul sat back down and nodded his head. 'Yes, it was.'

'And it was him who fired the shots that killed Glenn Barber?'

'As far as I know,' said Paul who then held his face in his hands.

'You've not done him any favours, Mr. Foster,' said Joe.

'Yes, I know that but surely you can see how I was fixed?' Paul pleaded. .

'Do you always chase married men, Mr. Foster?' Steve asked.

Paul looked up at him with utter disdain. 'He wasn't married when I met him.'

'Oh, so that's a recent development then, is it?'

'A few months ago.'

'What was the problem? He wanted to go back to the real thing? He'd had enough of the alternative lifestyle?'

'You're a homophobic bigot, Detective!'

'Now that's enough, Mr. Foster,' Joe warned.

'No it isn't when he stands there insulting me like that!' Paul retorted angrily. 'It's not nearly enough.'

'It isn't my fault you involve yourself in sordid affairs,' said Steve.

'My relationship with Jake is anything but sordid! I love the man and I wanted to give him a chance.'

'To escape justice?' said Steve.

'Look, Jake is one of the soldiers who risked his life to protect you. He was sent out to a country that's never been brought under control by anyone except dark forces like the Taliban. He was nearly killed on two occasions and when he came back there was no help for him. He needed psychological help but there was none for him.'

'Isn't that because he was dishonourably discharged after stealing weapons from his unit?' said Joe. 'Did he really deserve any help after doing that?'

'Yes, he bloody well did!' Paul raged.

'Calm down, Paul,' said Joe.

'Ah shut up and listen! Any fool could see that stealing those weapons was a symptom of the problem. Or is everyone still stuck in a time when we shot deserters and conscientious objectors? We'll treat you if your limbs have been blown off because that makes good telly but if your mind is broken then you're on your own.'

'Spare us the angry sermon, sir,' said Steve.

'Oh, I'm sorry, am I making it uncomfortable for you? The truth has a habit of doing that to people who haven't got the ability to think.'

'Mr. Foster, you lied to police in a murder investigation and you're lucky we're not charging you,' said Steve. 'That's something you really should think about.'

As soon as a distraught Paul got home he went straight next door to Kelly and Lydia's house.

'What's wrong with you?' asked Lydia.

'What's wrong? What is fucking wrong? Somebody dropped me in it to the police and I'm lucky I'm not on a fucking charge!'

'Hang on, hang on,' said Lydia, 'I don't follow. How could anyone drop you in it to the police?'

'Because I didn't tell them that it was Jake who was there the other night.'

'The night when you could've been killed?' said Kelly.

'Yes, the night I could've been killed but I wasn't,' said Paul. 'I'm still here.'

'Someone else isn't though, Paul,' said Kelly.

'Oh, so you want me to feel compassion for a lowlife loan shark? Don't make me fucking laugh.'

'Of course I'm not asking you to do that,' said Kelly. 'But I am asking you to think of the help that Jake needs.'

'What do you mean?'

'Well if they catch up with Jake then he'll get the help that you yourself have been saying that he so needs,' said Kelly. 'You did say that.'

Paul looked into his friend's eyes and then he knew. He didn't know why he hadn't thought of it before. Who else would know all the intimate details of his relationship with Jake? Some of his friends knew bits and pieces but only Kelly and Lydia knew it all.

'It was you, wasn't it?' said Paul.

Kelly swallowed hard. 'Yes, it was,' she admitted.

'Kelly!' said Lydia. 'Why didn't you tell me?'

'Of course it had to be you,' said Paul who was not just hurt about Kelly's betrayal but he was also very fucking angry. 'Only you and Lydia know what Jake means to me.'

'All I knew is that you gave him everything and got fuck all in return.'

'Oh well I'm sorry if my relationship with Jake doesn't fall into your narrow definition of what it should be! I'm sorry if it isn't like you and Lydia but what Jake and I have is the best that we can do. We love each other.'

'He's got a pregnant wife, Paul,' said Kelly.

'I'm well aware of that!'

'Paul, don't upset yourself, love,' said Lydia who went to put her arms round his shoulders but he stepped back.

'Too late for that, Lydia,' said Paul. 'Kelly, I could've been on a charge!'

'Paul,' said Kelly. 'You're an intelligent man and that's one of the reasons why we love you. But you've got no common sense especially when it comes to your emotions. I wanted to bring you to your senses, Paul. I'm scared for you. Jake is out there and I'm scared for you. I was being what a true friend should be.'

'Really?'

'Yes, really.'

'But it wasn't your decision to take!'

'Okay,' said Kelly. 'I'll give you that.'

'But you couldn't help yourself, could you? You had to go marching in because of course, only Kelly is ever right and the rest of the world is always wrong.'

'Now come on, Paul,' said Lydia. 'Don't say anything you might regret.'

'Speaking of which,' said Paul who then turned to Lydia. 'Has Kelly told you about a girl called Ursula who she met on that training course down in London last year? Oh I can see from the reaction on your face that she hasn't and why do you think that is? Something to hide perhaps?' he turned to Kelly. 'I'd stay around to hear you squirm your way out of that one but I've got far more important things to do. This is the first and last time you'll ever cross me.'

Sara walked into the squad room where Tim had constructed a white board with various pictures and notes relating to one of the most complex and disturbing cases any of them had ever come across. And all of them thought it was far from over yet.

'In short,' said Tim who then delivered the briefing. 'Leonid Sulkov is willing to testify that Lady Eleanor Harding was the real killer of Peter Jenkins in June, 1940.'

'According to what he was told,' said Steve.

'That's right,' said Tim, 'but the source was her ladyship herself so although it comes down to his word against hers, Leonid Sulkov has no reason to lie about it. We're going to bring her ladyship in for questioning and, hopefully, we'll be able to get a confession out of her. If an innocent man did go to the gallows because of her then it's time that justice was done.'

'Absolutely, DI Norris,' said Hargreaves. 'It's long overdue.'

'Sir,' said Tim, 'but that's not the only matter she can help us with. Moving up the years to the night in October 1974 when Ronald Harding was murdered, Lady Eleanor gave evidence at the time that it was her daughter who'd killed Ronald before disappearing, apparently into thin air. But there were two more people present who nobody knew about, as well as Dieter Naumann. Leonid Sulkov is one and Edward James Foster is the other. Foster was the boyfriend of Clarissa Harding and according to Sulkov he's now ready to come clean about that and about the struggle for a gun between Foster, Clarissa, and Lady Eleanor. Sulkov says the gun went off and Clarissa Harding was dead.'

'Sir, what's the connection between Leonid Sulkov and this Ed Foster?' asked Joe.

'Well they're friends and, like Lady Eleanor, they were both members of the British Fascist movement.'

'That doesn't make them bad people,' said Steve.

The rest of them turned and looked at Steve.

'What did I say?' he asked innocently.

'I'll go on,' said Tim. 'Clarissa and Ed Foster had a child.'

'Sir?' said Joe.

'Sulkov says the reason for the scene that night at the Hall was because Clarissa was angry at her parents for not accepting their grandchild. After the deaths of Ronald and Clarissa, a deal was made that Ed Foster would walk away with his son and promise never to contact Lady Eleanor again in return for her concocting the story about her daughter having shot Ronald and disappearing.'

'And they've all kept to that deal,' said Hargreaves.

'So why has Sulkov broken with it now?' Joe wanted to know.

'He's going along with the wishes of his friend, Ed Foster,' said Tim. 'Foster is close to death with cancer and he thinks the time is right to cleanse his soul. Sulkov is supporting him like he has done all the way through.'

'Are we going to charge him?' asked Steve. 'I mean, he not only withheld evidence but he didn't confess to being a murderer for nearly thirty years'

'That's true,' said Sara, 'but I'm not certain there's any value in charging him, Steve.'

'He broke the law, ma'am,' stated Steve. 'That's the value, surely?'

'We're going to caution him in exchange for his evidence,' said Sara. 'We have the chance to settle three murder cases, Steve, and to be able to clear the name of an innocent man. I think that's enough given the sensitive nature of what's going on here.'

'Yes, I agree DCI Hoyland,' said Hargreaves.

'Sir,' said Sara.

'Do we know what happened to Clarissa Harding's body?' asked Hargreaves.

'That's one of the things we need to question Lady Eleanor about, sir,' said Tim.

'So Dieter Naumann is innocent of all these going's on?' asked Hargreaves.

'It would seem so, sir,' said Sara. 'We were wrong. I was wrong. The extradition proceedings can now continue.'

'Right,' said Hargreaves. 'And in the meantime, we've still got a murder suspect on the run in the shape of Jake Thornton.'

'There are no traces of him anywhere, sir,' said Tim. 'He hasn't been back to his family home in Burnley, he hasn't used a debit or credit card, and he hasn't used his mobile.'

'Well he's somewhere, Tim,' said Hargreaves, 'and he has to be found.'

CHAPTER FOURTEEN

SARA IMMEDIATELY TOOK CONTROL when she sat down with Tim in the interview room across the table from Lady Eleanor and her lawyer. She switched on the tape recorder and went through the necessary preambles. Then it was down to business.

'Are you in favour of capital punishment, Lady Eleanor?' Sara began.

'The worse thing this country did, apart from joining Brussels, was to abolish the death penalty.'

'How did you feel the day Wilfred Jenkins was hanged, Lady Eleanor?' said Tim.

'The same as I did every other day,' said Eleanor, nonchalantly.

'And I wonder what he was feeling the moment that trap door was opened and his body dropped through. His neck probably broke within seconds and then he wasn't able to feel or think about anything anymore.'

'And why should any of that be a bother to me? He was a guilty man.'

'But he wasn't, was he?' said Sara, 'and why? Because you committed the murder that he was hanged for.'

Eleanor looked up at the ceiling and sniggered, 'you really are being preposterous.'

'Lady Eleanor, we have the sworn statement of Leonid Sulkov claiming that you confessed to the crime.'

Eleanor just sat there and didn't answer.

'Lady Eleanor? You'll help yourself if you answer the

questions.'

'You thought at one time that it was my darling Dieter who'd committed the crime and that I was protecting him,' Eleanor sneered.

'And now we know different,' said Sara.

'You'll be trying to blame someone else next week,' said Eleanor. 'Your incompetence is boundless. No wonder there's a problem with crime in this country.'

'The only problem with crime, Lady Eleanor,' said Sara, 'is when the wrong people are convicted and the guilty go free for seventy years.'

'And how long did it take you to think that one up? You really must be stretching your intellectual limits.'

'That's enough!' Tim shouted. 'Lady Eleanor, we've shown you every respect and courtesy and all you've done in return is either hide the truth from us or tell us downright lies. We want the truth Lady Eleanor, and we want it now.'

'You want, you want,' said Eleanor.

'My patience is wearing extremely thin, Lady Eleanor.'

'Then you should go on one of those, what do they call it these days? An anger management course.'

Tim slammed his hand on the table. 'No more games, Lady Eleanor!'

There was a momentary pause during which Tim and Sara noticed the capitulation written all across Eleanor's face. It was as if she'd regressed to her childhood and was being scolded by her father. Her eyes took on that wounded innocence of a little girl who couldn't understand why Daddy was shouting at her. Daddy had come back to tell her off. She could see his face all over the Detective's. The only man she'd ever listened to in her life was telling her it was time to finally tell the truth.

'I killed Peter Jenkins,' said Eleanor, softly. Her lawyer intervened to tell her to be quiet but she dismissed his entreaties. 'I killed him because his antics were going to get in the way of the agreement I was brokering for the British government with Hitler. I couldn't let that happen. I couldn't let his immature recklessness damage our chances. Then when Wilfred came into the room I knew he could provide me with my get out clause.'

'Even though he paid with his life?' said Sara, shaking he head in disbelief at Lady Eleanor's abominable selfishness.

'I had to do it for the greater good of what I was trying to achieve in the negotiations,' said Eleanor, 'you could call Wilfred one of those unexpected casualties of war.'

Sara scoffed. 'One that needn't have been, Lady Eleanor. The hanging of an innocent man was just a means of escaping justice for you.'

Eleanor tried to smile but she couldn't quite get there. She did however straighten herself up in preparation for the next confession.

'I suppose you want to know what really happened the night Ronald died too?'

'That's one of the reasons why you're here,' said Sara.

Eleanor then gave them an account of the October 1974 night and it was the first time in her life that she'd spoken the truth about it to anyone who hadn't been there. What she told them chimed perfectly with what Leonid Sulkov had told them.

'We will get a statement typed out that you can sign, Lady Eleanor,' said Tim.

'Very well,' said Eleanor.

'But just one more thing,' said Tim. 'What did you do with your daughter's body?'

'She's buried in the grounds of the Hall,' said Eleanor. 'If you send some people down I'll show them where.'

'And what about your grandson, Paul Foster, Lady Eleanor?' asked Sara as she moved in for the final round of questions. This was going to be the most satisfying arrest she'd ever made.

'What about him?' said Eleanor, her earlier defiance returning.

'What are you going to tell him about the mother he was never allowed to know?'

Marius Van Urk was nursing the hangover from hell. He'd been out the previous night with his workmates at the website office on King Street. Samantha and Dave were both about the same age as him and like him, they were both single. The three of them spent regular nights out on the town together but they were just mates. There was no romantic spark between Samantha and Dave or between Samantha and Marius. And as both of the boys were heterosexual nothing was going to go on between the two of them either. Marius hadn't always been single since he arrived in Manchester. He'd seen one or two girls but the last one he'd gone out with had turned out to be a complete control freak and he couldn't stand that. She'd tried to tell him what to do, what to wear, what time to be somewhere, all to fall in with the arrangements she'd made for the two of them and if he resisted she'd get all upset and start calling him a bastard. She was a pretty girl and when she wasn't trying to control his every move she could be really good company. But then he came home one day to find that she'd moved all the furniture around in his flat whilst he'd been out, she said that he had to admit that it all looked better the way she'd arranged it. That was enough. He'd told her it was over. There were tears, hysteria, she screamed obscenities at him but he really didn't need anyone to organise him. He could quite happily do his own laundry, cook for himself, keep the flat tidy and do the shopping. He wanted a girlfriend, not a mother. He had a mother who he loved very much but he didn't want another version of her.

Splitting up from his fiancé Yvette back in South Africa had been a painful experience and one which had affected both their families, but his new start in London hadn't ever felt permanent, even though he'd stayed there for three years. The people in Manchester reminded him of his mother's family in Nottingham. Their accents, to his ear, were similar and, mostly, they had the same no-nonsense way of looking at life. He'd always felt closer to his mother's British side of his family. Since he'd been living in the UK he saw them regularly, especially his grandparents. His father's Afrikaner heritage didn't mean much to him at all. But one thing the two respective sides of his family did have in common was a fondness for alcohol. And Marius had inherited it.

'You look how I feel,' said Samantha as she walked into Marius's office.

Marius rubbed his eyes with his fingertips. 'Why did we have those shots? I mean, hadn't we had enough by then?'

'I think we'd reached the point where enough was not enough,' laughed Samantha.

'Yeah, and I seem to be reaching that particular point with alarming regularity,' said Marius who then slumped over his desk. 'Let me die, please!'

'Not just yet, big boy,' said Dave when he joined them. 'You've got a visitor.'

'I have?' Marius questioned. 'Who the fuck wants to see me?'

'His name is Paul Foster,' said Dave. 'He's some sort of social worker.'

Paul was shown in to see Marius and they shook hands. Despite his mood Paul couldn't help noticing Marius in the way that men who like men do. He was a dead ringer for the footballer Jamie Redknapp with his short brown hair at the sides, gelled up at the front, dressed in a suit with an open necked shirt. He was probably straight though. Gay men rarely have that same glint in their eye that straight men do. Besides, pulling was the last thing on Paul's mind.

'So what can I do for you, Mr. Foster?'

'I want to tell you about what happens to a soldier when he's sent to fight a war against values instead of borders,' said Paul who then went on to explain everything about Jake. 'You can use his story as the centre of a piece about how we've failed these brave young men and women. We're not giving them what they need when they come back, Marius, and it's so wrong.'

'You're talking about the Jake Thornton who's wanted for questioning about the murder of Glenn Barber?'

'Yes,' said Paul, 'and I'm making the point that if he'd received proper help when he came back from Afghanistan then we might not be in this position now. Several other papers have speculated about Jake and his life but they've got it all wrong. Jake is a good man who was turned bad by his experiences in Afghanistan. I'm not making excuses for anything he's done. I'm just trying to explain the circumstances behind his actions. He's been damaged. He didn't come back in a body bag but he may as well be dead inside. He needs help and he has to get it.'

'You don't know where they might be able to find him?'

'I'm sorry but I don't,' said Paul. 'I wish I did.'

'He's more than just a friend, isn't he?'

'I want you to keep that side of the story out of your coverage.'

'Why? Isn't it part of it?'

'No,' said Paul, 'and if it did get out then it would become the story and it isn't the story. The story is about what he went through in Afghanistan. You've got to act at a higher level to your average tabloid hack. This is not about the salacious side of Jake's life even though nothing about our relationship was salacious. But it's not about that, Marius. It's not about that.'

'I see,' said Marius.

'Don't let me regret bringing this story to you,' said Paul.

'Why did you come to me?'

'Because I want the story to get out and you're the only journalist I know. I'm now trusting you to make a principled stand on what you reveal to the public. That decision will mark you out as either a great journalist or just another arsehole.'

When Sara and Tim got to Ed Foster's place in Blackpool, with the agreement of their Lancashire colleagues, any uncomfortable feelings they'd had about interviewing a dying man were amplified a thousand times. Ed Foster was clearly consumed with pain but they had to get a statement. This was one of the darker sides of police work and both of them would give it up if it didn't give them some degree of conscience.

They sat either side of Ed Foster's bed. Sara asked him to take as much time as he needed to give them his account of what happened on the now infamous night in October 1974. His voice was so weak and soft, they had to really concentrate to be able to hear him, but what they were able to discern was that he backed up everything that had been said by Leonid Sulkov and Lady Eleanor.

'I've been ashamed since the day it happened,' said Ed, his heart heavy with the weight of the past. 'I used to be friends with Dieter Naumann, or Gerald Edwards, until he tried to perform an abortion on Clarissa when she was pregnant with our son.'

'He did what?' asked Sara.

'Oh it was all at her ladyship's instigation,' said Ed. 'Clarissa went up to the Hall one night to appeal to her parents and they drugged her. I managed to get there just in time to save both Clarissa and our unborn child.'

Good God, thought Tim. Once a Nazi, always a bloody Nazi. It seemed to him that there were no depths to which Dieter Naumann wouldn't sink. The woman in the room with him had taken his baby away but that was of her own free will. He looked up at her. She looked away.

'Mr. Foster, we will have to arrest you for the murders of Ronald Harding and Clarissa Harding,' said Tim. 'But there will be no further investigation into the matter.'

'I'm sorry, detectives,' said Ed. 'I'm sorry that I kept quiet all this time. It doesn't make me much of a man, does it.'

'Well I wouldn't put it quite like that,' said Tim, 'but you understand that we have to follow a procedure?'

'Of course I do,' answered Ed, 'I needed to come clean

for the sake of my son Paul. He deserves to know the truth.'

On the drive back to Manchester along the M61, Sara's head was consumed with the latest ramifications of this most complicated case when a thought struck her.

'Tim?'

'Yeah?'

'Naumann said that he couldn't go back to Germany after his wife had been executed for treason because they would've executed him for the same thing, believing that he must've been in league with her?'

'Yes? That bit of his story is probably the most plausible.'

'But when the Nazi's were defeated at the end of the war, what would've stopped him going back to Germany then? I mean, what would it have mattered? He could've been reunited with his family in Munich. He didn't have to make himself a refugee.'

'Yeah, I see what you mean,' said Tim.

'I mean, he wasn't trapped in a foreign country like poor old Leonid Sulkov.'

'No,' said Tim, 'but Leonid Sulkov would probably know.'

'Let's make a detour on the way back to the office,' said Sara, 'there's a connection to be made between these two cases and we're going to make it.'

When they arrived at Leonid Sulkov's house they took him up on his offer of tea this time. They told him that the matter as far as Foster was concerned, the case was now closed. He'd been charged with the murder of Ronald Harding and Clarissa Harding but there'd be no trial, considering the circumstances of Foster's health.

'He will be relieved though,' said Leonid. 'I'm a few

years older than Ed. I've been a bit of an older brother to him. Oh he has his own brother, Doug, but he's younger. I've always looked out for Ed and I know this is what he wanted to do.'

'Mr. Sulkov,' said Sara, 'we've come back to see you because…'

'…oh indulge me and tell me it was my charm,' said Leonid. 'You're an attractive young lady and if I was fifty years younger I'd take you out for a good time.'

Sara smiled. 'Now there's an offer I couldn't refuse,' she said, 'if you were fifty years younger.'

'Ah, there's always a catch,' said Leonid. 'So what are you here about?'

'Well the thing is, sir, what we would like to know is why Dieter Naumann stayed in England at the end of the Second World War and we thought you might be able to tell us. I mean, why didn't he go back to Germany? The Nazis had been defeated so he would've been safe. He wasn't in the same position as you. Do you know the reason?'

'I think the police service should keep hold of you, young lady,' said Leonid, 'You have sharp and very accurate instincts.'

'Go on?'

'It was at the end of the war just after I'd started working for Lady Eleanor,' began Leonid, 'but again, I need to put things into context. Have you ever heard of the Lebensraum programme?'

'Wasn't that something to do with the Nazis?' said Tim.

'Oh yes,' said Leonid. 'They wanted to create the perfect Aryan race so they literally stole blond haired blue eyed kids from all across Europe, the countries they'd invaded and occupied that is, and took them back to Germany to the Lebensraum orphanages and then to be adopted by loyal Aryan German families. Their soldiers were also told to go out and multiply with any of the local blond haired girls who were willing to put it out for the German occupiers and collaborate.'

'But mainland Britain wasn't occupied' said Tim.

'No, but the British side of it is what I need to explain.'

'I didn't know there was a British side of it'

'Detective, Lady Eleanor Harding was the British side of it. She and Dieter Naumann were responsible for the disappearance from this country of about three hundred children.'

Tim and Sara looked at each other in complete disbelief.

'What?' said Tim.

'They paid poor impoverished folks across the North West for their blond, blue-eyed kids who were all then taken to Germany to join the rest in the Lebensraum programme.'

'Well what happened to these kids? Didn't anybody investigate?'

'They were all poor kids from poor backgrounds. In a lot of cases nobody really missed them. There was a war on. One less mouth to feed was a blessing and none of the parents informed the police. How could they when they'd taken money for them?'

'But what happened to them at the end of the war?'

'Presumably they were adopted by the German families they'd been given to,' said Leonid. 'But nobody ever found out.'

'But wait a minute?' said Tim. 'How did they get them

to Germany when there was a war on?'

'Well this is where it gets interesting,' said Leonid. 'You see, Lady Eleanor was as thick as thieves with the Duke of Windsor, the King who'd abdicated in 1936 so he could marry Wallis Simpson.'

'The King who later became known as the traitor King because of his closeness to Hitler and the Reich.'

'That's it,' said Leonid. 'It's fairly certain from what we now know that if Hitler had won the Battle of Britain then he'd have installed Edward back on the throne and deposed his brother, George VI, who'd ascended the throne after him.'

'So what did the Duke of Windsor have to do with these kids?'

'Nothing directly,' said Leonid. 'Or at least, nothing we know for sure. The thing is he was part of a network of British aristocrats that included Lady Eleanor and who all had Nazi connections. They were able to use that network to get the kids out of the country and into occupied France or Belgium from where they were then taken to Germany. Even after he'd been sent to the Bahamas to serve out the war there as governor, the British secret services kept a close eye on him and Mrs. Simpson. The couple maintained their contacts with their European friends as best they could.'

'No wonder they call him the Traitor King,' said Tim.

'Yes,' said Leonid. 'You see it's always been rumoured over the years but it is in fact true. The fortunes of many of the aristocracy had been built on investments in the countries of the empire and they were afraid that might all be cut off. That's why they wanted the deal with Hitler.'

'But I still don't know why Naumann didn't go back to Germany in 1945?' said Sara. 'Especially considering what he'd done here, I'd have thought he'd have wanted to escape. The Nazis had been defeated, so what was he afraid of?'

'It was because of his involvement in the Polish massacre,' said Leonid. 'He would've been charged if he'd gone back and he'd have probably been executed. So he blackmailed the British authorities with a threat to expose all the secrets of the British state that he'd found out when he was originally negotiating the pact with Hitler. But as it happened the authorities found out about Dieter and Eleanor's wartime activities and they narrowly escaped being charged with treason and going to the gallows. It was only Lady Eleanor's connections with the royal family that saved her and Dieter.'

Sara was appalled at the very idea of hundreds of children being sold by local families to help the Nazi war effort. It made her feel sick. She'd wracked her brains to think of how they could be traced but what would be the point after all this time? Those who were still alive would be old now and probably wouldn't even remember being a toddler in another land. They'd have children of their own; grandchildren, homes, lives. Then there's the fact that the families of the children actually sold them. They wanted them to go. They never wanted them to be traced. But maybe a crime of the past could bring about the conclusion of a crime of the present. Sara had nursed a hunch all the way through these investigations that something would appear that would bind them together in some way. And now she was sure she'd found it. She called a squad meeting and laid it all out for the rest of the team.

'Glenn Barber is someone the force have suspected for some time of being involved in other things besides just loan sharking.'

'It's a bit of a leap though, ma'am,' said Steve, 'to go from being a loan shark to abducting teenage girls?'

'On the face of it, yes,' said Sara, 'but this investigation has thrown up many surprises. I believe very strongly that there's a connection between these two cases and that the disappearance of the girls is what will lead us to it. Now, what do the families of all the missing girls have in common?'

'They're all on benefits?' said Steve.

'It's not as simple as that, Steve,' said Sara. 'Suppose they all borrowed money from Glenn Barber but were struggling to pay it back? What if he took the girls as some form of human collateral?'

The rest of the team looked at her with a mixture of bewilderment and the usual coppers' excitement when their noses could sniff something. She walked up to the white board and next to the picture of Glenn Barber she pinned one of Lady Eleanor.

'Lady Eleanor Harding,' said Sara, 'a cold, ruthless killer. A woman so ruthless she bought children for the Reich and organised their passage to Germany.'

'What did you say about Lady Eleanor's arrest back in 1945, Ma'am?' asked Joe.

'What does that matter now?' Steve wanted to know.

'It is significant because of what it leads to,' said Tim.

'The reason for their arrest isn't known,' Sara explained. 'No charges were subsequently brought. It all fits with what Sulkov claims about them being involved in the trafficking of children for the Reich but that somehow, through connections with the royal family, they were let off. I've been in touch with the Home Office and they'll neither confirm nor deny Sulkov's story – which means it's true. If the royal family brokered a deal to get them off the hook then the palace wouldn't want that getting out.'

'I'm surprised they didn't try to silence Sulkov and Ed Foster,' said Joe.

'Yeah, they appear to have left a flank open there,' said Tim. 'Until now. Let's not forget that Sulkov and Foster kept it all to themselves for all this time. But who knows how those people work. They've always been a mystery to me.'

'Who, the Home Office?' Steve questioned.

'No, the royals,' said Tim, '…but also the Home Office.'

'Well I think we should make a start by going back to the parents of the girls who've gone missing and see if they all owed money to Glenn Barber,' said Joe. 'Starting with Shona Higgins parents. Hit them with it and see how they react.'

'Excellent,' said Sara. 'Thanks, Joe.'

'We know that people sell their kids for money,' said Joe. 'Unfortunately, we've all dealt with such cases.'

'Sadly that's true, Joe,' said Sara, 'except that I don't think these kids today were sold. I think they were taken. Although we know what happened to Shona Higgins, God only knows what's happened to the rest of them but I'd bet my life that her Ladyship does.'

'But why though?' said Steve. 'If she was a Nazi sympathiser then I can square that with what she got up to in the war years…'

'… I'm glad you can,' said Sara.

'Ma'am, only in respect of her wanting to do anything to help the cause back then,' Steve explained. 'But what would be her motivation for doing it now? I assume she must be making money out of it somewhere along the line but she doesn't need it.'

'Your guess is as good as mine on that one, Steve,' said Sara.

'That is what I'm struggling to get my head round, ma'am,' said Steve.

'And how could she do something so sick?' said Joe.

'How could a man keep his daughter and grandchildren in the cellar of his house for all those years without anybody finding out?' said Sara. 'How could a woman, who was also a mother, get herself involved with a paedophile ring? If a mind is that warped then the person it belongs to won't see what the rest of us do.'

'Good point, ma'am,' said Steve.

'We're bringing her back in for questioning,' said Sara. 'Her days of getting away, literally, with murder, are well and truly numbered.'

CHAPTER FIFTEEN

PAUL LET HIMSELF INTO his parents' house and knew straight away that he was too late. The air was still and cold but somehow peaceful. He went into his parents' room where his mother was standing by the bed. His father had passed away.

'He's gone,' she announced.

'When?' asked Paul, looking down at his father's still face.

'About seven this morning,' his mother answered flatly. 'The doctor's just left. The undertaker will be here any minute. Your Uncle Leonid has just gone round to the shop.'

'How come Uncle Leonid is here?'

'I called him,' said Mary. 'He was your father's best friend. He'd have wanted him here.'

'Why didn't you call me?' he asked, not being able to read her emotions at all.

'You were coming anyway so it wasn't worth the cost of a phone call.'

Paul felt his heart break into little pieces. He rubbed his hand across his mouth and looked intensely at his father who was now free of the pain that had so wracked him these past months. He leaned down and kissed his father's forehead.

'Bye, Dad,' he whispered, 'I love you.'

'There are things to be done,' said Mary, bluntly, cutting across Paul's emotions like a bullet cuts through someone's skin.

'They can wait.'

'No, they can't.'

'Is our Denise on her way?'

Without looking at him she replied, 'she's very busy today.'

'Oh so you rang her?'

'She had a right to know.'

'She's not been near him throughout his illness!'

'She couldn't bear to see him in such pain,' said Mary 'Same as she couldn't bear to see him lying here like this. She's doesn't like playing the hero like you do.'

'You unspeakable bitch!'

Paul was exasperated with her. He walked out of the bedroom and stood in the hallway. He leaned against the wall to steady himself. He felt the most incredible loneliness, like there was a cold wind blowing all the way through his soul. Then his mother came out of the bedroom and brushed past him.

'Mum?'

She carried on through to the kitchen and he followed her.

'Mum, for God's sake!'

'He's barely cold!' she snapped, 'don't start anything now.'

'Mum, can't we be at peace just for one day. Is that really beyond you?'

'Don't talk to me like I'm one of those failures you spend your life looking after.'

'Mum, for crying out loud will you stop sticking the knife into me!' he pleaded desperately. 'Please, just for today. I'm breaking up here.'

'And I should care?'

Paul walked out of the kitchen and into the lounge where he sat down and put his head in his hands. He sensed when his mother came into the room but didn't look up.

'On second thoughts maybe today is the day to start something,' said Mary.

'What the hell are you talking about?'

'You've never belonged in my family,' she snarled. 'My Denise was only three when your father had his affair with your mother.'

Paul felt light-headed. He didn't think he'd be able to stand up if he tried. 'You've gone crazy. You're talking nonsense.'

'Your father, your big hero, left me for your mother but when you came along and her family rejected all three of you I, like the stupid fool I was, took him back and took you as my son too. I've regretted the decision since the day he walked up the path with you in his arms. I hated the sight of you then and I still do. If it hadn't been for your mother getting her rotten claws in, we'd have been happy as a family of three. Denise would've wanted for nothing. But then you came into this house and ruined everything. Your mother destroyed my marriage. You destroyed the rest of my life.'

Paul drove home and went round immediately to Kelly and Lydia's house.

'I'm sorry,' he said after Lydia had opened the door. 'I didn't know where else to go.'

'It's alright,' said Lydia as she opened her arms and he fell into them.

'I don't know what to make of anything,' he said.

'Well come in,' said Lydia, 'we'll help you sort it all out.'

He walked into the living room where Kelly was stood

waiting for him.

'I shouldn't have said what I did,' said Paul.

'And neither should I,' said Kelly. 'Come here.'

The three of them locked into an embrace. Paul was relieved that they'd forgiven him for his spitefulness. He really needed his friends now.

'I lashed out because I love Jake, Kelly,' said Paul, 'and I'm petrified for him.'

'I know,' said Kelly. 'I know all of that, love. But you've got to deal with the loss of your Dad first. Paul, it's all true. Mary isn't your mother. Your mother was Clarissa, the lady who gave your Dad the watch that he gave you.'

'He told us when we went to see him the other day,' said Lydia.

'He told you but he didn't tell me?'

'Don't be angry with him, Paul,' said Lydia. 'I'm sure he had his reasons.'

'I'd like to know what they are,' said Paul. 'He said that this Clarissa would want me to have the watch but I didn't know what he meant. Now, I do. Christ.'

Kelly handed Paul the letter his father had given them. 'He asked us to give you this once he'd... once he'd gone. He said it'll explain everything.'

Paul wiped his mouth with the back of his hand. 'I don't know what to say. I don't know what the hell to even think.'

'Read the letter, Paul,' said Lydia. 'We'll leave you to it. We'll be in the kitchen.'

Paul ripped open the envelope and was immediately comforted by his Dad's familiar handwriting. Then he started to read what it said.

Dear Paul,
There's so much I have to tell you about that I almost don't

know where to start. You're probably annoyed with me because, no doubt, you now know that Mary isn't your mother and, to put it mildly, it will have come as quite a shock. But there's a lot more to it than just that, son, and I hope that by the time you finish reading these words, you'll be able to understand that I did what I thought was best at the time.

When I was younger I was a member of the British Fascist movement. We believed in reclaiming British society for the white British race and we didn't hold with accepting other cultures. We did things, Paul, that now I'm not proud of, but I can't wipe them out. I was a fascist. I believed in the supremacy of the white race. I sympathised with Hitler. I know you have views that are opposed to this perspective, Paul, and I've never admitted my involvement before, but I'm admitting to it now and I seek your understanding. I didn't want any immigration. I didn't want the Jews controlling everything, including worldwide sympathy for the Holocaust. I believed in self-reliance. I thought that apartheid was the best way of creating racial harmony by keeping the races apart with one, the white race, as superior. That's how I got on so well with Lady Eleanor, your Uncle Leonid, and Dieter Naumann.

I went out with your Uncle Leonid for a few pints one night and met Clarissa in a pub near Glossop. It was love at first sight for both of us. We became friends but we couldn't resist the rest of the journey. I was married but not happily, in fact, I was desperately unhappy. It's an age old classic story of unhappily married man meets nice girl in a pub one night but I really did love your mother more than I can put into words. She was a lovely young woman, strong but with a nice, gentle temperament and I've always seen so much of her in you.

Your mother and I had to keep our relationship secret from her parents because they didn't approve. Not because I was married. Oh no, they had no such simple scruples as that. Lady Harding and her husband didn't approve because I was from a class that they considered beneath them. It was okay for me to organise things in the British Fascist movement for them and be useful to them in that way. But I mustn't get above myself and think I could get involved with their daughter. Oh no, that was unthinkable. I was bloody annoyed at the time because after all I'd done for them I felt like they were slapping me in the face. You can understand that, can't you?

Anyway, love wasn't something they believed in and in any case, they didn't give a damn about your mother. But when I met your mother and we fell in love, I'd have done anything to please her. She wanted me to have nothing to do with fascism and I gave it all up for her. She needed me, Paul. I was one of the only people to show her any kindness, to show her that she was worth someone's affection and devotion. We were in love and in our own little world we were happy. But hell wasn't far away.

I eventually left Mary and moved into a flat with Clarissa. Her parents were vehemently against it but we didn't care. Then when we found out that your mother was expecting you and we were on top of the world. She went home to tell them. That's when it turned ugly. They locked her in her room and Dieter Naumann drugged your mother and he was about to perform an abortion when me and your Uncle Leonid got there just in time and stopped him. We took your mother back to our flat in Urmston and that's where she stayed until you were born.

After you were born we were even happier. It was only a tiny flat we had but we got it looking really nice. I was aware that it was all way short of what your mother was used to but she didn't mind. We were content in this little world we'd created with the three of us. But your mother wanted her parents to acknowledge her happiness and to acknowledge you. She took you to see them. I went with her of course. After what had happened last time I wasn't going to let her go on her own. You were only a few weeks old. She was so proud. She was so happy to have had you, Paul, and whatever you think, you've got to believe that and hold onto it.

Anyway, suffice to say that she had an almighty row with her parents and something must've snapped in me. I shot Ronald Harding. I feel as if it had happened yesterday. You were crying your heart out in your pram. I'd shot Ronald Harding. There were even droplets of his blood on your pram. It was the most hideous, the most evil scene I'd ever come across. Then your grandmother struggled to get the gun off Clarissa. I waded in to help. But then the gun went off and your mother was dead. Did I have my finger on the trigger at the time? Yes is the answer to that one. But I was trying to save your mother, Paul. You must see that?

I was in a mess, Paul. Your Uncle Leonid arranged for me to take you away on condition that I never contacted her Ladyship again. Your Uncle Doug and Aunty Sheila who, as you know, have never been able to have children, suggested that they adopted you, but son, I couldn't go through the pain of losing both you and your mother. That's when I went back to Mary and took you with me. Looking back, I should've let Doug and Sheila adopt you, or I should've brought you up by myself. I made the wrong decision, son, and I've bitterly regretted it ever since. I hope you can forgive me that.

Paul, because of your birthright your grandmother, Lady Eleanor, will be contacting you and before you make any hasty decisions, I ask you to remember that your heritage comes through your mother who was an angel and a woman who'd have been the best mother in the world to you had she got the chance. You owe it to her not to just turn your back on what you've gained from being her son.

I kept a lot of photographs of your mother and of you with her and of the three of us together. They're with my solicitor and naturally I've left them to you in my will. I know that photographs can't ever replace what could've been but at least they'll give you something of a time when the three of us were together and so very happy.

Don't think badly of me, son. I know I should've told you all this when I was still around for you to ask me all the questions that must be springing into your head right now. But it was hard for me, Paul and in time you may come to understand that. You know how proud of you I've always been and I know your mother would've been proud of you too. You've always had steel in your character that you must've got from your mother's side and you'll really need it now and for whatever lies ahead. This has all been dropped on you, Paul, I know, but I also know you'll find your way through it because you've got that strength.

Keep me in your heart, son and please, please don't hate me.
With love,
Dad

When Kelly and Lydia came back into the room they found Paul on the floor, in a heap, crying his heart out. Paul kept himself quiet for a couple of days. He was trying to digest everything and had read and re-read his father's letter so many times that the paper was starting to flake. His life had suddenly changed and without hint or warning. His beloved father had kept so much from him and not that he was beyond the grave he couldn't go to him for answers. All he did know was that a firm of Manchester solicitors who catered to the rich and famous had been trying to contact him. His status as a member of society had changed but he didn't feel it. His heart didn't beat any faster at the knowledge of what he was now a part of. He'd have to deal with it. They would keep on at him until he did. But he was going to keep them at arm's length until he'd worked out how he was going to deal with it all.

He'd also read up about the British Fascist movement and all the trouble they'd caused when his father was involved and he was ashamed that his father had been part of it. He couldn't reconcile the father he knew with the man who'd organised for stones to be thrown at immigrant children on their way home from school. His father was right. It was the sort of activity that Paul abhorred. Then when he came to think about himself it made him wish that his father had let his Uncle Doug and Aunty Sheila adopt him. That would've saved him a lot of physical and emotional harm at the hands of his step-mother.

But what did infuriate him one afternoon was when his sister Denise sent a message to say that she wouldn't be able to make it to her father's funeral. He rang her to find out why and she said that it was because 'George is getting his bonus from the bank this month and we've got a holiday booked to Mauritius, flying first class, five-star hotel and everything. It really can't all be undone at such short notice.'

'You selfish bitch.'

'I beg your pardon?'

'Well, are you going to let your mother come and stay with you for a while? She's on her own and despite her shrugging the shoulder act she's grieving, Denise. You're her daughter and she needs you. God knows, I don't know why I'm trying to help her because I've enough reason not to. But she is grieving, Denise. Surely you realise that?' He heard his sister sigh down the phone. 'Denise?'

'Well it's just that it's not very convenient for me at the moment.'

'Oh well death isn't very convenient! Especially when it's your own father! You knew, didn't you? You knew that you and I didn't share the same mother?'

'Of course I knew,' Denise crowed. 'You were the only one in the dark.'

'Oh don't bother showing me any sensitivity.'

'No, I won't.'

'It would be a first if you did,' said Paul. 'You used to stand by whilst she beat the hell out of me. You watched, you even laughed sometimes when I thought I was going to pass out with pain. That makes you just as evil as she was.'

'It's always so good to talk about our childhood days with you, Paul, but I must go,' said Denise. 'And anyway, George would be more than happy to advise you on your investment potential now that you're filthy rich.'

'Oh, really? Well let me tell you something, sister dearest. Now that I am wealthy I may use some of it to influence the promotion decisions of the bank where George works.'

'You wouldn't dare!'

'Oh? So you can dish it out but you can't take it? How weak you are. Well if I choose to make hell for you I will because now I can. I can settle some scores now that I've got the resources, so I wouldn't be so fucking smug if I were you. I suffered at your hands for years and you'd deserve anything I chose to do to you. Enjoy Mauritius. Next year it might have to be an off-season caravan in Margate.'

The morning of the funeral Paul took a picture of his mother, one of the ones his father had been saving for him, to the chapel of rest and placed it in the coffin with his father. He'd been able to reunite them at last. He'd done his duty as their son. It had broken his heart but it was the best he could do.

Fall From Grace

He did find it rather uncomfortable walking behind his father's coffin with Mary but he took a deep breath and got on with it. On top of the coffin he'd placed a Liverpool FC scarf and had even managed to get the team to sign a farewell card to his Dad who'd supported the club throughout his life. The sight of the scarf made his Uncle Doug break down. They'd been supporters since they were small boys and Paul promised to go with his Uncle from now on.

'You'll be too busy,' said Doug, tearfully.

'I'll never be too busy for you, Uncle Doug,' said Paul, equally as emotional. 'I want you and Aunty Sheila to always remember that. I'm your son now.'

As they walked towards the grave he glanced behind him at his Uncle Doug and Aunty Sheila, followed by his Uncle Leonid, Kelly and Lydia and the rest of the mourners just behind them. Paul had managed to read the eulogy at the service without breaking down but he didn't know how long he'd be able to last.

The coffin was lowered into the ground and he saw that Mary was crying. The sight made him furious. Her sister Alma, who Paul had always detested, had come down from her home in Keswick and passed her a hanky to wipe her face with. Mary was going to go back with Alma after the funeral for a couple of weeks. He saw her to Alma's car.

'Are you alright?' he asked.

'Yes' said Mary, her face set, 'I'm alright.'

'You don't deserve to be,' said Paul.

'Oh what do you know about anything?' she sneered.

'I know about all the pain and misery you caused me! I understand you chose to make my life a living hell because you were too stupid to see beyond your own pain. That's why you took it out on me. For Dad's sake I wanted to try and help you but I can't do that. I just can't get past the memories of what you did to me and I can't forgive you. If you'd have had any dignity at all you'd have divorced my Dad, a man who clearly didn't love you anymore and saved us all a lot of unpleasantness. But instead you decided to hold onto him and to be cruel to an innocent child. You disgust me and after today we're out of each other's lives for good. Oh and by the way, that goes for that slut daughter of yours as well. Goodbye, Mary'

'Now you just wait a minute,' said Mary, attempting a fight back. 'I'm owed by you as well! You're going to be rich now and I want mine!'

Paul felt all the anger of what she'd done to him over the years rise up inside him and fill his voice. 'You have the nerve to bring that up at my father's funeral! Well let me tell you, I owe you nothing! Now get out of my sight and stay there or so help me, I will not be responsible for what I do to you.'

Kelly and Lydia didn't want Paul to be alone that night but he insisted he'd be fine and that he wanted to have some space to think.

'Anyway, you'll only be next door,' said Paul. 'I'll knock on the wall if I need you.'

'Keep your phone right beside you,' said Kelly, 'and pre-programme it for a 999 call. Just in case you get any unexpected visitors and need help fast.'

Paul knew that she meant Jake and what he hadn't told anyone was that he'd seen Jake that day. He was standing a good fifty metres away, beside a clump of trees, in the cemetery when Paul's father had been lowered into the ground. He'd smiled and nodded at him before Jake had disappeared. But at least he'd come and paid his respects to

Paul's Dad. And Paul was grateful for that.

He did jump though when he heard a knock at the front door. Immediately he knew it wouldn't be Jake. Someone on the run like that wouldn't just walk down the street and knock on his door as if he'd just gone down to the off license for a bottle of wine. And it wouldn't be Kelly or Lydia because they've both got a key. He looked at his watch and saw that it a little after nine o'clock. So who was it at this time?

He opened the door to his Uncle Leonid.

'Uncle Leonid?' said Paul as he let his visitor in and closed the door, 'I thought Kelly took you home?'

'She did,' said Leonid, 'but I decided to come back. I thought perhaps you and I should talk on our own.'

'Uncle Leonid, you should've just stayed. You know I don't like you using the buses and walking the streets when it's dark.'

'Yes, yes, I know,' said Leonid. 'You're a good man, Paul. Your father was very proud of you.'

'Well I shall make up the bed in the spare room,' said Paul. 'You're not going home on your own. I'll drive you back in the morning.'

'Paul, it's only a couple of miles, you know.'

'Uncle Leonid, I'm not going to argue with you.'

Leonid smiled. 'Very well' he said, 'if it pleases you.'

'It does,' said Paul. 'Now come and sit down and I'll get you a drink. Your usual?'

'A vodka would be very nice, thank you.'

'I'll go and get the bottle out the fridge.'

Paul poured a vodka for Leonid and a scotch for himself. He came and sat down with his uncle in the living room.

'Why did he lie to me all my life, Uncle Leonid? Why

didn't he ever tell me the truth?'

'He was scared, Paul,' said Leonid. 'He was scared of how you'd react. You've always been so close and he just didn't want to risk that.'

'But I'm more ashamed because he kept it a secret,' said Paul. 'If he'd come clean about his involvement with those bloody fascists then I'd have been angry beyond words but I would've had time to come to terms with it. As it is I want to get hold of him by the scruff of the bloody neck. I mean, when I think of your life story, Uncle Leonid, and your support for the Germans during the war, which was understandable given the circumstances your country was in, the fact that you and Dad were such good friends perhaps should've led me to put two and two together. It wouldn't have taken a great leap of the imagination.'

'No, perhaps it wouldn't,' said Leonid, 'but you mustn't forget that he gave it all up for your mother and the life he was wanting to build with her and you.'

'I realise that, Uncle Leonid.'

'Then send him the peace he deserves to have on the other side,' said Leonid, 'he gave it all up for the love of a woman, your mother.'

'A woman he shot.'

'That really was a terrible accident, Paul,' said Leonid, reliving every moment of that awful night.

'They've found my mother's body,' said Paul.

'Have they?'

'Yes, it was badly decomposed of course but they've managed to identify it. She was just a few metres back from Gatley Hall, just before the start of the woods on the southern side. I'm going to arrange to have her buried next to my Dad.'

'She would like that.'

'You will come to the service?'

'Of course I will,' said Leonid.

'Do you know how my mother got hold of that watch, Uncle Leonid? The one she gave to my father who then gave it to me?'

'Yes,' said Leonid, 'it was given to her by a Royal Prince.'

CHAPTER SIXTEEN

JOE AND STEVE WENT ROUND to see Lorraine Cowley and this time she gave them a lot more than the time before. She felt like she could talk with more freely now that she was certain Glenn Barber was dead and her story coincided with what the parents of Shona Higgins had finally told them.

'He took our Michaela because I couldn't make the repayments he'd set,' said Lorraine, crying. 'I begged and pleaded with him but he wouldn't listen.'

'And when did he say he would release her?' asked Steve.

'When he considered my debt to have been paid,' said Lorraine. 'It was entirely in his control. I had no say just like I've had no say in anything to do with my life.'

Steve rolled his eyes up impatiently to the Heavens. Joe offered Lorraine a handkerchief which she took.

'Thanks,' said Lorraine, wiping her eyes.

Joe took one of the chairs around the kitchen table and brought it up close to her. He sat down on it and placed his hand on Lorraine's shoulder.

'Come on now, Lorraine,' said Joe. 'We'll do our best to get her back but you've got to level with us and we've wasted enough valuable time as it is. We're here to help you, Lorraine. But to do that you must try and help us. Do you have any idea where Michaela could've been taken by Barber?'

'No,' said Lorraine who now was sobbing. 'I just couldn't afford to pay him back.'

'Look, with Barber dead that must mean that the chances of finding all the girls we know he'd taken, are good,' said Joe. 'So come on, if there's anything you can think of, you've got to tell us.'

'All know is she went to school that morning and never came back,' said Lorraine. 'And I blame that blasted Paul Foster.'

'Paul Foster the social worker?' Steve questioned. 'Why do you blame him?'

'Because if he'd have left us alone in the first place and not tried to interfere on this estate then we might not be in this mess now.'

'So you'd rather owe money to the likes of Barber than to a collective credit union?' said Steve. 'Isn't that what he was trying to get started?'

'Credit union,' Lorraine sneered, her tears temporarily dried up. 'It's all Foster's fault and nobody is going to tell me otherwise. He's messed up the lives of all my kids.'

'Oh you've probably done a pretty good job of doing that yourself,' said Steve.

'Look, I've got one daughter missing, one forced into doing a stupid job and my son is in care. None of that is down to me!'

'You're their mother, Lorraine,' said Steve. 'Now can you tell us anything of any use or are we wasting our time here?'

'He usually came round with someone called Jake,' said Lorraine. 'The same one who's being dished up in the papers as some sort of forgotten war hero or something. It makes me sick.'

'There's a procedure that will now fall into place,

Lorraine. A family liaison officer will be appointed to you who will provide you with the necessary support whilst we continue to look for Michaela.'

'Can they get me any money?' Lorraine asked.

Joe paused before answering. He thought Steve had been a bit tough on her before but with that response she'd lost him now too.

'Emotional and practical support to do with the investigation, Lorraine,' said Joe. He sighed wearily, 'you never know, you might just find it useful and if you're short of money then ask the social for an emergency loan. We'll get you that liaison officer, Lorraine. That's all we can do whilst we look for Michaela.'

When Paul went back to work after his father's death, he stared at the photograph of his mother that he'd put in a silver frame and placed on his desk where she could see him and he could see her. It was a lovely picture of her. His Uncle Doug had told him that his Dad had taken it when she was pregnant. He could see the joy and the happiness in her eyes and he held onto her in that joyful state. He hoped that she'd help him mend his shattered heart. He wished he'd known her. He wished they could've been close. He wished he could talk to her now.

'I thought you might need this,' said Anita as she brought him in a mug of coffee and one for herself.

'Thanks, Anita,' said Paul. 'I didn't have any breakfast this morning. I couldn't be arsed with it.'

Anita produced a packet of chocolate biscuits. 'Fancy one or two of these then?'

'Ah, magic!' Said Paul, taking the packet from her and

diving in. 'Why don't you sit down and talk to me for a minute?'

'Okay, then,' said Anita before adding with a grin. 'I've never sat down with a Lord before.'

'Now enough of that you,' said Paul, pointing his finger at her.

'So are you dead minted now?'

'Anita…'

'…I know, I know, you're always saying it isn't about money it's about values, I know, I've always been listening.'

'And I was saying it when I didn't have any money as well as now that … well, anyway, I'm only a Lord on paper, on inheritance, and I've no idea how much money there is in the bank.'

'But you know it's a lot.'

'Yes,' said Paul. 'But I haven't seen any of it yet so let's change the subject. Are you really starting to enjoy working here now?'

'Oh yeah,' said Anita, 'it's boss.'

'Well you're doing really well,' said Paul who watched over the last few weeks as Anita had travelled from being an insolent, defensive, sulky little cow into someone who was starting to grow up. She was now ironing her clothes before coming to work. She was showing due respect to other people and wasn't nearly as volatile as when she'd first started. In fact, her volatility had largely gone and been replaced by an eagerness to learn and understand. 'I'm proud of you, we all are.'

'I wish my Mum was.'

'She'll come round eventually,' said Paul.

'Oh she's alright on a Friday night when I give her some money out my wages for my board,' said Anita.

'She can't be easy to live with.'

'You're not kidding,' said Anita, 'flaming impossible at times.'

'You've come to a lot of realisations whilst you've been here,' said Paul. 'I mean, when we first met you were wedded to all her ways.'

'Working here has so opened my eyes,' said Anita. 'To what's important and to what I've missed out on.'

'What was your mother's own upbringing like?'

'She didn't really have one I don't think,' said Anita. 'As far as I know her Dad left, her Mum left, she was brought up by someone, some relation I don't know.'

'So she's probably chronically insecure,' said Paul. 'Which is why she's such a control freak with her family.'

'Still makes it a pile of shit to live with, Paul,' said Anita. 'No matter how you try and understand it.'

Paul smiled. 'Oh yes' he said. 'I know.'

'Well I don't care anymore,' said Anita, staring into her coffee. 'I just want to get on for me and Candice.'

'Good for you,' said Paul. 'Go for it, girlfriend!.'

'I've got an appointment this afternoon about getting my own flat.'

'Oh brilliant!' said Paul. 'Do they want a guarantor? I'll do that for you. And don't worry about furniture and all that. We'll sort all that out.'

'Really?'

'Absolutely,' said Paul. 'I can't guarantee what it will all be like but we'll get you some things to get you started. I might even throw some paint on your walls for you if you're good.' Anita looked like she was about to start crying. 'What's up?'

'It's just... since I started working here I've never known so much kindness shown to me.'

'You're worth it, sweetheart.'

'I never knew that before.'

'Well you do now,' said Paul, 'despite what your daft mother says.'

'You know, I've never known what it is to have a Dad,' said Anita, 'but you're as good as.'

'I'm not old enough to be your Dad, you cheeky cow.'

'How old are you?'

'Thirty-five.'

'And I'm only seventeen, so you are old enough,' said Anita.

'Well alright, I'll give you that one,' said Paul, laughing. 'But only just.'

'Paul, I know you were dead upset about your Dad and that but you see, I've never met my Dad. I don't know his name, I don't know what he looks like and I haven't even got a photograph or anything. But if I could choose a Dad it would be you.'

Paul felt humbled by Anita's words, 'well I'd say I'd adopt you but I think I already have.'

'You're not getting rid of me now,' said Anita.

Paul faked a weary sigh. 'Oh God what have I started?'

'I could do with getting a bloke as well as a flat.'

'Very good but no more babies for a few years,' said Paul, 'one step at a time. Have yourself a bit of cock but make sure there's a dress code.'

Anita laughed, 'A what?'

'A dress code? Make sure he wears a jacket? A condom?'

'Oh, right, I didn't get you at first,' said Anita who was still smiling at Paul's use of the word 'cock'. 'I won't make you a Granddad again just yet.'

They both fell into fits of laughter that was a welcome relief from all their worries.

'You're the best medicine, Anita.'

Anita smiled and then stood up and made for the door. Then she stopped.

'What is it?' Paul asked.

'She blames you, you know,' said Anita. 'My Mum. She blames you for everything.'

'Now why doesn't that surprise me?'

Paul went round to Lorraine Cowley's house and when she opened the door he was struck by the same familiar defensive stare.

'Can I come in, Lorraine?'

'Seeing as it's you I don't suppose I've got any choice.'

'You've always got a choice, Lorraine.'

Lorraine led him into the house and folded her arms defensively. 'So? Have you come to tell me I've thousands of pounds in unclaimed Benefits stashed away? Because that's the only thing you'd have to say that would interest me.'

'I'm here to offer you a job, Lorraine.'

'You what? Have you not listened to a single word I've ever said?'

'Have you not listened to a single word I've ever said?'

'You've only ever talked rubbish.'

'Lorraine, do you have any idea? Do you have any idea about what it's like for soldiers who are out there making it safe for you to go and spend your benefit money in the Arndale Centre? Do you? I mean, do you?'

'What's that got to do with me?'

'Well that's the bloody point!'

'No need to get so fucking aggressive.'

'There's every fucking need! You sit around on your fat arse blaming anybody you can lay your hands on for the mess you've made of your life and yet you don't have a fucking clue about what real sacrifice is all about.'

'I've never had anything in my life!'

'Wrong, Lorraine! You started off with nothing and you'll end up with nothing unless you start to take some fucking responsibility. You can't change what has happened in the past, Lorraine, none of us can, even though we all wish we could. But you can make things different in the future if you open your eyes to yourself.'

'Why are you laying this on me now?'

'Because I know you blame me for everything you perceive to be wrong in your life at the moment,' said Paul, 'and I won't accept that.'

'Well you wouldn't.'

'Lorraine, we don't need a revolution for those at the top. We need one for folks like you who expect the rest of us to keep you afloat. It's not good enough, Lorraine. It's not good enough for you and it's not good enough for those soldiers out there risking their lives on your behalf. You need to show yourself and them some fucking respect.'

Lorraine had never been spoken to like that before.

'Are you upset about something?' she asked.

Paul laughed. 'Upset? That doesn't go anywhere near covering what I'm feeling at the moment.'

'Do you want a coffee?'

'Yeah, I want a coffee.'

'You've got a job for me?'

'Yes, I have.'

'I can't read or write.'

Paul immediately felt like a complete idiot. Why hadn't he spotted that? She didn't take any interest in her son Sam's reading abilities because she couldn't. And her only way of dealing with it was to set herself against it and him. She'd never got a job because she couldn't fill in an application form. Her only way of dealing with life was to have babies and to avoid facing up to what the real challenge in her life was. It was so fucking obvious it might as well have leapt up and slapped him across the face.

'I'm sorry, Lorraine,' said Paul. 'I should've realised.'

'It's too late now.'

'No it isn't too late,' Paul insisted. 'Lorraine, it is not too late.'

Lorraine didn't look at him as she cried. 'I can't do it now.'

'Yes you can, Lorraine. Do you hear me?'

'I can't.'

'You can,' Paul repeated. 'You just need the right kind of help.'

'I don't know where to get it, I don't know where to get a job, I don't know where to get nothing!'

'You can come and see us at the centre, Lorraine,' said Paul. 'Isn't that what I've been trying to tell everyone on the estate all these months?'

'I don't like.'

'What don't you like?'

'I don't like talking to people who are going to look down on me.'

'They won't, Lorraine,' said Paul. 'Your own daughter works there.'

'She looks down on me now.'

'No she doesn't, that just exists inside your own head.'

'She does look down on me!'

'Alright, you win, but why don't you do something to make her proud of you instead?'

'I need somebody to help me.'

'I'll help you, Lorraine,' said Paul. 'I'll help you.'

'What's this job you've got for me?'

'I want you to turn up at the social services centre at ten on Monday morning where you'll be officially employed as a cleaner,' Paul announced, 'hours to suit and we will fix your reading and writing classes around it. Okay?'

'I'm not talking to any posh people.'

'Lorraine, there are lots of people in your situation and there won't be any posh people there.'

'You're smiling.'

'I'm smiling because you're sounding so bloody absurd.'

'What does absurd mean?'

'It means you when you're resisting any kind of change,' said Paul, holding up his now empty coffee mug. 'Will you make me another one? I'm not sleeping at the moment and I need all the help I can to stay awake during the day. Oh and will you lay off Anita? I know you're giving her a hard time but she doesn't deserve it.'

Lorraine took the mug from him and emptied a spoonful of coffee granules into it from the jar.

'I don't think you and I can ever really be friends, you know?'

'Oh no,' said Paul, smiling. 'Now that really would be absurd.'

Paul drove away from Lorraine Cowley's house realising that revolutions didn't always have to involve the chopping off of heads.

'This is becoming a rather detestable habit, Detectives,' said Eleanor as she sat in the interview room again with Sara and Tim. Her lawyer was again next to her.

'You were very busy during the war years, weren't you, Lady Eleanor?' said Sara. 'Not in a way that helped the war effort for our own side, of course. You were busy helping the enemy, weren't you?'

'Oh what do you want to know now?' said Eleanor, wearily. 'I really have had enough of all this.'

'How many children did you buy for the Reich?'

'The total was two hundred and fifty-six.'

Sara was taken aback at her Ladyship's candour. 'You're not even going to try and deny it?'

'Why should I? I was proud of what we did. Do you hear me? I was proud of what we did to try and make Germany victorious. Those children were born into nothing. They were urchins. They had families who were happy to part with them for cash. We sent them to be part of the glorious Reich and they've probably led better and more productive lives in Germany, despite the post-war nonsense, than they ever could've led here.'

'You just don't see it, do you?' said Sara, shaking her head in disbelief at her Ladyship's bare faced audacity. 'You bought children and sold them to the enemy!'

'Oh save me your puritan values,' Eleanor scoffed. 'I'd do it all again if the situation arose. And if I'd been able to facilitate the rise of a fourth Reich then I most certainly would've done.'

In the interview room next door, Steve and Joe were trying to get the truth out of Dieter Naumann.

'You talk, I procrastinate,' said Dieter. 'I don't have

much time left and you have to secure some kind of confession. What fun we shall have!'

'You think the issue of buying children is fun?' demanded Joe, angrily.

'Well if the Nazi's were guilty of everything we'd been accused of in the war, then the buying of children for the Reich is nothing,' said Dieter. 'I mean, it really isn't. It's just a little something that happened.'

'Not for the children involved,' said Steve.

'Oh they were only babies most of them,' said Dieter, dismissively. 'All two hundred and fifty-six of them.'

'How many?' Joe asked, astonished.

'Eleanor and I were perfect Nazi's so we kept perfect records,' said Dieter.

'So you can hand over those records and reveal the identities of all the babies involved?'

'Oh no,' said Dieter. 'We destroyed all the records when the Polish woman identified me and this whole process began to take shape. Sorry to excite you and then disappoint you, Detective. Sorry to have you licking your lips only for them to go dry again with equal suddenness.'

'You've recently got back into the child trafficking business, Lady Eleanor,' said Sara. 'Do you want to tell us about it?'

'Not particularly.'

Sara wanted to slap the bitch but she pressed on regardless. 'We can't do anything about the children you bought during the war years, Lady Eleanor. But we can do something about the trade you're engaged in today. Your business relationship with Glenn Barber. Why don't you start your explanations there?'

Eleanor paused before responding. 'I have mixed with many criminals over the years. Oh I'm not interested in the petty thief. I'm only interested in the ones who keep pushing it and pushing it until they've had way more than their fair share of everything. The ones who become leaders in their community.'

'By leaders you mean those who rule by fear and intimidation,' said Sara.

'Most people are so stupid they need the strength of firm, hard leaders.'

'Like Adolf Hitler?'

'Like the beloved Fuhrer.'

'Like Glenn Barber?'

'Glenn Barber was known to an associate of mine who introduced us,' said Eleanor. 'He needed some investment in his business and I needed teenage girls for some of my friends who still know what it's like to have some fun. They like the girls to dress up for them and be playful.'

'It's the oldest perversion in the book!' Sara scoffed.

'I didn't take you for a prude, detective.'

'I'm not a prude,' said Sara, 'but neither am I an abuser. What goes on between consenting adults is nobody else's business. But the key word there is consenting. And only adults can consent to activities within the law.'

'If you say so, my dear.'

'So everything was all your idea? You thought of a plan to take teenage girls off of families who couldn't repay their loans?' asked Sara.

'Well Glenn Barber wouldn't have had the brains to come up with it,' said Eleanor, haughtily. 'But he had his way and he knew what I needed so he'd target the families with the suitable girls accordingly. I saved the state a lot of money by taking those girls out of it.'

Sara sat back in her chair in absolute revulsion. 'I don't follow?'

'Well they would never have amounted to anything,' Eleanor insisted.

'At least one of them is dead!'

'Well she would've been the same drain on the state for the entirety of her sad, stupid life as any of the others.'

'How did you make them do what you wanted?' asked Tim who was equally as sickened as Sara at what he was hearing.

'Drugs,' answered Eleanor, simply. 'They were drugged into compliance. Their parents should never have had them in the first place but of course, we let the wrong sort breed these days. You could say that I was doing my bit to put that right.'

'So you have no remorse for what has happened to these girls at all?' Tim pressed.

'None whatsoever,' said Eleanor. 'I'd be a liar if I told you otherwise.'

Even the uniformed police officer assigned to the room was aghast at what was coming out of Lady Eleanor's mouth. What none of them could get over was the brazen candour with which Lady Eleanor was admitting her culpability in such heinous crimes.

'Where are these girls being held, Lady Eleanor?' Sara demanded.

'I don't know,' said Lady Eleanor.

'You expect us to believe that?'

'It's the truth,' Eleanor insisted. 'I didn't get involved in the where, just the how and the why.'

'What happened to Shona Higgins, Lady Eleanor?' asked Tim.

'It was simple,' said Lady Eleanor. 'She was costing us money.'

'How?'

'She needed more drugs to maintain her compliance,' said Lady Eleanor. 'Once the cost of those drugs met the income figure we were getting for her, then she started to cost us money. It was our policy that when that happened the girls had to be got rid of. Her novelty had worn off. Our clientele weren't asking for her anymore.'

'And because of that she had to die?'

Eleanor shrugged her shoulders. 'Her parents are the ones to point the fingers at,' she said. 'They shouldn't have got themselves into such a financial mess.'

'A mess that you were charging them an indefensible amount of interest for!' retorted Sara, angrily.

Eleanor shrugged her shoulders again. 'That's what's called the market.'

'And Glenn Barber committed the murder?'

'Yes,' said Eleanor, 'or at least, I gave him the instruction so I suppose he must have.'

'Lady Eleanor, why did you get involved with all of this?'

'Because I could and because I like making money.'

'But you already had more than you'll ever need.'

'I wanted more.'

'How do you sleep at night?'

'In my bed with a clear conscience just like every good Catholic who goes to confession every Sunday to absolve herself of her human sin.'

CHAPTER SEVENTEEN

SARA DROVE INTO WORK the next morning and paused before getting out of her car. She still couldn't get over how someone like Lady Eleanor had actually sat down and planned such heinous crimes. She'd dealt with two serial killers in her career so far and both of them had been able to justifiably claim at least a measure of insanity as part of their defence. They'd both been able to point to events in their lives that had twisted their emotions beyond any reason or perspective and contributed to turning them into killers. Not that any of it could excuse what they'd done and it certainly didn't inspire her to have any sympathy for them. But it did explain some of the psychology behind their crimes and helped Sara try to work out how they'd come to commit them whereas Lady Eleanor wasn't even trying to claim that she might've been driven to such evil by events further back in her life. On the contrary, she saw everything she did as a stroke of genius to be celebrated. It was beyond Sara to even try and understand the workings of a mind like that.

She asked the custody sergeant to open up the cell where Lady Eleanor had spent what Sara hoped would've been a very uncomfortable night. And she was right. Her Ladyship looked as rough as a stray dog.

'Good morning, Lady Eleanor,' Sara said, in greeting, 'I don't expect you're used to such surroundings but I hope they've served their purpose in inspiring you to talk.'

Lady Eleanor looked up at Sara with eyes that were those of a predator who was desperate to unleash her savagery on her. 'You will most certainly pay for this.'

'No, I'm hoping that you'll finally pay for your crimes, Lady Eleanor.'

'I've told you that I don't know where the girls are being held!'

'And I don't believe you.'

'Then you're wrong'

'Who's taken over the Glenn Barber side of your business, Lady Eleanor? Now that Barber is dead. Who's your executioner of choice now?'

'Jake Thornton was working with him,' said Eleanor, flatly. 'You should start there but of course, he's on the run and you don't know where he is.'

'I don't think we need to go that far away from home, do we? I'll be driving out to see your head of household, Colin Bradley. I'm sure he's got a tale to tell.'

'When are you going to let me go?'

'You're helping us with our enquiries, Lady Eleanor,' said Sara, lightly, 'and we've a few more hours yet before we have to give you back to your life of luxury. So sit back and take in the scenery. Oh and I suggest you choose tea. The coffee in this place really isn't up to much.'

'Do you really think you can get one over on me? After all this time?'

'Oh I think the law has finally got one or two over on you, Lady Eleanor. Let's recall, you've been charged with one murder, one case of accessory to murder, and the abduction and sexual exploitation of underage girls. You could go home on conditional bail now, only because of a concession to your age and only if you told me where the girls are being held.'

'And I told you that I don't know!'

'I'll give you a few more hours to think again about your answer,' said Sara who then turned on her heels and made for the door.

'Where's my Dieter?'

'At home, waiting for you.'

'You won't get what you want by dividing us!'

'We'll see.'

'I'll destroy you when I get out of here!'

'Make anymore threats like that and you never will get out of here, Lady Eleanor, believe me,' warned Sara, 'I'm the one with the power here and neither you nor anybody else is above the law. This isn't 1940.'

Paul was driving west along the elevated stretch of Mancunian Way on the south side of the city centre, heading for home, when his mobile rang. He was glad that he'd finally fitted the hands free kit the other day, even if the earpiece did make him look like a twat. He saw from the caller display that it was his friend, Colleen Price. He pressed the answer button.

'Colleen? How are you?'

'Not very good,' said Colleen, solemnly.

'Colleen? What's up?'

Colleen struggled to stay calm. 'Oh Paul, something terrible has happened.'

'What, love?'

'Somebody came into the school and… everything's destroyed, Paul. They've smashed all the computers, the language lab looks like a battlefield, and the windows of all the class rooms are in shards scattered everywhere…' she started to cry. '…I don't know what to do, Paul. I've sent the kids home but I don't know how I'm going to clear all this up.'

'I'll be straight round,' said Paul. 'Sit tight.'

When Paul made it round to the school he noticed a group of local lads standing across the road looking pleased with themselves. He couldn't help himself. He walked over to them.

'Do you lot know anything about who did this?'

'Don't know what you mean, mate,' said Tyrone, Lorraine Cowley's nephew.

'Don't fuck with me,' said Paul.

Tyrone and the rest of them started laughing.

'Do you think it's funny? You've destroyed everybody's hard work and you think that's funny? You're sick, pal, sick and twisted in the head.'

Tyrone didn't quite see the funny side of that and moved up close and threatening to Paul, the rest of his mates forming closely behind him. At this point Paul wondered if he should've challenged them. They could pull a knife on him or anything. But he wasn't going to back off. They weren't going to intimidate him especially this streak of shit who was acting like the big, hard man.

'Watch your mouth, social man,' Tyrone threatened, 'it could get you in a lot of trouble.'

'You don't deserve it,' said Paul. 'You don't deserve for people like Colleen Price to try and get you to believe in a future. There's people all over the world going out onto the streets to demand their freedom and liberty. And what do you do? Sit around like slobs all day waiting for the next handout, throwing away all the rights and responsibilities that people throughout history have fought to get for you. You're not worth it. You're not worth anybody's sacrifice.'

Paul turned and walked into the school, not looking behind him and noting the silence that followed him.

Once inside he stood with Colleen in the computer science room, or what was left of it, it made him so bloody angry. Colleen had fought tooth and nail for the funding to buy the computers and get them set up and now some… some little shit had come along and smashed all of her good work away. She'd been really making a difference with these kids. She'd been determined to get for them the same facilities that schools in more advantaged suburbs benefited from and she was succeeding. Or she had been.

'It beats me why some people choose to be so destructive,' said Colleen, her heart breaking with all she could see around her.

'It doesn't beat me,' said Paul. 'Whoever did this doesn't want this community to move on. They want it to stay in the pits because they're too idle to take advantage of what people like you are trying to do for them.'

'But what am I going to do, Paul?' Colleen pleaded. 'How am I going to get all this back for the sake of the kids?'

Paul put his arms round her and pulled her close. 'Hey, hey, it'll be alright.'

'How will it?'

'Colleen, we'll rebuild,' said Paul. 'We'll get the funding and we'll show them that you're not beaten.'

'The insurance will cover most of it,' said Colleen.

'Well there you are then.'

'But it's just that it's happened at all! Somebody has come along and laid into everything I've done to help the kids round here. It's not fair!'

'I know, love, I know,' said Paul, holding her tight. 'But one way or another we'll sort it.'

They were shaken out of their embrace by the sound of a single gunshot. Their first instinct was to get down but they managed to make the way, crawling along the floor, to one of the smashed in windows. What they saw was Tyrone lying dead on the ground, with blood pouring out of a wound in his head. Some of the assembled crowd were looking down at him whilst the rest were looking in the direction of a man who was running down the street and heading further into the estate.

Sara and Joe went down to Gatley Hall only to be told that Colin Bradley had gone off duty two days previously and that although he was due back today after his days off, he hadn't shown up for work. This was unusual by all accounts. He hadn't missed a day since starting at the Hall almost twenty years ago.

'Where's he gone, Mr. Naumann?' Sara asked, impatiently.

'How the hell should I know?'

'You're lying!'

'If you weren't a police officer I'd slap your stupid face!'

'Oh go ahead, sir. In fact, feel free. You must be so out of practice after leaving your storm trooping and torturing days behind? In fact, what did it feel like to cure people of their pain, rather than being the one who was causing it? That must've been quite some transition.'

'I have given decades of service to this country as a medical professional, young lady.'

'Then I appeal to that… that side of the man you are. Help me to save those girls, Mr. Naumann. Help me to do the decent thing for once in your life.'

'Go to hell.'

'Oh I don't think I'll be going there, sir,' Sara snarled, 'but I think you might.'

After their encounter with Naumann they drove to the terraced cottage in Bollington, up in the hills east of Macclesfield, where Colin Bradley lived.

'I always feel dirty after I've been in that Nazi's company,' said Sara.

'I know what you mean,' said Joe, 'both him and her Ladyship are quite something.'

'He really believes he's done no wrong,' said Sara. 'That's the really hideous thing about it. There's nothing to link him with the relationship between Glenn Barber and her Ladyship but I bloody wish there was. Anyway, let's see what Bradley is up to.'

There was no reply when they knocked on the door and when Sara peered through the window there was no sign of life. Then one of the neighbours emerged from next door, a short, plump woman in a knitted cardigan and a tweed skirt. Her hair was going grey and was in no discernable style, just short and wavy.

'Are you looking for the Bradley's?' she asked.

'That's right, madam,' said Joe. 'I'm Detective Constable Alexander and this is Detective Chief Inspector Hoyland.'

'Police?' said the woman, her hand against her chest. 'I'm sure it's nothing to do with the police.'

'What isn't?' asked Sara.

'Well they left here in a taxi yesterday morning. Colin and Monica and the two boys. You should've seen the taxi. I thought its suspension was going to go with all the stuff they were taking with them. Come to think of it, it did look like they were going on more than just a holiday and even that surprised me because I thought they were supposed to be broke.'

'Where did they say they were going, Mrs...?'

'Treadwell, Julia Treadwell.'

'Mrs. Treadwell.'

'Well all they said was that they were on their way to catch a flight at Manchester Airport,' said Julia Treadwell. 'There wasn't time for them to tell me where to before they sped off.'

'And what time was this, Mrs. Treadwell?' asked Joe.

'It was just before eight o'clock,' said Julia Treadwell. 'I was just on my way to work.'

'And you say they were broke?'

'Oh, they were always broke,' said Julia. 'That's why I thought it was strange that they were going on holiday all of a sudden.'

When they got back to the station Sara ordered a check on the passenger lists of all flights departing Manchester Airport yesterday. Superintendent Hargreaves then asked her to come to his office.

'Close the door, Sara,' said Hargreaves, 'and then you'd better take a seat.'

'I don't like the sound of that, sir,' said Sara. 'Have you got some bad news for me?'

'You could say that,' said Hargreaves who was sat behind his desk. 'You're to drop all charges and any pending investigations involving Lady Eleanor Harding.'

Sara was aghast. 'I don't understand, sir?'

'Whatever we find out about her activities, past or present, will have to be dropped.'

Sara felt like she'd been hit with a cricket bat. 'Say that again, sir?'

'Instructions that have to be obeyed, DCI Hoyland,'

said Hargreaves. 'No questions, no compromise, just absolute obedience.'

'And this is from the Home Office?' she demanded rather sharply. The look on Hargreaves face said it all. 'Sorry, sir. It's just a bit of a shock'

'It's alright,' said Hargreaves.

'So did this come from the Home Office, sir?'

'Yes but they would be acting on instructions from elsewhere,' said Hargreaves.

'Where?'

'The palace probably,' said Hargreaves. 'That's the way these things usually work.'

Sara paced to the window and rubbed the back of her neck. All that work. All that pushing to get a confession out of both Harding and Naumann was now all going to be pissed down the drain because those who sit at the top table of the British establishment always look after their own. It made her sick. She'd never been a revolutionary but she was wondering about it now.

'All is not lost though, Sara'

Sara turned back to him. 'How do you mean, sir?'

'They tried to impose a news blackout on all this,' said Hargreaves. 'But they were too late. Someone had already leaked the story to the press.'

Sara could see the obvious look of pleasure on the Superintendent's face and she returned it with a smile. 'And that will prove very inconvenient to those with something to hide.'

Charlie Mason was only doing his job at the petrol station to earn some extra cash for his intended trip next year. He planned to get a working visa for Australia and maybe even settle there permanently. Since his mother had died, his father had married 'the bitch' with unforgivable haste – his mother hadn't even been dead three months before she marched his Dad into a register office and tied the knot with him. They'd been having an affair for years before Charlie's mother had been killed in a car accident. Now he had to listen to them at it all night and every night through the thin walls of their terraced house on the east of Oldham. Their love-in had frozen him out and he felt alone in his own family home where once he'd felt safe and happy. It was as if his mother had never existed. The bitch had changed everything she could into the way she wanted it and his father had raised no objections. He hated his father now. How could he have been so indecent? His father wasn't an old man, only just into his forties, and Charlie had wanted him to be happy. But not like this. Not with someone who wanted to take over his life and freeze out everyone who'd gone before. His Aunts and Uncles, especially on his Mum's side, had all noticed and had even offered him a room at theirs when it got too much. His maternal grandparents didn't want him to go to Australia. They'd lost their daughter and didn't want to effectively lose their grandson, too. But they understood that he had to find his own way and promised to go and see him if he did end up settling there.

But all of that was still a few months away. He had to save some more cash first. He liked doing the early shift. If there was no overtime going in the afternoon he'd usually spend the time walking on the moors close to where he lived. The open space and the peace it offered made him feel close to his mother. He spoke to her out there on the moors. It felt like she was all around him. He still missed her like crazy even after all this time.

It was just before half past nine and the busy period had just passed. Those who refused to use the trains to commute into Manchester usually started their journey around this time and would often curse for not having filled up the night before. They could be quite temperamental by the time they got to pay and Charlie had to ask them to put their pin number into the card machine. But Charlie never let it get to him. It was like water off a duck's back. They could all just go and fuck themselves. He wouldn't give them a second thought when he was lying on a Sydney beach in a few months time with some hot girl beside him. Like his father and the bitch, he would be a million miles away in his own world.

He didn't see the man come out of the bushes on the other side of the garage forecourt. He didn't notice him marching up purposefully to the shop where Charlie was engaged behind the cash desk. He didn't see him take the gun out of his pocket and blast Charlie's dreams of a future in Australia into the next life.

Paul had just got back from a meeting with the head of Salford social services when Anita told him he had a visitor.

'She says her name is Tiffany?' said Anita. 'She says you'll know her? She looks heavily pregnant. It can't be long before she drops it.'

Paul's heart sank. He really didn't need this just now.

'What's up?' asked Anita. 'You've gone as white as a sheet.'

'No matter,' said Paul. 'Thanks Anita. You can show her

in.'

When Tiffany stepped through into Paul's office he didn't know quite what he'd been expecting but it wasn't the girl who was stood before him. Yes, she was pregnant but she carried quite a bit of weight on her anyway. She was a big girl. She wasn't classically beautiful. Her cheekbones weren't high and her mouth was small giving her face a kind of pinched look. She was quite ordinary and if it wasn't for the wonders of make-up it struck Paul that she was just the sort of girl a soldier chooses to keep the home fires burning whilst he's out there risking his life for Queen and country. Someone to push out a couple of kids for him and make him feel like the returning hero as soon as he walks through the door. Sexually she was probably pretty ordinary, he guessed. But she no doubt knew enough to fill in the gaps for him between tours of duty. Her hair was breast length and dyed a bright copper colour which Paul didn't think suited her very white face. He hated himself for appraising her like this but he couldn't help it. Sizing up the opposition was always too tempting to resist despite the circumstances.

'Tiffany?'

'Yes, I'm Tiffany,' she answered. 'Jake's wife.'

She emphasised the word 'wife' as if she was slapping him across the face with it.

'Any news on Jake?' he asked.

'No,' she said. 'You heard anything?'

'No,' said Paul.

'Mind you, I don't know who he'd contact first,' said Tiffany. 'You or me.'

'I don't know.'

'Suppose it depends on which one of us he was into at that particular moment.'

'You should be sitting down,' said Paul, gesturing to the chair in front of his desk.

'I'd rather stand, thank you.'

'Tiffany, for fuck's sake you shouldn't be standing for too long and neither should you get yourself upset.'

Tiffany put her hand on her hip. The affected drama of the move almost made Paul burst out laughing.

'You've got a sodding nerve. If you didn't want me upset then you shouldn't have been sleeping with my husband!'

Paul's momentary flash of humour was quickly replaced by anger. 'I was going out with Jake for nearly four years before he married you.'

'Really?' she scoffed.

'Yes, really, and instead of being a grown up and telling me he didn't want me anymore he just stopped contacting me for months. I was going out of my mind with worry when he was building his little love nest with you so if anybody's got a right to be upset it's me!'

'So you say,' she said dismissively.

'Yes, I say! So sit down and we'll talk but I'm not taking a lecture from you, Tiffany, because I don't deserve it.'

Tiffany waited a moment and then she did sit down. Her back was aching. Her legs were too and she really shouldn't have worn these shoes. The heels were too high considering the bump she was already balancing.

'How long before the baby is due?'

'I'm seven months gone,' she said. 'Do you love him, Paul?'

'Yes, I do,' said Paul.

'Well at least you're being honest.'

'It's the only way to be,' said Paul, 'no point pretending now.'

'When I read about your friendship with him in the paper I just put two and two together. It was a shock but then so much has been a shock lately. I never expected my husband to be into men as well as women, but I had no idea he was working for a gangster either. Then when the police said they were looking for him in connection with Glenn Barber's murder I just didn't know what to do.'

Tiffany started sobbing and Paul couldn't help going round and putting his arm round her.

'I've moved back in with my Mum since we found out,' said Tiffany, between sobs. 'Why has Jake done this to me?' she cried.

'He hasn't done it to you,' said Paul in measured tones. Her self-obsession was annoying him. 'He's done it to himself.'

'But I'm the one who's got to live with it.'

'Don't you think he has too?'

'I don't know what he thinks and I'm not sure I care anymore.'

'He should've held on,' said Paul. 'We could've put into his defence everything about the traumas he went through in Afghanistan. That's where he changed, Tiffany. That's what we need to understand.'

'But he's a murderer,' she wailed. 'He murdered Glenn Barber.'

'I know but the lawyers could've argued mitigating circumstances, Tiffany, that's what I'm saying.'

'I'm too ashamed to face anyone I know,' she said. 'That's another reason why I moved back in with my Mum.'

Oh so it's back to being all about you, thought Paul. 'I don't see why.'

'But what am I going to tell the baby?' she pleaded.

'How can I tell it that it's father is a murderer?'

'You don't tell the baby that,' said Paul who was struck by the weirdness of a situation where he was sitting here trying to reason with the wife of the man he loved. 'You tell the baby that it's father was a heroic soldier for his country but that his experiences led him to do some bad things.'

'My Mum never wanted me to marry him but I loved him, Paul.'

Tiffany cried her heart out on Paul's shoulder although he didn't feel that disposed towards her. He didn't like thinking it but she was clearly too thick to have been able to cope with someone as complex as Jake had become.

'Look, Tiffany, you've got to focus on the future for yourself and the baby now.'

'And how am I going to do that?'

'I'll make sure you've got enough money and I'll make sure you've got everything you need for the baby.'

'You'd have taken Jake off me if you'd had half the chance.'

'Tiffany, either accept my help or don't accept it,' said Paul who was tired of trying to get through to this child. Jake was out there somewhere and what with that and everything else that was on his mind he really didn't have time to indulge someone who should've been able to at least try and save Jake.

'But you would've taken him off me,' said Tiffany. 'Don't lie. You would've done if you could have.'

Louise Cooper tried her best to convince all the girls she worked with in the travel agent's on the edge of Bury town centre that she wasn't a gold digger. But they all knew that she was. The thing was that although she'd grown up on one of the town's council estates, her family had been given a taste of the good life through her father's £200,000 lottery win but her parents had splashed it around like the proverbial confetti and now, five years later, it had all but gone. They were back living on benefits and Louise badly needed her roots doing. But that was something else. She'd grown used to going to the top hair designer in Manchester and now she couldn't contemplate going anywhere else. It was all part of the image she'd built up around herself. So she had to save up and though she'd been at the travel agents a while she wasn't paid that much. She'd been passed over for promotion twice in the time she'd been there and though she would protest till the cows came home that she was quite happy out on the desk serving the customers, the reason why she hadn't been promoted was that she lacked the ability for a supervisory or management position. She was thick. Exceptionally pretty on the outside, thanks to some very expensive make-up that she now struggled to keep on buying, but on the inside she was like a house with no furniture in it, a table laid but no food in the bare cupboards. Her accent was so affected it made her workmates cringe at times and she could always be heard above all other noise wherever she was. She knew they laughed at her behind her back. When her family had money she couldn't have cared less. These days she'd been getting more sensitive about it.

Her current boyfriend was called Raymond. He wasn't just in fine furnishings. He owned a chain of furniture shops across Northern England and they went to all the right places to eat and drink. He'd told her that he hadn't had sex with his wife for five years and explained the existence of his two-year old daughter by having given in to his wife on her birthday once. Still, he gave her a good time in fancy places before she had to open her legs and try and keep up with his voracious appetite. She'd never known anything like it. He could keep it going for hours. She always told the girls at work all the details the next day whether they wanted to know or not.

But at least Raymond was helping her get over Justin. That really had been traumatic for her. She'd had to break up with him just days before their wedding when she'd woken up one morning and realised that she just didn't love him anymore. It was the morning after he'd told her his business was about to collapse and that he'd have to declare himself bankrupt, meaning that he'd probably lose his six-bedroom detached with electric gates in Altrincham where Louise had made herself very comfortable. But of course that was just a coincidence and nothing to do with her feelings having changed at all. The girls in the office had seen through it all though. One of them now went out with Justin. She was helping him re-build his life and didn't care whether or not he owned his own business. She just loved him and wanted to make him happy.

Louise liked to sit at the front desk just inside the window and often came in early to reserve her place. But this morning when she looked up and locked eyes with the man standing on the street looking in, she wished she hadn't. In a split second she saw him produce his gun and fire it through the window, killing her instantly with a volley of bullets.

CHAPTER EIGHTEEN

THE CLOSER PAUL GOT to Gatley Hall, the more nauseous he felt. He'd driven down the A34 out of Manchester city centre many times to go and see his friends Alan and Richard in Cheadle but this time his destination was rather different. He'd finally given in to all the calls and he was on his way to validate his own history, his own bloodline. He was going to see a grandmother he never knew he had, a woman who was nothing more than an evil criminal. He was still fielding calls from the press who'd tried to interview him at work and who'd turned up outside his house at all hours. It was starting to become a nightmare, especially once they had broken the story about how his grandmother and her Nazi boyfriend weren't going to answer for their crimes.

When he got to the Hall he looked up at an edifice to everything he hated about the class system. There was even a fucking Union Jack flying above the front door. He wasn't against that per se but he detested the way the flag had been hijacked by the far right and it was such hypocrisy for his grandmother to fly it considering everything she'd done against the country. He took a deep breath. He could hear his bowels. They were angry. But then he told himself off. He had nothing to be ashamed of. Those who should be ashamed were already inside this glorified prison.

He was greeted at the door by a member of his grandmother's staff and led through to where she was waiting for him.

'Well now,' said Eleanor as she looked him up and down, 'here you are then. You finally responded to my calls.'

Paul took a deep breath. It made his skin crawl to think that he was related to this woman who wouldn't know shame if her life depended on it.

'I didn't want to but my father brought me up to show due respect.'

'Then he brought you up well.'

'You should be grateful to him.'

'Yes, well, we have important matters to discuss but firstly, I had my staff prepare us some drinks,' said Eleanor, waving her hand across the tray of drinks on the table in front of her. 'I understand you're partial to a gin and tonic?'

This was weird, thought Paul. She was his grandmother but she was also an unreconstructed fascist who harbours Nazi war criminals. She was a woman who'd screwed up the lives of his mother, his father, and himself. He hadn't known quite what to expect but apart from her frailty, what struck Paul was the menace in her eyes. They were the coldest and most disturbing pair of eyes he'd ever seen.

'Do you think I've come here to talk about good times over a drink?'

'Oh God, you're going to be tiresome,' said Eleanor, 'your mother was the same.'

'I buried my mother yesterday.'

'Well you had good weather for it.'

'You didn't bother to turn up to your own daughter's funeral!'

'I had other things to do.'

'That was more important? I don't think so'

'Look, having a conscience has never been one of my failings, Paul,' said Eleanor.

'Never a truer word spoken,' Paul spat back.

'Alright,' said Eleanor. 'If that's how you want it. Look Paul, when it came to your mother, I neglected her when she was a child. I was selfish and I saw her as an irritating distraction from whatever I wanted to do. She and Ronald took to each other even though of course he wasn't her father. But I let them get on with it. There was nothing in it for me in playing happy families.'

'My God, it's true what they say. You really are heartless.'

'Then when she was grown up and we might've had things to talk about, it was too late. We didn't know each other and we didn't like each other. When she met your father I could see how happy and in love she was but I didn't believe in love across the social classes and I still don't.'

'So you were happy to use someone of the lower classes to further your cause of fascism but your daughter mustn't marry him?'

'Your way of putting it.'

'You destroyed my parents' happiness and my chances of growing up with my own family!'

'Oh for heaven's sake, stop being so dramatic.'

'You let an innocent man hang for a murder you'd committed,' said Paul.

Eleanor paused. 'Wilfred Jenkins… if there'd been a scandal then it would've destroyed any chance I had of facilitating a deal with Hitler to bring an end to the war.'

'But you'd have done that without any regard at all for the Poles, the Belgians, the Dutch, the French, the Norwegians. I've read all about how the British aristocracy wanted Chamberlain to sell out the continent to protect the empire.'

'Paul, there was a war on and people did what they thought they had to do.'

'To protect your own wealth!' Paul charged. 'You were prepared to sacrifice everyone on the continent for that. Then there's the murder of six million Jews, gypsies and homosexuals in the camps. Did you not consider their suffering at all?'

Eleanor raised her eyes to the Heavens as if she was so irritated by the triviality of these stupid questions. 'Oh the Jews, the Jews, the Jews, when will they ever shut up. Look, when they knew what was happening, and they knew in the early thirties what would surely come, they should've just left Germany and gone to America or some other such place.'

'So it's all their fault for not having up rooted themselves?' asked an astonished Paul. 'The Reich wanted to eliminate a whole ethnicity. How could you not be disgusted by that measure of evil?'

'The Jews were responsible for the murder of our Lord Jesus! They finally got what had been coming to them for centuries.'

'So you really think that Jesus himself would've approved of that? The Nazi's systematically murdered nearly six million of them'

'Look, Germany worked under the Reich,' Eleanor asserted. 'Hitler may have got a little too expansionist towards the end which was ultimately his downfall but I cannot say that I didn't admire the way he led his country. The Queen herself supported us all in our endeavours to protect our trade routes with the empire'

'The Royal family sent their own cousins to their

Bolshevik executioners when they refused to give sanctuary to Tsar Nicolas and his family,' said Paul 'It doesn't surprise me to have it confirmed how selfish they've always been. The British people should've had more guts. We should've had our own revolution.'

'That's your point of view I suppose,' said Eleanor, flatly.

'You and I may as well be at opposite ends of the universe.'

'Don't you think you can ever make peace with who you are?' asked Eleanor in a quieter voice that nevertheless made Paul take notice.

'Oh I've made peace with it,' said Paul, looking straight at her. 'In memory of my mother whose life you destroyed. But are you going to make peace whilst you've still got time?'

She looked at him sharply. 'What do you mean?'

'The location of where all those poor girls are being held?'

Eleanor looked up at the heavens and laughed. 'So you're just a stooge for all those idiots who call themselves police officers.'

'There are teenage girls who're missing and you must know where they are!'

Eleanor stared into him like a drill going into metal. 'I tell you I don't know!'

'Nonsense! What has happened to those girls? Who are these pervert friends of yours who've been abusing them?'

'You don't demand things from me!'

Paul was exasperated. 'Do the right thing for once in your life!'

'Aren't you going to even try to understand me, Paul?'

'Understand? You bought children and gave them over

to the Lebensraum programme. You did it for four years and God knows what happened to all those children. Don't you feel any shame?'

'No,' said Eleanor, flatly. 'I don't because I did it for the Reich.'

'And you know where these missing girls are today, don't you? This could be your last chance to do the decent thing and let the police know. So if you want to do something that will go some way towards some kind of redemption, and God knows you damn well need it, then tell the police where these girls are.'

'Paul, I really don't know,' said Eleanor. 'I like making money and I like the criminal mind. I put the two together as one last throw of the dice.'

'That's all you've got to say for yourself?'

'Don't you dare stand there and judge me!' Eleanor thundered.

'Judge you? I don't need to judge you. The evidence is all there and it's conclusive.'

'That's enough!' Dieter demanded as he came into the room. 'I will not let you speak to your grandmother in this fashion!'

'Well here he is,' said Paul. 'The other side of this farce. So what are you going to do if I don't stop? Because if I could get away with it I'd kill you right now and I'd have the souls of all those in that Polish village cheering me on. But that would be too easy. You need to know what it means to suffer.'

Dieter laughed sardonically before sitting down next to Eleanor who still wanted Paul to try and understand her actions.

'Paul, Dieter and I are children of the Reich,' said Eleanor.

'You're making a point of some kind?'

'All those years ago we were sorting out the Jewish problem and if we'd been victorious then there would never have been a 9/11 because we'd have sorted out the Muslims before they could've done us any harm too,' said Dieter. 'Germany and the Reich would've built a Europe based on our Aryan values, free from all forms of human imperfection.'

'I can almost feel hell freezing over as you say that.'

'White, Christian, Heterosexual, and ruled from Berlin,' said Eleanor, firmly.

'You're absolutely insane.'

'Paul, I said that's enough!' Dieter demanded.

'What about the watch?' asked Paul. 'It was stolen, wasn't it?'

'It was taken from the undeserving,' said Eleanor.

'It was taken from a Jewish family before they were murdered,' said Paul. 'Well I know a member of that family who survived and I'm going to make sure he gets it back.'

Eleanor smirked. 'If you want to play the boy scout.'

'Why not? Are you scared I might implicate your royal friends in the theft? After all, it was one of theirs who gave it to you, wasn't it?'

'I don't answer questions I don't care for.'

'Paul, can't we just sit down and talk?' said Dieter. 'Wouldn't you prefer that?'

'What shall we talk about? The weather? Murdering people?'

'That's enough, Paul,' said Dieter. 'I've warned you already.'

'Oh no, I haven't even started yet!' Paul shot back. 'You both make my skin crawl.'

'I told you before that's enough, Paul,' said Dieter,

sternly.

'This is pointless,' said Paul. 'I don't like you and you don't like me. There's no use in us continuing this fascinating exchange. I'm going home.'

'You already are home,' said Eleanor.

'What are you talking about?'

'Well I told you we had important matters to discuss. I've signed everything over to you, Paul. The money, this Hall, the title. It's all yours.'

Paul didn't quite know how to react. He'd suspected that she'd pull some kind of stunt. He'd had a few days to get his head around what his destiny had in store for him but he hadn't expected it to be this death of the witch's death.

'Why now?'

Eleanor took hold of Dieter's hand. 'Our time is done,' said Eleanor. 'Dieter and I will not be around to see you fill this place with whatever it is you want. We still have our love after all these years and now that's all that matters.'

'You mean that I can do what I want?'

'You are now the Earl of Gatley and a very wealthy young man,' said Eleanor. 'I know you don't value such historical traditions but it's your time. Dieter and I have been let down and betrayed…'

'…you've done some terrible things. For people like you to feel the pain of betrayal is beyond all reason.'

'That's your view,' said Eleanor, 'but we wish to wash our hands of everything and just be together.'

'You don't deserve it'

'That's also your view.'

'And what's your view, Mr. War Criminal? Or do you always let the woman do the talking?'

'At least I know what it is to be a man with a woman.'

Paul threw his head back and laughed. 'Is that the best you can do?'

'Don't be too smug,' said Dieter.

'Well now,' said Paul as the most wonderful idea dropped into his head. 'I can be as smug as I like in my own house.' He turned to his grandmother. 'Now will you tell me where those missing teenage girls are or not?'

'You've already asked me that and my answer is still the same.'

'Very well,' said Paul. 'I want you both to pack your bags and leave here tomorrow.'

'You can't mean that,' said Eleanor.

'Oh I do mean it.'

'But this has been my home all my life,' Eleanor protested.

'Which you've now signed over to me,' said Paul. 'And I owe you nothing. I would never give any of my heart and soul to a fascist.'

'Mind your tongue,' said Eleanor, her words spitting out of her mouth like the venom of a snake. 'Your own father was a fascist.'

'Yes but he gave it all up for the woman he loved,' said Paul. 'Just like your friend the traitor King who gave up the British throne for a woman he loved.'

'Edward was a true patriot!'

'He barely disguised his admiration for fascism! He'd have delivered the British people to Hitler if he'd had the chance. He was a traitor and so were you.'

'I'm all you have!' said Eleanor.

'By blood,' said Paul, 'but not by character and my friends mean more to me than you ever will.' He then turned to Dieter. 'You've still got your house in Glossop. I suggest you go there first thing.'

'You can't throw us out, Paul,' Eleanor pleaded, 'we're family.'

'Oh don't play the family card with me! You destroyed my family. I'll be back first thing and if you're not gone I'll throw you both out myself.'

'But Paul, how can you be so cold?'

Paul fixed her firmly in the eye.

'It must be in the blood.'

★

The next morning Paul was woken by a call from John Carpenter, his grandmother's lawyer. He said he had some sad news. He was sorry to have to inform him that his grandmother and Dieter Naumann were both dead. They'd committed suicide.

'Well, well, well,' said Paul to himself after he'd ended the call, 'so they've had the last fucking laugh.'

Kelly and Lydia went down to Gatley Hall with Paul. He'd made his peace with his two best friends and he was so glad of that now.

'It must be hard to take it all in,' said Lydia as they wandered through the Hall.

'In a way,' said Paul.

'You seem to be taking it in your stride,' said Kelly. 'I don't think I would be.'

'Well my Dad sort of prepared me for something like this in his letter,' said Paul, holding back the tears as he thought of his father. 'I don't think I quite expected it to be done in the way it was, but then I was dealing with a wicked old witch. However she's gone now and I've got a responsibility to this estate and to all the people who work here. I've just got to get on with it.'

'So how did they do it?' Kelly asked.

'They each took a cyanide pill,' said Paul who was beginning to feel exhausted with everything that had happened. 'I might've known. That was the classic Nazi method of doing away with yourself. They even made their own children do it in Hitler's bunker in Berlin during those final hours of the Reich when the Russians were closing in.'

'It makes me go cold just thinking about it,' said Kelly. 'Do you think they planned it?'

'Yes, I do,' said Paul. 'I told them they had to leave by this morning. Maybe that pushed them into doing it but, you know, I'm not going to beat myself up over it. They were bad people. They did some evil things. But they left this world together after a long life.'

'They were actually lying on the bed in an embrace?' Lydia questioned.

'They were, yes,' said Paul.

'Well it's quite… well romantic in a pretty twisted, dark sort of way.'

'Oh they were in love alright,' said Paul.

'They didn't deserve that kind of feeling,' said Kelly.

'They'd loved each other for seventy years,' said Paul, 'but what really frustrates me is that their end was too quick and clean. They should've ended their days as painfully as possible as far as I'm concerned. Where's the justice for all those people they made suffer? Where's the justice for all of their victims in what they did?'

'They'll get their justice alright,' said Lydia, her Catholic upbringing coming through despite her lapsed application to it. 'I'm sure they'll be going downstairs.'

'I hope so,' said Paul, 'it's what's due to them.'

'You're not wasting any tears then?'

'Not one,' said Paul. 'Naumann's body will be taken by his family once the coroner is through with it. They can feed it to the birds as far as I'm concerned. As for her... well I'll be burying her in the local churchyard but there'll be no fuss. I'm not even going to put her title on the gravestone.'

'Some people might say that's vindictive, Paul,' said Lydia.

'Lydia, I'm really not in the mood to be sugar and spice and all things nice about the old witch and I'm not going to rewrite history just because she's dead. She deserves nothing from me and that's exactly what she's going to get. As for this place, well, things are going to be very different round here from now on.'

'Having all this to deal with,' said Lydia, looking all around at the splendour of the surroundings. 'I wouldn't know where to start, Paul. How many rooms are in this place?'

'About two hundred apparently,' said Paul. 'Give or take.'

'So where do you start?' asked Kelly.

'With the people who've been running this place long before I came along,' said Paul. 'I'm not the expert.'

'But there's all the grounds as well,' said Lydia. 'I suppose there's people looking after those too?'

'There are nearly thirty people working here,' said Paul. 'They look after the house, security, the grounds. I'm just going to leave them to it whilst I get on with washing all that dirty money clean that I've inherited.'

'How are you going to do that?' Kelly enquired.

'I'm going to see to it that certain debts are repaid.'

'You're thinking of the Jenkins family?' said Kelly.

'Yes,' said Paul. 'I'm going to make sure that Wilfred

Jenkins' good name is restored. It's not just about getting him a posthumous pardon. I'm going to do more than that.'

'But you weren't responsible for what your grandmother did,' said Lydia.

'No but I'm responsible for this estate now,' Paul insisted. 'I'm going to rename this place too, after my mother.'

'That's a lovely touch,' smiled Kelly.

'You sound like you're getting a lot of things worked out,' said Lydia.

'Yes,' said Paul. 'I think the fog is clearing.'

'And how are you feeling about Jake?'

'I'm sick with worry about him,' said Paul, his heart falling to the ground as he thought about Jake. 'But there's no change there. I just hate to think of the whole city being on alert because of him. This is the man with whom I've shared all the tender moments you expect from being in love. But now he's the most wanted man in the country and it sends a shiver down my spine to think of those poor souls he shot dead in cold blood. It's hard. It's just so fucking hard.'

'And he's still out there,' said Kelly.

'Yes,' said Paul, 'and that scares me more than anything.'

CHAPTER NINETEEN

SUPERINTENDENT HARGREAVES JOINED the rest of the squad to look over the CCTV pictures from the petrol station and the travel agent.

'There's no doubt about it, sir,' said Tim. 'That's Jake Thornton, clear as day on both images. It's a gift, sir. It's like he's wrapped it all up in coloured paper and handed it to us with a big blue ribbon bow.'

'I see what you mean,' said Hargreaves. 'Where are the reports from the areas at the time of the attacks? The petrol station didn't have many people in it and the travel agent shop isn't in the centre of town. We're not talking about great crowds of people here.'

'In both incidents, sir, people seemed to have frozen,' said Sara.

'Usual story,' said Hargreaves, 'and understandable considering gun fire was involved.'

'That's right, sir,' said Tim. 'One or two people are being treated for shock and trauma after witnessing the incidents but after both of them, Thornton was able to just run off and lose himself in the local surrounding areas. He wasn't pursued by anyone and by the time the police arrived on the scene in both cases he was long gone.'

'He wanted us to know it's him,' said Hargreaves.

'You could almost call it a cry for help, sir,' said Joe. 'Our friend Thornton here is desperately in need of getting his head sorted. He doesn't think anyone cares about what he or any of his comrades went through out in

Afghanistan.'

'Did Paul Foster concur with this?' asked Hargreaves.

'Yes, sir,' said Joe, 'and he has had an intimate relationship with him.'

'So he is best placed to comment,' said Tim.

'So Thornton feels like he's got nothing to lose from randomly shooting innocent people to somehow draw attention to the plight of the men and women out there? Is that what you're saying?'

'Yes, sir,' said Tim.

'I mean, I presume there's no link between these two victims?'

'No, sir,' said Steve. 'We've checked it out and there's nothing.'

'Sir, there's been a manhunt underway for Jake Thornton ever since the murder of Glenn Barber. The whole city is on alert for another sniper incident and all the usual services are standing by.'

'Christ, the press conference is going to be fun,' said Hargreaves, 'the public are right to expect answers and quickly before someone else is shot.'

'Sir, we've got to try and take Thornton,' said Sara, 'he may be the only one who can tell us where the missing girls are.'

'What happened with Colin Bradley?'

'He and his family boarded a Singapore Airlines flight at Manchester on the morning they left their house, sir,' said Sara. 'They had a connection to Melbourne, Australia and according to the immigration authorities down there, Bradley gave an Australian address that was his brother's house in a place called Scoresby about an hour's drive east of Melbourne. The local police have been there to interview him but as yet they've not been able to make contact. It seems pretty certain to me, sir, that Bradley had been asked by Lady Eleanor to take over from Glenn Barber but he lost his nerve and ran.'

'Taking the proceeds from the loan shark business with him,' said Hargreaves.

'Yes, sir,' said Sara. 'We've checked his bank accounts and credit cards. He wouldn't have been able to afford his trip around the world if he hadn't taken the money from somewhere.'

'Yes, I agree, DCI Hoyland,' said Hargreaves. 'Is Paul Foster still okay about taking part in the press conference?'

'Yes, sir,' said Tim. 'When we put it to him earlier this morning he almost jumped at the chance. He feels guilty for not coming clean about Thornton right from the start and he wants to make amends.'

'You don't think he's lying to us anymore then?' said Hargreaves.

'No, sir,' said Joe. 'We believe him when he says he doesn't know where Thornton might be.'

'I have to disagree, sir,' said Steve.

'With what, Steve?'

'With the way we're handling Foster. Sir, with all due respect I think that Foster is the one who's going to lead us to Thornton. He and Thornton have been intimately involved and still could be. If he's going to try and contact anybody it's going to be Foster.'

Hargreaves turned to Sara. 'DCI Hoyland?'

'We have discussed this at some length, sir,' said Sara, looking at Steve with barely disguised irritation. 'Foster's life has become very complicated and very high profile lately and we don't think that Thornton would risk any contact.'

'I see that, DCI Hoyland,' said Hargreaves, 'but I also think that DS Osborne has got a point. I'm not going to mount a full-scale surveillance operation on Foster. But I will ask the local uniforms to make his house and his place of work part of their patrols.'

'Sir,' said Steve who was happy enough with the partial victory but still wasn't completely satisfied.

'So we're down to finding the missing girls and locating a sniper before he's able to kill anyone else,' said Hargreaves.

A call from the reception desk downstairs informed them that Paul Foster had arrived and that the press were beginning to gather in the conference room. Hargreaves put on his uniform jacket and buttoned it up. He then led them out and down to where Foster was waiting in an interview room. They briefed him and told him to just relax and talk to Jake as if he was there.

Once the press conference started, Superintendent Hargreaves opened proceedings sat at the makeshift desk with Sara Hoyland on one side and Paul on the other. Paul looked around. He'd seen this sort of thing hundreds of times before on TV with a backdrop advertising Greater Manchester police behind where they sat before three microphones.

By the time it came for Paul to speak he cleared his throat and hoped he'd be able to make it through to the end without getting emotional. Kelly and Lydia had been allowed to come with him and were sitting at the back behind the twenty or so journalists. Because the ramifications of the case meant that it had now turned into a hunt for a sniper, even the national television networks were there.

'…I've known Jake Thornton for four years and in that time I've known what an honourable soldier he's been, on duty for his country in Afghanistan. Since returning though I'd noticed a complete change in his personality. He seemed to have been consumed by the terrible memories of what had happened to him and his friends out there and I'm not making excuses for him because he needs to answer for his crimes. So Jake, if you're listening to this, I'm begging you to turn yourself in. Please don't let another family suffer. Turn yourself in and take responsibility for what you've done. I'm also appealing to anyone with information about Jake's whereabouts to please come forward and contact the police. Jake, it's time to do what's right. And that means turning yourself in. So, please do it before anyone else gets hurt and so that you can get the help you need.'

Julie Loudon had walked into too many doors. Any statistician would say that nobody in a whole lifetime would walk into as many doors as Julie had done and she was only thirty-seven. If it was only a question of walking into doors then she would be able to cope with everybody's questions about where her bruises came from. But it wasn't a question of walking into doors. Same as it wasn't a question of missing the bottom step when she ran down stairs to answer the phone or slipping in the shower or just simply not looking where she was going.

Her marriage hadn't always been like that. When she and Barry had first got together he was as sweet as he could be. Julie had always been the nervous sort. She'd never had much in the way of confidence. She'd been bullied at school because they said she was too fat. She was a bright girl who'd never been given the chance to realise her full potential. Her father had left home when she was seven and after that her mother had almost given up on life. Her father had married again and had two more daughters but he rarely went back to see Julie. She was alone a lot of the time. Her mother slept a lot on account of the pills she took for her depression and mostly Julie had to take care of herself. She used to try ringing her Dad. But he was either never in or when he did come to the phone he always sounded like he was too busy to talk to her. She did find out from him though that he and his new family lived in a nice bungalow overlooking the sea at Bridlington in Yorkshire. Julie never saw the sea when she was growing up. She and her mother never went on holiday. After her mother developed agoraphobia they never went anywhere. So Julie gave up on school. Later on in life she wished she'd had more drive to achieve. But she hadn't.

Barry had first hit her on their wedding night. His card had been rejected when he'd tried to buy a round of drinks at the hotel bar. She'd stepped in and handed over one of hers but later, when they were on their own in the honeymoon suite, he'd accused her of humiliating him in front of their family and friends and slapped her once, twice, three times. It had now been fourteen years since she realised that Barry wasn't her Prince Charming after all and whenever anything went wrong for him he would take it out on her. It had almost become a pattern. Between these times he was a good husband and a good father to their three kids. But when the darkness descended she knew she would be in for a beating. His parents knew what he was like but they never offered her any support. They turned a blind eye. Except for a bizarre conversation she'd once had with his mother in which she told Julie that Barry's father had sometimes slapped her about a bit but she hadn't made a fuss because that's what men do. And women just had to accept it.

She was sitting waiting for him in the car outside the shops. Barry was picking up his dry cleaning. With the pain of her latest beating giving her a lot of discomfort across her back she didn't notice the man point his gun at Barry as he approached the car and when she heard the shots she swung her head round and saw him fall to the ground with blood pouring out of the back of his head. In that split second she decided to let him spend the last few seconds of his life on his own. She wasn't scared anymore and now she would tell both her two sons and her daughter that it wasn't ever acceptable for violence to be part of any marriage.

'So,' said Lorraine Cowley as she watched Anita pack her things and those of her daughter Candice, 'you're leaving me.'

'I'll only be down the road, Mum,' said Anita. 'You can see my place from here.'

'But you won't be here with me,' Lorraine insisted.

'No, I won't, Mum, but I won't be far.'

'Then what's the bloody point!'

'To be independent, Mum! To do things my own way!'

Lorraine started crying. She slid down the wall and onto the floor. She was disconsolate.

'Mum?' said Anita as she went to her. 'Mum, please don't get upset.'

'Everybody leaves me,' said Lorraine, unable to stop the sobs from overwhelming her. 'Everybody goes. My Dad. My Mum, and now my own kids.'

'I'm not leaving you, Mum,' said Anita. 'I'm just going

to live somewhere else.'

'You won't want me anymore.'

'What do you mean?'

'You've got your posh friends at work now.'

'They're not posh, Mum,' said Anita. 'They're just ordinary people getting by just like the rest of us. They have to rob Peter to pay Paul, they're broke at the end of the month before they get paid, they've all got credit card debt. Mum, everybody has their struggles. That's the biggest thing I've learned since I started work.'

'What?'

'That we're not the only ones,' said Anita, 'but we can make it better if we try and if we want to and that's why I'm so proud of you for agreeing to go to those reading and writing classes.'

Lorraine let herself be held tight by her daughter whilst she recalled the emotional pain inflicted on her by her deadbeat Dad and her deadbeat Mum and all the deadbeat men she'd used to get pregnant. Her eldest son had gone. Her youngest son had gone. Her eldest daughter was about to go and her younger daughter was caught God knows where and that was all her mother's fault for borrowing money from Glenn Barber. Not much to show for thirty-five years on this earth.

'I just don't want to be left,' Lorraine cried.

'You won't be,' said Anita. 'I'll be round here every day.'

'You promise?'

'I promise,' said Anita, 'and are we friends again, Mum?'

'You're all I've got left.'

'And me and Candice want you to be our first visitor to our new home,' said Anita. 'Will you do that for us?'

'And sit on the furniture that Paul Foster has bought for you? You must be joking.'

'Aw, look Mum, I thought you'd made your peace with Paul?'

'I'll do what he asks because I've no flaming choice!' Lorraine declared.

'You just keep picking at it, don't you? Well Mum, Paul has been a good friend to me and I'm not giving that up'

'You are so lost to me.'

'I'm not it's you who's pushing me away!'

'You've fallen under the influence of that Paul Foster good and proper,' said Lorraine.

'Mum, we've all got to turn over a new leaf. We've got to start again and I know you're scared about going to those reading classes but you don't need to be. Everybody will help you.'

Lorraine started sobbing. 'Do you think they'll be able to find Michaela?'

'I hope so, Mum,' said Anita, doing her best to comfort her mother. 'They're doing their best and I really hope so.'

Paul was working late at the centre. He'd had to take so much time off lately that he felt guilty about neglecting his duties. Everybody told him that was nonsense but he couldn't be convinced. He had a stack of reports to write and it was strange when a large building given over to a constant traffic of people all through the day came to rest at night. It somehow didn't seem right that it was all so quiet. The doctor's surgery had even finished the evening session and was now closed until tomorrow. He looked at his watch and saw that it was ten past eight. Another five minutes and then he was going to pack up and go home. He was hungry but he didn't feel like cooking so he planned to pick up a curry on the way home. He fancied some butter chicken with saffron rice and a cheese naan bread. Yummy!

He looked up when he saw a flash of headlights cross the extreme of his vision. His office was behind the administration area where four desks and four computer screens lay idle. The reception desk for the building was in front of that and Paul's office door was open, giving him a view right across to the main entrance door. For a moment he froze. Nobody would be driving into the car park this late. Perhaps he was an idiot to stay behind on his own when Jake was still out there. He didn't think that Jake would do him any harm but he was unpredictable and he didn't know what Jake might do if he was cornered.

He walked out in front of the reception desk and into the corridor. He moved toward the main entrance door that worked automatically. But the mechanism had been turned off just like it always was at the end of the day. A pole handle ran from top to bottom of the almost entirely glass door and he looked all around him before taking a deep breath and opened the door wide.

But it wasn't Jake who stepped out of the darkness.

'Damn the bastard!' stormed Superintendent Hargreaves.

Two PC's on patrol in the area of Salford behind the tall, grey shopping precinct recognised the shifty looking man heading towards one of the council tower blocks of flats as Jake Thornton but by the time they'd got themselves moving he'd noticed they were on to him and he'd ran. They leapt out of their car and gave chase but it was no good. He was a soldier and he was used to slipping away whenever he needed to. They lost him in the labyrinth of alleyways and housing blocks.

'You just tell those two jokers that they will be in my office tomorrow morning and they will answer to me for their sheer fucking incompetence!'

'Sir, at least we know he's in the area,' said Tim, trying to calm things down.

'Yes, well that's all very fine DI Norris but it's hardly going to make the citizens of Greater Manchester feel any safer, is it?'

'No, sir,' said Tim who was getting irritated by the Superintendent's tone, 'but it's a start in trying to catch him.'

Hargreaves leaned forward and placed his hands palm down on Tim's desk. He liked Tim. He always had done. Tim was a good copper in Hargreaves' eyes. But for fuck's sake he could come out with some meaningless shit sometimes.

'I'm glad you've worked that out, Tim,' said Hargreaves. 'Where is Steve Osborne by the way? Isn't he supposed to be here for this briefing, Tim?'

'Yes, sir,' said Tim, 'but we can't get hold of him.'

'I've tried ringing him on his mobile, sir' said Joe. 'But it just keeps going to voicemail.'

'Well he's another one who'll be answering to me,' said Hargreaves..

Sara came into the squad room with a printout of an email that had been received from Thornton that gave the names of over a hundred men ranging from celebrities and politicians to judges and high ranking police officers. They'd all 'bought' the time of the girls who were forced to dress up as schoolgirls and were drugged and raped into submission.

'It's just like Lady Eleanor said, sir,' said Sara, wondering if the Superintendent had noticed the name of a chief constable and the name of the husband of another one. She watched his face change when he did.

'Good God,' said Hargreaves. 'I used to work with that guy over in Yorkshire. And I know this guy's wife very well. I wonder if she knows what her husband has been getting up to whilst she's been catching criminals. Where was this sent from?'

'An internet café near Salford university, sir,' said Sara.

'The ramifications of this… well, the individuals concerned should've thought about that before. But he still doesn't give us a fucking location, damn him!'

Their attention was then taken by the door opening and Kieran Quinn, the PC who was Sara's lover, came in. She felt that usual twitch in her groin whenever she saw him. The first time he'd come round to her flat they'd kept their clothes on for barely an hour before they were naked and she was leading him by his erection to her bed. They'd both had the next day off and they stayed in her bed for almost thirty hours. Kieran had stamina alright and he had imagination. They wrestled with each other when he was inside her, each of them fighting to be the one on top when he came. He groaned loudly with pleasure when she inserted her set of love beads up his bum and then pulled them out in tune with his orgasm. He liked her to cuff his hands to the bed head too and ride him like a horse. It was these visions that they were both trying to ignore as he stood there, trying not to lock eyes with her.

'Well come on, Constable,' said Hargreaves. 'Some may think you're a pretty picture to look at but I don't. What is it you want?'

'Sir, a man answering Jake Thornton's description was seen running from an isolated farmhouse a few miles north of Nantwich in Cheshire…'

'… When?' Tim asked.

'Early this morning, sir, just before six,' said Kieran. 'Cheshire police investigated and found three males downstairs in some kind of office space. Two white, one black, aged between thirty-five and fifty, they'd all been shot dead. The officers then went upstairs. Twenty rooms, all small, all with a lock on the door that could only be turned from the outside, all with a double bed and a shower unit and all with a terrified young girl cowering inside.'

'What's happened to them now?' said Sara.

'Ambulances were called and they've been taken away to the local hospital,' said Kieran. 'They're either screaming out with fear or terribly withdrawn.'

'Bastards!'

'There were also various items found associated with the sex trade, ma'am.'

'Do they know if Thornton, if indeed it was Thornton, was acting on his own?' asked Joe.

'Well, the initial report from our Cheshire colleagues suggests that the three men were all shot using bullets from the same gun, sir,' said Kieran, 'which probably means he was.'

'Well if he's been seen hanging about in the Salford precinct area and he sent that email from a place near to Salford university then my guess is that he is trying to get to Paul Foster,' said Hargreaves. 'Never mind their history, Thornton is unpredictable and Foster could be in great danger.'

'Let's get down there,' said Tim, 'and where the hell is DS Osborne?'

CHAPTER TWENTY

'IT'S DETECTIVE SERGEANT OSBORNE, isn't it?' said Paul. 'What are you doing here at this time? Have you heard something about Jake?'

'I'm not here on official business,' said Steve who was intent on showing the rest of the squad, especially Sara Hoyland, that he was capable of getting a result, even if he had to go out on a limb to get it. He was going to break the will of this shirt-lifter into telling the truth. He was going to deliver the whereabouts of Jake Thornton.

'Then why are you here?' asked Paul who hadn't liked this Osborne character first time round and didn't want to waste any time on pleasantries.

'I came to remind myself what a liar looks like.'

Paul was taken aback. 'I beg your pardon?'

'You know where Jake Thornton is, don't you?'

'Of course I don't know where he is.'

'Well I think you do.'

'Look, it's late and I was just about to head home,' said Paul who was furious at this idiot's accusation. He could really do without this. 'So if you're not going to say anything sensible then I suggest, seeing as you're not here on official business, that you do one.'

'Love can make someone do things that they know are wrong,' said Steve. 'It's part of the human condition.'

'Really? You don't strike me as being the sort who'd watch Oprah'

Steve broke into a smirk. 'You're protecting Jake

Thornton.'

'That's absurd.'

'Is it?'

'You know it is.'

'No, I don't,' said Steve, 'because you're a liar. You make up that very touching little act during that TV appeal but that's just what it was, an act. You were lying through your pretty pink teeth.'

Paul stepped up close to his adversary. 'What is it with you, eh? Nobody lets you play the big man so you come round here trying it with me? Aren't you enough of a man to work for a female boss?' He saw the reaction in Osborne's eyes. 'Oh so that's it. Your prick is too small to work for someone who doesn't have one. Well take your attitude and stick it where the sun don't shine.'

Paul turned to go back into the centre but Osborne called him back.

'I'll make a deal with you, Foster.'

Paul turned back around and squared up to Osborne again. 'This should be good.'

'You let me know where Thornton is and I'll say I got an anonymous tip-off.'

'You are so fucking desperate! Do you really think I would let those people be killed if I could've stopped it?'

'I don't know what you're capable of.'

'Anymore of this bullshit and I'll put in an official complaint, Osborne!' Paul raged. 'Now in case you didn't hear me before, do one!'

A shot rang out.

Paul was consumed with shock as he watched Osborne's eyes bulge wide open and saw blood come seeping out of his mouth.

A second shot rang out.

Osborne's body fell forward and Paul couldn't help but put his arms out and catch it. He was covered in Osborne's blood when he looked up and saw Jake standing there with the gun still in his hand.

'Oh my God, Jake,' said Paul who started to cry, 'what the hell have you done?'

'He was going to hurt you.'

'No he wasn't,' said Paul, the tears streaming down his cheeks. He was on his knees, cradling Osborne's torn head in his lap. He'd seen too much death recently and he was staring to lose it. 'You shouldn't have done it, Jake.'

'He was going to hurt you like that useless youth outside the school.'

'That was you?'

'Glenn Barber wanted me to kill you.'

'I know.'

'I couldn't protect Richie and Errol but I could protect you.'

'But Jake? All those other people?'

'They needed to learn.'

'What did they need to learn, Jake?' Paul demanded emotionally.

'That we can't just be forgotten about,' said Jake. 'We were out there doing it for all of them and they couldn't give a stuff.'

'That's not true, Jake!'

'It is true,' said Jake who felt strangely calm. 'They say they care when they ring in to TV programmes and put some loose change in a collection pot for heroes. But they don't really. They cross the road when they see a soldier who's only got stumps where his legs used to be. They don't know what to say. They get too embarrassed. Or they patronise us with their shallow, meaningless words about how brave we are and how they're thinking of us. It's all bullshit! The politicians send us out there playing their little power games and they don't even make sure we've got all the right fucking equipment!'

'Jake, we can make them all sit up and take notice,' said Paul, 'but all this has got to stop. Please, Jake.'

'Then it was your grandma who really did it'

'What do you mean?'

'When all charges against her were dropped,' said Jake. 'I saw it all over the papers. It's never going to change, Paul. She kills and gets away with it because of who she knows. I kill and I'm the most wanted man in the country. Her and her Nazi should've had justice served on them.'

'I know, Jake, I know, and I agree but this is not the way to change any of that.'

'I didn't care,' said Jake. 'I mean, what's the fucking difference? They send me out to kill Afghans for their reasons. It's okay if you're killing for Queen and country. But you come back home and you're driven to kill because the people couldn't give a shit about what you've been through. Well, nobody is going to drop the charges against the likes of me. I'm just a soldier, a piece of equipment to fight their wars for them.'

'Oh Jake, Jake…'

'…that stupid youth who was giving out to you outside the school was a fucking useless excuse for a human being. Never done a day's work in his life and yet still expects everything to be given to him on a fucking plate. He was pissing himself about that head teacher friend of yours. I had to do something, just like I had to do something about the missing girls.'

'You know where they are?'

'They were down Nantwich way in a farmhouse. I

freed them this morning. They'll be alright. You'll be alright. I'm the one who needs to get out.'

'What do you mean?'

Their was taken by the screeching to a halt of several police cars. An Armed Response Unit had been called and in seconds Paul could see several guns pointing at Jake's head.

'Jake, don't give them reason to shoot you!'

'I've got to give them a chance to kill a British soldier.'

'What... who? Jake, you're not making any sense to me.'

'Put your weapon down!'

Paul was frantic to stop them from killing Jake.

'Jake, think about your child!'

'We don't think about the children,' said Jake. 'We never think about the children when we drop our bombs to protect our oil. We never think about their children. We only think about ours.'

Jake turned and when he stepped forward they opened fire. Paul could only watch in horrified shock as Jake fell to the ground.

After all the difficulties of the evening, when Sara got back to the station she sat down at her desk and buried her head in her hands.

'Sara?' said Superintendent Hargreaves as he entered her office and closed the door behind him. 'Are you okay?'

'About as okay as I can be on a day like this, sir.'

'Come on,' said Hargreaves, 'you're not to blame for Steve Osborne. He went out on a limb of his own accord, Sara. Nobody could've stopped him.'

'He was under my charge, sir, so with all due respect, I

am responsible.'

'Okay, I'll give you that,' said Hargreaves, 'but don't punish yourself. Anyway, we got a result.'

'We may have got a result, sir, but where's the justice? I was able to prove that a load of dead people committed certain crimes but where's the justice for their victims?'

'Maybe the fact that all the perpetrators of those crimes are now dead is the justice, Sara,' said Hargreaves. 'Try to look at it that way.'

Sara sat back in her chair. 'But then I think of those kids who were sold to the Nazi's in the war and what could've happened to them.'

'They might've ended up leading very happy lives,' said Hargreaves.

'With no recollection that they were actually English,' said Sara. 'So many crimes stretching back to the war, sir. It's hard to get your head around.'

'The world is very different from nineteen forty-five, Sara,' said Hargreaves. 'You have to earn your stripes these days. Deference is not entirely dead but it's not the automatic right it used to be.'

'And do you agree with that?'

'I'm like a lot of British people, Sara,' said Hargreaves. 'I'm more concerned about how much tax I pay than in any kind of social injustice.'

'Well I used to think like you, sir, but this case has made me think,' said Sara. 'We missed our chance in this country. We should've had a revolution.'

'Sara, we could never have had a revolution in this country because all we Brits would do is argue about who was going to pay for the guillotine.'

Sara laughed. 'You could be right there, sir.'

'So let's just move on from these events,' said Hargreaves,

'and everything that went with them. You know, we're very much alike, you and me, Sara.'

'We are, sir?'

'I'm sure it will become apparent to you as your career progresses,' said Hargreaves as he opened her office door. 'It was a good result, Sara, despite the difficulties. I'm pleased with it and so should you be and Steve Osborne wouldn't want us to think any different.'

Paul had been given tranquilisers to get him through the day and sleeping pills to make sure he didn't lie awake all night reliving the events outside the centre when Jake checked out of this world. The drugs, along with Kelly and Lydia, had held him together through his darkest days. It was a darkness that almost made him feel separate from the world he was living in. There'd been so much death, so much pointless, needless death, so much unnecessary heartache for so many people. He had to try and mend some of it. And he knew where to start. He went down to Rubinstein's jewellery shop on St. Peter's Square with the watch his father had given him.

'Mr. Foster,' Saul Rubinstein said, greeting him warmly, 'how nice to see you. Please, come through to the back.'

Paul followed Mr. Rubinstein through to his back office and handed him the watch. 'This belongs to you and your family, Mr. Rubinstein,' said Paul. 'I've discovered through an investigation by certain experts that my grandmother had quite a collection of gold and jewellery that has been verified as having been stolen by the Nazi's. Some of it, I have to say, was given to her by a member of our own royal family, and some of it came into her possession by her own misdeeds both during and after the war. It's been valued at about a million pounds. I'm planning an auction and the entire proceeds will go to the Simon Wiesenthal centre in Vienna. I hope you think that's some kind of poetic justice.'

Saul Rubinstein took hold of Paul's hand and, tearfully, he said, 'thank you. You are a big man, Paul Foster and only big men can deliver real justice.'

'Mr. Rubinstein, my family have been involved in some evil things but it's up to me now to bring an end to it all. I just hope this goes some way to putting things right.'

'From your mouth to God's ears,' said Saul.

CHAPTER TWENTY-ONE

ONE MONTH LATER

PAUL WAS NERVOUS as he got into his suit. The day had finally dawned and it was going to be good for his soul. A cleansing of the past and the name of a good family restored. He'd been a multi-millionaire for the best part of a month before he'd turned over most of his money to the Wilfred Jenkins foundation that he'd set up. He'd kept some back and he considered he was due something from the old witch. Yet he still felt there was more than enough left over for him to be comfortable for the rest of his life and able to help out his friends whenever they needed it.

'Hi!' said Lydia as he came into the bedroom, 'don't you scrub up well?'

'You've seen me in a suit before, Lydia.'

'I know, darling, but today is a special day,' she smiled Lydia, 'what's wrong?'

'My stomach is going round and round like a bloody washing machine.'

'Well some nerves are good,' said Lydia. 'It shows you've still got a heart beating in there.'

Paul was perched on the end of his bed and looking down at his folded hands in his lap. Lydia knew there was something more going on than just nerves.

'Come on, what is it?'

Paul started crying and he wiped his face with his

hands. 'Tiffany came to see me yesterday.'

'And?'

'Little Callum… just days old but he's the spitting image of his Dad.'

'But what did she do to make you so upset, love?'

'She said… she said that she didn't want me to have anymore contact with her or Callum.'

'Why?'

'She said that it would confuse Callum and make it difficult when she met somebody else.'

'Oh Paul, darling,' said Lydia. 'It must've broken your heart.'

'It's like I've lost Jake all over again, Lydia,' said Paul, 'and breaking my heart doesn't even come close to it.' Paul broke down again and wept on Lydia's shoulder.

'But hang on, love,' said Lydia. 'The trust fund you've set up for Callum and the monthly allowance you're giving her? Is she still taking that?'

'Yes,' said Paul.

'Then she's taking you for a ride, Paul.'

'Lydia, she's quite right when she says I've got no right to see Callum though,' said Paul.

'Well then she's got no right to your money.'

'Lydia, I promised and I can't go back on that now.'

'But she's taking the piss.'

'I know but I… like I said, I just can't go back on the promise I made, Lydia but I've lost Jake, the only man I've ever truly loved and now I've lost contact with his son and I'm just getting a little tired of putting on a brave face and pretending everything's alright when it fucking well isn't.'

'Now listen,' said Lydia, taking hold of his shoulders. 'Lesser men would never have thought of doing what you're doing today. They'd have just taken the money and run for the hills.'

'Yeah, well I don't feel very noble.'

'Paul, you didn't have to do it, you chose to do it.'

'So what are you trying to say?'

'That the pain in your heart about Jake won't go away for a very long time but that you should feel proud of what you're doing in the rest of your life. It gives you a reason to go on.'

'It wasn't him who committed those awful murders, Lydia,' said Paul, 'if you'd have seen his eyes in those final moments…'

'…he wasn't the man that we'd known, love, I know that.'

'How's Kathy Jenkins doing?'

'She's downstairs having a cup of tea with your Uncle Leonid,' said Lydia. 'I think he's chatting her up.'

'Good for her,' said Paul, 'and good for him. You and Kelly have been so good to Kathy though.'

'She's a sweetie,' said Lydia, 'but I can understand why she didn't want to move to another flat like you wanted her to. She wasn't slighting you, Paul.'

'Yeah, I know that,' said Paul. 'She's got her neighbours and she'll be okay if we keep an eye on her or if Uncle Leonid does. Do you know she'd never even had her hair done until you took her to the hairdressers yesterday? She'd never thought anything about herself at all.'

'Today will help to make up for all that she lost, Paul.'

'I hope so, Lydia. I really do.'

'Well go in the bathroom and wash your face,' said Lydia. 'You don't want people to know you've been crying.'

'No,' said Paul. 'I'll see you in a minute. And thanks, Lydia.'

'Me and Kelly are here for you,' she added, 'always will be.'

There'd always been a community centre on the Tatton estate, it's just that it had never been used. The windows had all been boarded up, there was graffiti on the walls, and most of the residents didn't even register anymore that it was there. But it was in a prime location at the start of the estate, just off the A6 that ran like a vein through the heart of Salford.

Kelly drove Lydia, Paul, Kathy Jenkins, and Paul's Uncle Leonid to the estate and parked in the newly resurfaced car park outside the community centre. Leonid was proud to be there. Paul had promised to use his position to campaign for official recognition of the Holodomor that the Ukrainians went through during the 1920's and 1930's. They'd talked a lot recently, mainly about Paul's father, but Paul had also floated the idea of trying to re-unite Leonid with his family in the Ukraine. Leonid thought it was too late now, too many decades had passed and it should all just be left alone.

Paul couldn't believe how many people were there. He'd chosen a Saturday to launch proceedings so that as many of the estate's residents, including all the children, could take part in the ceremony. But he hadn't counted on virtually the whole estate turning up. He looked at the expectant faces. He wanted it all to change for the sake of the children. He had to make it all work for them. Sam Cowley had settled happily into his new foster home over at Eccles with a couple who were giving him the right support to learn that he'd sorely needed for so long. But he couldn't take them all away. Some of them had to be helped from where they were.

'I hope I can pull this off,' said Paul.

'Well it's up to them now,' said Kelly. 'You've done all you can.'

As soon as they got out of the car Paul was besieged by the press. He answered their questions carefully and then Anita Cowley managed to get both him and Kathy inside where the leader of the council and the city's MP, a woman whom Paul had met before and liked for the way she didn't stand on ceremony, were both waiting for them. So were Superintendent Hargreaves and DCI Hoyland whom Paul had invited to be part of the whole event.

'This is all going mental,' said Anita, 'even me Mum is here.'

It had been difficult getting Lorraine Cowley to see a future for herself after what had happened to Michaela. She'd blamed herself but with the right kind of counselling she was now coming through it and had finally settled into her reading and writing classes after going sick for the first three. Michaela, like the rest of the girls who'd been rescued from the Cheshire farmhouse, was still in a psychiatric unit working through the trauma she'd endured. But the doctors were hopeful and every day she was making progress according to Anita.

'I've had to keep the front doors locked to keep them out,' said Anita.

'Well you're the estate manager, Anita,' said Paul. 'So it's your decision.'

Anita pulled a frightened face. 'Right,' she said, 'look, Paul, do you really think I can do this?'

'Yes I do,' said Paul 'You know the estate inside out and you know the people here. I didn't want to get anyone in from outside who didn't have the first idea about how life works on an estate like this. I've every confidence in you. I believe in you. You've got to believe in yourself.'

'I'm bricking it today, Paul.'

'You and me both, kid.'

She kissed him.

'What was that for?' He asked.

'For all of this,' said Anita, 'for giving me this chance.'

Film crews from both the BBC Northwest and ITV Granada filmed the whole ceremony, from Anita's faltering start before she found her groove and got stuck in, through the congratulations received from the leader of the council and the praise from the MP who said it was just the direction that communities should take in owning their regeneration, to the tearful expressions of thanks from Kathy. Paul then wrapped things up with his own speech.

'...Ladies and gentlemen, I'm delighted to be able to launch the Wilfred Jenkins foundation, a non-profit trust that will begin its work with the purchase of all the properties of the Tatton estate. The purpose of the foundation is two-fold. One, it is a way of restoring the good name of Wilfred Jenkins who was wrongfully hanged for murder back in 1940 on the false evidence of the real perpetrator of the crime, my grandmother, Lady Eleanor Harding. We've also now applied for a posthumous pardon for Wilfred and I'm proud to make this announcement in the presence of his daughter, Kathy.' He waved his hand in Kathy's direction and she blushed as she took her applause. 'Kathy, I wish to publicly apologise for the terrible crime inflicted on your family by mine and I hope that today will be the start of putting all that sorrow behind us.'

Paul didn't know if it was the applause he got for his remarks but he was starting to feel quite emotional. He took a few deep breaths before carrying on.

'…and that's not the only apology I have to make. More than twenty girls were taken from their homes and put through hell by evil men and the whole plan had been masterminded by an evil woman, my grandmother. So I say to them and to the children who were bought from their families during the Second World War… I say to them all that on behalf of my family I am truly sorry. But friends, criminal charges against my grandparents were dropped because the police were ordered to drop them. The powerful should no longer be able to use their connections to escape the law in this day and age so I urge everyone to join our campaign to remove all the privileges of the establishment once and for all. Only then could we say that a truly fair society is within our reach.

'But now to the working remit of the foundation which will be to invest in the kind of social projects that will be of benefit to people who've never shared in the wealth of our society. The people of the Tatton need a new start and the Wilfred Jenkins foundation is going to provide them with it. People all over the world are waking up to the power they have and we're bringing that dynamic to the Tatton and to all the other estates we'll be taking over in the next few months.'

Once the speeches were over the crowds dispersed and Paul was whisked into a side room by Marius Van Urk for an 'exclusive' interview.

'Paul,' Marius began, 'you inherited millions when your grandmother signed over her estate to you but now you've given over most of it to the Wilfred Jenkins foundation that you've created and which you head. Why did you do that?'

'I had to wash the money clean,' said Paul, 'it struck me

that this was an opportunity to do something positive that could affect the lives of a lot of people as well as doing something to right the wrong that had been done against the Jenkins family. That's why I decided to set up the foundation in Wilfred Jenkins' name. We need to start a revolution from the bottom up and show people who've never believed in themselves that they can make it to wherever they want to go. I take my inspiration from the Reverend Jesse Jackson in the United States who tells disadvantaged people to keep believing that they are somebody despite their current circumstances and that they do have a right to a better future. But of course, they themselves have also to put in the effort too. That's where the tough love comes in.'

'And you've turned over the ownership of Gatley Hall to the foundation?'

'Well it's now been re-named Clarissa Harding Hall.'

'After your mother?'

'Yes.'

'She'd have been proud.'

'I hope so,' said Paul. 'The hall will become the headquarters of the Wilfred Jenkins foundation and the rest will become a conference and events centre under a separate management team. We've managed to secure all the jobs of those who work there now and we'll be looking to recruit more people too. I'll keep my own private apartment there and I'll be the Chair of the foundation.'

'Well coming back to the work of the Wilfred Jenkins foundation,' said Marius. 'The tenancies of the residents of the Tatton estate have been re-written by the foundation after it took them over. Tell us more about that?'

'Well, it is a condition now of the tenancy that nobody borrows money from doorstep lenders. We know that loan sharks have been targeting estates like the Tatton, playing on the vulnerability of residents who can't be part of the normal loan market, and charging them ludicrous amounts of interest for the privilege. We've set up a credit union for residents of the estate where they'll be able to borrow money at much lower and more affordable rates and which will be a community initiative that nobody profits from.'

'But there is one aspect of the new tenancy agreements that is somewhat controversial?'

'Well, yes, we've said that we have the right to instruct social services to take children into care at the earliest sign of abuse,' said Paul. 'There have been far too many cases recently of little kids ending up dead because those who could've rescued them didn't. We've been too timid to condemn bad parenting. That's something we won't be timid of at the foundation. Also, if any child on the estate is accused of a crime then we will call the parents in and ask them to explain how the situation could've arisen. Parents have to take an interest in what their children are up to.'

'You've also set up a nursery in this community centre, what's the intention there?'

'It's a full-on children's centre that takes care of all aspects of children's welfare and is linked to the social services centre that I manage just up the road in Broughton. It's about giving people the support they need whilst also allowing them to take advantage of opportunities with regard to finding a job. One of the problems on the estate is the absence of a culture of work but the children growing up here need to see that going to work is about earning money to live. The Benefits system is there to help support people on low incomes. It shouldn't be seen as a lifestyle choice.'

'And are the residents buying into all that?'

'The job of the foundation will be to assist the residents in that process.'

'You've also been on the receiving end of some sharp criticism from people who say you're basically taking control of the residents, taking away their free choices and their liberties. What do you say to that?'

'Well, the people who say that are mostly middle class sitting around their tables in nice leafy suburbs and who've never been anywhere near the Tatton and certainly never spoken to anyone living here. Look, I'm a social revolutionary. I don't accept that things can never change. I adopt a tough love approach because here on the Tatton there are problems that require it.'

'Such as?'

'There are too many children having children for a start,' said Paul. 'We have fathers and mothers who can't get a job because they can't read and write, people who are becoming grandparents at the age of thirty without ever having worked. Now people in the wider community who work hard are growing tired of subsidising that kind of behaviour. What we need is realism and honesty instead of softly, softly kid gloves. And also, it's about the waste of human potential which is a crime in itself in this day and age. Unless someone takes firm leadership of the situation then all of the people on these estates will remain at the bottom of the heap and I don't think that's good enough for them or for the wider community. You see, it's not just about the gap between rich and poor in society although that is important. But it's also about realising the value of education. If people in developing countries can see education as the means to get out of poverty then why can't our people here?'

'So you do support early intervention in so-called

problem families on the estate?'

'I certainly do, yes, because I'm thinking of the rights of the children. There are cases right across the country where if social services had intervened earlier then children's lives might have been saved. It's not about the Nanny state. It's simply about saving lives. We also need to recruit more social workers from estates like the Tatton, people who've got firsthand experience of living in a community that never goes beyond its own boundaries, never goes to the cinema or into town or on holiday, never engages with the rest of society. We need people who know what it's like to live on estates like the Tatton and can deal with the residents because they're one of their own. We need to look into how we can achieve that because middle-class do-good solutions don't work on estates like the Tatton.'

'Creating the big society?'

'No,' said Paul, firmly, 'creating the truly fair society where everybody recognises their responsibilities as well as their right to a fair go.'

'You sound like you're on a bit of a crusade?'

'I don't like the word crusade but I do want to do something to stop the tide of wasted lives. We're also working with Colleen Price who did a fantastic job as Head of Tatton High School only to see her hard work destroyed by a mindless vandal. We're working with her to repair the damage done to the school and she'll set standards of education in the area higher than they've ever been.'

'And what's the other dimension to what you're doing at the foundation?'

'Well we've set up at Clarissa Harding Hall a residential clinic for members of the armed forces who've returned from active duty in Iraq and Afghanistan with combat stress. Now that could mean anything in terms of how their behaviour changes but the clinic will be there to give them the necessary treatment.'

'You've given up your title of the Earl of Gatley and with it your right to sit in the House of Lords. That's a lot of history to give up.'

'I'm not interested in titles,' said Paul, 'I never have been and I don't see any reason to change now. I've never been in favour of the hereditary principle and I don't think that anybody should be in the second chamber of parliament unless they've been elected to it. People talk about a democratic deficit in the EU but the biggest democratic deficit for British people is a House of Lords that remains unelected. It's what I felt before I inherited the title and I don't see any reason to change my view now.'

'Despite the change in your personal circumstances?'

'Especially because of the change in my personal circumstances. You have to put your money where your mouth is or else your values are nothing more than meaningless posturing.'

'And what about your campaign to remove all remaining privileges from the establishment? How is that going to be more than posturing?'

'I want to shame those at the top of our society into recognising that privilege has no place in a modern country like ours. I want to see an end to all titles and I want to see an end to the monarchy. I've been given a profile that wasn't of my choosing but I'm going to use it as a means of waking the people up to what's been done to them for centuries. The royals and the aristocracy don't give a damn about ordinary people. That's the message I want people to understand and then do something about it.'

★

A couple of evenings later, Paul had just got home to his Salford home when he received a visitor. The man on his doorstep must've been in his late fifties with thin grey hair parted on the left hand side. He was dressed in a sombre looking dark grey three-piece suit and his shoes were so highly polished that he could almost see his reflection in them. He was taller than Paul and he had that commanding presence that couldn't be ignored.

'My name is Charles Bartlett,' he announced as he reached out his hand and Paul shook it. 'Major General Charles Bartlett. I work for the Crown. May I come in?'

Paul was bemused. 'Of course,' he said, 'but what do you want with me?'

'I'll explain inside.'

Paul stepped back to let him through and gestured for him to sit down in the lounge armchair. Paul sat on the sofa at right angles to him.

'So?' said Paul. 'What can I do for you? Is it about me giving back my title?'

'In a roundabout way, yes,' said Bartlett who then opened his old-fashioned style leather briefcase and brought out a pile of papers.

'I don't understand.'

'Then I'll explain,' said Bartlett.

Something about Bartlett's voice made Paul feel a shiver go down his spine. What the fuck was this all about?

'I need you to sign this,' said Bartlett as he handed Paul a two-page document.

'What is it?'

'Well you don't need to concern yourself with all the details,' said Bartlett. 'But what it basically means is that you relinquish your right to be part of the line of succession.'

'The line of succession? Major Bartlett, what on earth are you talking about?'

'You're entitled to a place in the line of succession because of who your grandfather was.'

'My grandfather was a Nazi war criminal.'

'No, he wasn't,' said Bartlett. 'Dieter Naumann was not your grandfather. Your grandfather was a Prince, the brother of King George.'

'I beg your pardon?'

'And it means that you're a second cousin to her majesty the Queen.'

'Edward?'

'I'm afraid I'm not at liberty to confirm that,' said Bartlett. 'We let things go too far with your grandmother and I'd be the first to admit that. The situation should never have got as far as charges being made. But now we're moving much more quickly.'

'Oh my God.'

'The document includes a confidentiality clause,' said Bartlett. 'You must never reveal your heritage to anyone.'

Just when Paul thought he couldn't be given anymore shocks that would make the ground shake beneath his feet, he received another one. He didn't know whether to be relieved that he wasn't related to a Nazi war criminal after all or to be horrified at the reality of being related to the world's most dysfunctional family. But now it made sense why his grandmother rejected his mother. If Naumann had been her father then she would've been their love child. But he wasn't. And Paul's grandmother, for reasons he'll never know, had a child she didn't want by a man who probably didn't love her. He was married and living in exile then. The monarchy probably couldn't have withstood another scandal so soon after the abdication. So Paul's mother had to suffer to save their pathetic skins.

'I won't sign anything,' said Paul.

'You don't have any choice.'

'Yes I do and I won't sign anything.'

'Look here, I do hope you're not going to cause us any trouble?'

'And what will happen if I do?' Paul retorted angrily. 'Will I have a car accident in a tunnel late at night where the car that made contact with mine is never traced? Will you make it so that the ambulance takes twice as long to get to the nearest hospital than it would do usually? I mean, isn't that how you deal with family members who show the royals up for the emotional illiterates that they are?'

'And talk like that won't get you anywhere, Mr. Foster,' said Bartlett, a flash of annoyance running across his face. He held up the document and a pen. 'Now please sign this.'

'I said no,' said Paul, defiantly. 'I will not acquiesce to some kind of royal command. I'm a republican. I don't believe in the Crown or in titles which is one of the reasons I gave mine back. I'm not interested in being part of any line of succession, Major Bartlett. You can run back to your boss and tell her that.'

'I should warn you that your refusal may have consequences.'

'And what is she going to do? Send me to the tower and have my head chopped off? Watch the news, Major Bartlett. People all over the world are finally realising the power that they have to remove all those at the top who've kept them down for too long. It will happen here.'

Bartlett looked up with his eyes fixed into Paul's. 'Sign the document, please.'

'No wonder they all sympathised with Hitler. They're

all fascists!'

'Just like your father, I understand.'

'Get out! Go on, get out of my house!'

Bartlett screwed the top back on his fountain pen and collected his things. He stood up and made for the door but then he stopped and looked at Paul.

'People like you come and go but the British state remains timeless.'

'People like me?'

'People who think they can change things,' said Bartlett. 'Do you really think that we would ever tolerate the social order of this great nation being challenged? Oh, every politician that comes along claims they can make it better for everyone at the bottom with talk of progressive this and progressive that but they all get sucked in eventually. The establishment of this country is more powerful than any elected mouthpiece. The lower classes will be kept down there by the system and we will maintain the social hierarchy on which our history and traditions stand. Nobody will ever change things fundamentally and anybody who tries will be dealt with in one way or another. The poor will always be too stupid to realise what the monarch really thinks of them. They'll continue to buy the tea towels and wave the flag on royal wedding days. Their stupid belief that the monarch actually cares about them is what keeps her there and what will keep her successors there. You made a fine and fancy speech the other day but you should know from the example of your late grandmother that we will have our way and you never will.'

'If you don't get out of my house I will throw you out.'

'Oh don't worry, I'm going,' said Bartlett. 'But you will be hearing from us again.'

CHAPTER TWENTY-TWO

SARA SLAMMED HER HAND against the filing cabinet in her office. 'I can understand your anger, Sara,' said Hargreaves, 'but there's nothing that you or I can do.'

'Sir, Paul Foster came to me twice, once when his house had been broken into and once when he was convinced he was being followed. He told me that a man who said he was representing the Crown had visited him and more or less threatened him with dire consequences if he didn't keep his mouth shut. This man, Major General Bartlett, isn't known to any of the agencies we deal with or to the palace. They're denying all knowledge of him because it's part of the cover up, sir. Now I know that Paul Foster was about to go to the press with all this but then low and behold he ends up dead in a car accident late at night. We know that his brakes had been cut and that he only had one drink in the bar he went to. But the autopsy said that the amount of alcohol in his bloodstream would've meant that he would barely have been able to walk, let alone drive a car.'

'You make a very convincing case, DCI Hoyland,' said Hargreaves, 'but it won't go anywhere.'

'He was murdered, sir.'

'I agree it looks very much that way.'

'I'm a law enforcement officer and I should be out there finding who did it.'

'But you never will find them, Sara,' said Hargreaves,

'we both know that.'

'And all because we've been ordered not to proceed with the bloody investigation.'

'It will go down as a tragic accident.'

Sara snorted. 'Yeah, and they're not even being original with that one.'

'DCI Hoyland, if you try and proceed with this then it will be the end to your career,' said Hargreaves. 'Now I'm warning you. Forget Paul Foster and forget this case. I know it's wrong but if you don't then I will not be able to protect you.'

'This absolutely stinks, sir,' said Sara.

'Yes it does,' said Hargreaves. 'Look, I'm as frustrated as you, Sara, believe me I am. I don't like anything about this and what's frustrating is that nothing can be done about it. We've got to let it go, Sara. I'm sorry but that's just the way it is.'

'Sir, I'm employed to uphold the law of this land,' said Sara, 'but what's happening here, is that faceless people who I can't identify are forcing me into being complicit in their breaking of that law. I didn't think I lived in that kind of country.'

By the time Sara got down to the pub she was in a foul mood. The last person she wanted to see was Tim and if he hadn't seen her, she'd have turned on her heels and left. He was just getting himself a drink and he bought her one too. Then they went and sat down at a table at the other end of the bar.

'The Paul Foster business?'

'How did you guess?'

'It's been winding you up since we were told not to investigate it.'

'It's wrong, Tim,' Sara insisted. 'It is so wrong.'

'I know but the Superintendent is right,' said Tim. 'We have to let it go.'

'Paul Foster was one of the good guys, Tim,' said Sara. 'We should be getting justice for him.'

'But we can't,' said Tim. 'I'm as angry about it as you but are we going to risk our careers over it?'

Sara sighed. 'No,' she said. 'I don't suppose we are.'

'So how's it going between you and Kieran?'

'That's a bit of a change of subject.'

'Well it's pointless talking about the Paul Foster case,' said Tim. 'It's been taken out of our hands by people much more powerful than us. So how is it going?'

'Very well as it happens.'

'The sex is good then?'

'Jealous?'

'What? Of a kid fresh out of training college?'

'Look, let's just talk about something else'

Tim sipped his pint. 'Like what? The weather? How the boys are doing in the Ashes test down in Perth? What it's like to have sex with a boy instead of a man?'

Sara picked up her jacket that had been lying beside her and stood up. Tim was really doing her head in and she just wasn't in the mood for it.

'I may have ten years on Kieran but I tell you something, Tim,' said Sara, 'he's a lot more mature about personal relationships than you. And he wouldn't be winding me up like this when he knows the kind of day I've had.'

Tim grabbed her wrist. 'Don't go, Sara.'

Sara slumped back down on her chair. 'I don't know what you want from me, Tim.'

'I don't know either,' said Tim. 'The answers to a lot of unanswerable questions about our baby, I suppose.'

'You were getting married to Helen, you were happy…'

'…and all the time I had a son,' said Tim, 'and he's out there somewhere and he doesn't know that his Daddy would give anything to hold him in his arms.'

'Tim?'

Tim and Sara both turned round to see a shocked looking Helen standing above them. It was only then that Tim remembered he'd asked his wife to join him at the pub. He immediately stood up and reached out to her but she backed away. The looks she exchanged told them that she had heard every word. She started crying and ran out of the pub.

Tim stood up and ran after her, leaving Sara alone.

THE END

BEAUTIFUL CHILD

Canon Brendan O' Farrell of Holy Saints Catholic Church, Salford, is nearing retirement when a series of gruesome murders takes place among his congregation.

In this the second of David Menon's DCI Sara Hoyland mysteries, the detective finds that the trail of clues leads to questions that may be a little too close to home.

BUY IT NOW AS AN E-BOOK AT AMAZON KINDLE, APPLE iBOOKS AND FOR ALL OTHER DEVICES.

PAPERBACK PUBLISHED AUTUMN 2012

www.davidmenon.com
www.empire-uk.com

Other novels from Empire

TEABAGS & TEARS

ISBN: 1901746 917

£8.95 - PAPERBACK - 256 PP

PUBLISHED: 1ST JUNE 2012

Sandra Partington has led a dog's life. Abused by her husband and humiliated by her sister, she finds the strength to take revenge on both with spectacular consequences.

In her fifth novel, Karen Woods deals with issues as diverse as domestic violence and celebrity culture in a way which will make you laugh and cry.

ORDER THIS BOOK NOW FOR JUST £6
WWW.EMPIRE-UK.COM

Other novels from Empire

BAGHEADS

"An author Manchester should be proud of"

CRISSY ROCK

As heroin addict Shaun Cook lies comatose in hospital following a suicide attempt, his family come to terms with his life and their part in his downfall.

At turns funny and heart-breaking, Karen Woods' fourth novel sees her return to familiar territory to craft an indictment of modern society that will make you laugh and cry.

ORDER THIS BOOK NOW FOR JUST £6
WWW.EMPIRE-UK.COM

Other novels from Empire

BROKEN YOUTH

A novel by Karen Woods

"Sex, violence and fractured relationships, a kitchen sink drama that needs to be told and a fresh voice to tell it."

TERRY CHRISTIAN

When rebellious teenager Misty Sullivan falls pregnant to a local wannabe gangster, she soon becomes a prisoner in her own home. Despite the betrayal of her best friend, she eventually recovers her self-belief and plots revenge on her abusive boyfriend with spectacular consequences.

This gripping tale sees the impressive debut of Karen Woods in the first of a series of novels based on characters living on a Manchester council estate. Themes of social deprivation, self-empowerment, lust, greed and envy come to the fore in this authentic tale of modern life.

ORDER THIS BOOK NOW FOR JUST £6
WWW.EMPIRE-UK.COM

Other novels from Empire

BLACK TEAR$

A NOVEL BY KAREN WOODS

"MANCHESTER'S ANSWER TO MARTINA COLE"

WITH EVIL GORDON locked up in Strangeways for 5 years, the characters from Karen Woods' debut novel 'Broken Youth' come to terms with life without him.

Misty, now married to Dominic, gives birth to Gordon's child, Charlotte. Her former best friend Francesca also gives birth to one of Gordon's children, Rico, while staying with Gordon's heroin addicted brother Tom.'

Meanwhile, as the clock ticks down on his sentence, Gordon broods on the injustice of his situation and plots sweet revenge on those on the outside.

ORDER THIS BOOK NOW FOR JUST £6
WWW.EMPIRE-UK.COM

Other novels from Empire

NORTHERN GIRLS ♥ GRAVY

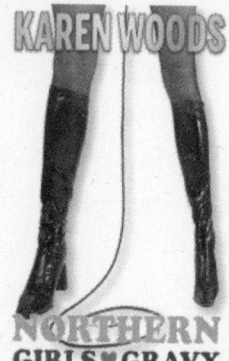

A NOVEL BY KAREN WOODS

"Victoria Greybank had everything a woman could ever dream of but as she stood tall in the full length mirror she pulled at her expensive clothes and hated her life."

Trapped in a loveless marriage Victoria soon discovers her husband's late nights at the office are excuses to engage in sado-masochistic sex.

Bewildered, she falls in with a lesbian overseas property developer who comes up with a big plan to make them both very rich...

Karen Woods' third novel deals is sexy, saucy and very, very naughty.

ORDER THIS BOOK NOW FOR JUST £6
WWW.EMPIRE-UK.COM

Other novels from Empire

THE CARPET KING OF TEXAS

PAUL KENNEDY

"TRAINSPOTTING FOR THE VIAGRA GENERATION"
SUNDAY MIRROR
"DRUG-TAKING, SEXUAL DEPRAVITY... NOT FOR THE FAINT HEARTED."
NEWS OF THE WORLD

This shocking debut novel from award-winning journalist Paul Kennedy tells the twisted tales of three lives a million miles apart as they come crashing together with disastrous consequences.

Away on business, Dirk McVee is the self proclaimed "Carpet King of Texas" - but work is the last thing on his mind as he prowls Liverpool's underbelly to quench his thirst for sexual kicks.

Teenager Jade Thompson is far too trusting for her own good. In search of a guiding light and influential figure, she slips away from her loving family and into a life where no one emerges unscathed.

And John Jones Junior is the small boy with the grown-up face. With a drug addicted father, no motherly love, no hope, and no future, he has no chance at all.

The Carpet King of Texas is a gritty and gruesome, humorous and harrowing story of a world we all live in but rarely see.

ORDER THIS BOOK NOW FOR JUST £6
WWW.EMPIRE-UK.COM

Other novels from Empire

ONE MORE TIME...

A NOVEL BY MICHAEL DILWORTH

Falling in love was never easy for Liam Kirk, until he met valerie Walters. Their relationship – if you could call it that – was strained, least of all because she was still the girlfriend of an old mate. This, however, didn't stop them embarking on an affair which ended rather abruptly.

Fast forward 13 years and Liam has just completed his first novel based on his relationship with val – without changing her name. This wouldn't be such a problem if she hadn't just gate-crashed liam's life for a second time and was now reading his account of their relationship.

Will they have the happy ending liam wished for all those years ago? or will val get the better of him one More Time? Set in various Lancastrian pubs and Californian coffee bars, this wry novel marks the writing debut of Michael Dilworth.

ABOUT THE AUTHOR

Born and raised in Silverdale, Lancaster, Michael Dilworth always loved telling stories. Having spent a fair few years writing for football fanzines, Mick decided to take his writing to the next level by writing a novel. Listing his biggest influences as Nick Hornby and Bill Bryson, he started to write a book loosely based on his own youthful antics. Mick currently resides in heysham with his wife and two children.

ORDER THIS BOOK NOW FOR JUST £6
WWW.EMPIRE-UK.COM